Shayne
Love you
Mich
Hope you Love
Story

DIS BONNE NUIT

Angela Daniel

Dis Bonne Nuit Table of Contents

Credits:

Cover art creation by Angela Daniel

Fractal art - (*Mardi Gras Spiral*) by permission: Artist Peggi Wolfe

www.deviantart.com/wolfepaw

Back Cover Photo - Life Captures Photography

www.instagram.com/scottjohnedwards

About the author drawing – Noveastar www.instagram.com/noveastar

Editor - Danny Daniel Jr.

Print Formatting/Editing - Zara Kor (Author of *Under Tomorrow's Alleged Sky*)

2111 Post Office Road

Galveston, TX 77550

www.fromtheheart.gallery

Very special thank you to From the Heart Gallery in Galveston, Texas. Your support and involvement in this book have been so valuable to me. The continued support of my writing throughout, though, has been *PRICELESS.*

Thank you for providing me a place in this world to exist.

Dis Bonne Nuit is a work of fiction that takes place elsewhere in the Multiverse. While places, names or other things may seem familiar...they are not of this world. So, relax and enjoy.

ACT ONE – BEFORE THE END BEGAN

Before the End Began

It could have been any day on Bourbon Street. The busy hustle of shop owners, beggars, and cons truly never ceased. It was, after all, a never-ending celebration. Noon had long since passed but dusk was still a bit off. The light of sunset spilled through the Quarter, creating blinding rays followed by ominous shadows.

Loud music blared from all around. Different styles and sounds blending together to form a dissonant crescendo to set the mood. Each sounding with the hopes that it would entice the passers-by to come in. The pungent smell of beer and vomit mixed with the sweet smell of confectioners' pastries created a nauseating aura.

Smokers hovered outside doors to get the last puff before entering any one of the never-ending stores. The pockets of smoky plumes seemed to meet just a couple of feet above head, creating a hazy shield to the streetlamps. As the sun sank lower and lower in the sky, the shadows crept further and further out encroaching all the way to the streets and creating the illusion of gobbling up things like random bike tires as it went.

The sudden wafting scent of natural gas indicated that the lamps had been lit. Dusk had arrived. The witching hour, as various faith healers, traiteurs and anyone with a pack of cards and an elementary understanding of what they meant pounced on tourists.

From the shadows the old haggard woman sat, taking inventory of passers-by and watching for quick hands and unsuspecting pockets. Drawing heavily on the crushed cigarillo between her teeth, she rocked back and forth on a weathered, creaky, pre-war era rocking chair.

After what must have been decades of chain-smoking cigars and chewing tobacco, her voice had been mangled into a half growl, half wheeze. "Get on!" the old woman yelled as she lashed her gnarled cane out and made contact with the forearm of a dirty young man.

The surprise in the eyes of the mark was almost more overwhelming than the fear in the eyes of the would-be thief. Both scurried away in opposite directions. The old woman nodded to no one in particular.

From time to time she would call out from her dark corner, ever vigilant at her self-appointed post as the "Eye of the Quarter". Locals who weren't smart enough to just avoid the entire mess altogether had their theories on the old woman's past.

No one really knew anything about her except that she made her meager living giving old world readings and had become a cult tourist attraction. She had never been proven wrong on her predictions on a baby's gender, length of a marriage or even who was secretly dancing with whom. She lived in the one room loft above her tiny corner storefront, in as bad disrepair inside as out.

It was Friday night. Any families that might have been out enjoying one of the trendy restaurants or shops had long since retreated back to their homes, leaving the streets of the Quarter to the inebriated mix of tourists and social refugees. Everyone was here to remember or forget. Either was possible.

Peering over the rim of her obscenely oversized drink, Hana tried to sink into the shadows. The mix of rum and whatever else they were slinging as the server came by had started to catch up to her. As she witnessed the scene across the street, a small chuckle escaped before she could bring it back.

She had no idea why it amused her. Quickly scanning the tables and stools around her, Hana had concluded that no one had heard her laugh. Because it seemed that she still cared what people might think, she groaned and waved her hand in the air attempting to catch the bartender's attention.

The unspoken order was filled within minutes and a different server set the glass in front of her. "That's going to be seven fifty, hon." The southern belle act was transparent on the young, perky blonde.

For the fifth time, Hana retrieved a ten-dollar bill from her wallet. "Keep the change," she muttered without looking up. She had rented a room right in the middle of the action and could see her front window from where she was sitting. She could crawl to the flat if she had to. She was planning on needing to.

Drowning her memories and incapacitating her thoughts was becoming harder and harder. The liquor didn't pack the punch it used to. Somehow, she had gone from the joyful lightweight to the cynical drunk without the spiral in the middle. Or maybe there had been a spiral, she just didn't remember anymore. Everything felt like sinking.

Pressing a cigarette between her lips that she had recovered from the crumpled foil pack at the bottom of her hand bag, she dug frantically for a lighter. Realizing how ridiculous she looked, she scanned the room again. She hadn't noticed that the background noise had grown to a low rumble; the place was packed.

From behind her, the familiar sound of a lighter sparked. She turned towards the sound and knocked her bag over, spilling much of its contents across the floor. "Fuck it," she mumbled, leaning in towards the flame being offered. As she drew in she managed to breathe out, "Thanks."

"Need some help?" The tall figure motioned towards the various cosmetic and hygiene items strewn around. Without waiting for her to answer, he knelt down and started to pick up her things.

Jumping from the chair as though she had been shocked, she clutched the filter of her smoke between her teeth and obviously annoyed, said, "I've got it. Jesus." She snatched the lipstick and hand sanitizer he was holding. Scrambling to collect the rest of the contents of her purse, she stumbled over an invisible obstacle.

The handsome, if not handsy, stranger reached out and plucked her from her fall. "Calm down." The embers on the cigarette were so close to his face, it was almost uncomfortable. Even with the wind catching errant tiny cinders and flinging them towards him he didn't flinch. "So, do you need some help?"

It was an understatement. She tried to contain the guttural laughter that threatened to creep up. "Why not." Regaining what she could of her dignity, she sat carefully in the chair, crossed her legs and straightened out her skirt. "What did you want to do? Help me get drunk?"

"It doesn't look like you need any help with that." He paused before pulling out the chair across from her at the tiny bar table. "Would you mind if I..." The neon lights from the bar reflected the ring on his left hand in almost prismatic fashion.

"Knock yourself out," she agreed apathetically. The rumble of the growing crowd inside the bar spilled out onto the sidewalk patio. She flattened the non-existent wrinkles in her blouse and then again in her skirt and then stood and gathered her things. "It's all yours."

Slinging her bag over her shoulder created a tiny impact which threatened to topple her. She attempted to correct the movement and over did it, swaying the other way. The man watched without reacting. He was trying to hide the amusement in his eyes. Quite unsuccessfully.

"Are you sure you're okay?" The concern in his voice sounded genuine.

She wasn't. She wasn't okay at all. But that wasn't what he meant. "I'm a big girl," she slurred as she took each of her shoes off individually, steadying her stance. Clutching the sling backs in one hand she shot the peace sign in the air, aimed towards him. "I got this."

The crowds had gathered out into the streets, singing loudly and badly along with whatever was playing within the walls they had recently inhabited. Jaywalkers crossed from the curb at any point they wanted. Hana slowly and deliberately made her way to the metal barricade blocking traffic from going any further down Bourbon Street.

The man kept an eye on her from his newly acquired chair. One he obviously hadn't expected to be sitting alone at so soon. She turned back just before stepping off the curb. For a brief moment she contemplated walking back into the bar and having an actual conversation with a human being for a change. Instead she stepped off the curb, her bare feet contacting loose gravel and other debris.

Rather than stepping back up she lightly tread forward, heading directly towards the corner shop where the old woman was perched, keeping watch. Slowly the old woman expelled a breath, "Je t'attendais." Then she translated, "I been waiting for you." She was looking directly at Hana.

Hana attempted to look everywhere but where the crumpled, dirty woman was. She increased the speed between her steps with purpose, even if she was a little wobbly. But she didn't move fast enough. A gnarled wooden cane shot up, blocking her from reaching the curb.

"What? You got no manners? I said I been waiting for you."

"What do you want?" Hana stumbled over the words. "Money? Is that it?" She retrieved the last ten-dollar bill she had reserved for the sixth cocktail she did not order and shoved the crumpled paper towards the woman's face.

With a snarl comprised of several missing teeth the woman quickly slapped Hana's hand holding the money. Her accent was a confusing sloppy mush of heavy Cajun French and island dialect. One of the two had been for show lifetimes ago, it was possible even *she* couldn't remember which one was hers. She managed to almost moan out, "Nope, ain't got no manners at all." Shaking her head, she stood and lowered her cane.

Hana took the opportunity to try to usher herself past the woman. The fusion of fragrances from different incenses mixed with the odor her body was emitting wafted up in a sickeningly sweet aroma. The woman stepped into her path again. "I can see you." She drew out the "I" longer than necessary.

"Yes. I can see you too." Mumbling under her breath a little louder than she thought she added, "And smell you."

The woman cackled and swirled her cane around in the air. "You got some spirit. I like that. But you got something else." She craned her

8

face in, almost touching her nose to Hana's. "That darkness is no place for a girl to be hiding." The mixture of the smell of rotting teeth and stale cigars almost caused Hana to gag and she recoiled.

With only one corner to cross to reach the reprieve of her vacation apartment, Hana attempted once more to walk around the woman. She was not afraid of her, but her head was spinning, and she was getting irritated with the show. Finally stepping aside and letting her pass, the woman whispered, "Le mal vient dans le noir." [Evil comes in the dark.]

Hana crossed the street, spying the entrance to the lofts she was heading for. The unpleasant woman behind her, she shuddered a bit. The same feeling that she got when she turned her back on a suspicious character. The feeling she was being followed stuck with her even after she made her way into the building and hurried up the stairs. The elevator had been out of commission the whole week she had been here. She suspected it had been out for a very long time.

Before exiting the stairwell at the second floor, she turned. There was no one behind her. The business below had long since closed, but the street still sounded the eternal party and it leeched through the walls echoing directly into her brain.

Fortunately, the apartment she'd rented through Air B&B was over a legal office that closed well before the nightly debauchery began.

"Best criminal defense attorney in all of Louisiana," the reviews said. It was odd that his rental review included repeated mention of his practice, but it didn't take a genius to realize those were left by his friends and cronies. The room reviews were not as glowing, but she didn't care. The clean if not shabby accommodations were fine for her.

She changed into a t-shirt but abandoned the shorts as she stumbled several times to raise her leg into them. The clock on the microwave flashed 2:03. It appeared to be keeping time, even though it was flashing. It took a moment for her to realize that someone was knocking ever so lightly on the front door. "Really?" she muttered to herself and tiptoed towards the door, attempting to peek out and see who might have followed her.

Three soft raps came again from the door as she slowly peered out of the peep-hole, extended all the way on her tip toes. It was the man from the bar. *IT WAS THE MAN FROM THE BAR. Of course* he had seen where she had gone. As she saw who it was, she shifted her weight, accidentally pushing on the door slightly. Her cover had been blown—he knew she was looking.

The darkest parts of her mind imagined the scene advancing by a gun firing through the hole, through the door, maybe through the wall. As she held her breath waiting for the assault to begin, her legs began to betray her. She could not stand on her toes any longer.

Positive something horrible was about to happen, or maybe wishing it was, she croaked, "What do you want?"

"Hana Patel?" he questioned from the other side of the door.

How did he know her name? She began to shake a bit. "Go away."

The light underneath the door shifted and the shadows changed. Watching the floor, she was surprised when something came sliding through. It was her driver's license. "Shit," she exclaimed louder than she meant to. She had obviously missed it when she gathered everything up that had dumped so gracefully at the bar.

The mystery man leaned his head in towards the junction where the outer frame met the door. In a drunken whisper he said, "I just wanted to get that back to you." From the way the light shifted, he had stepped away from the door. She could hear the tap of his shoes on the hard hallway floor. He was retreating.

His footsteps stopped as she fumbled with the chains to unlock the door. Before turning the thumb bolt, she hesitated. She could really use the company. A handsome, nameless and possibly drunk man was standing right outside the door. It wasn't a bad scenario.

"Wait," she called as she poked her head out the door, "You want a drink?" She thrust her right arm out the door, in her hand she was clutching a bottle of spiced rum.

With a soft chuckle he whispered again playfully, "Do I have to drink it out here?"

Without a word she shoved the door so that it swung out into the hall. Turning, she walked away from the door towards the living area. As she strode away from him, she ordered, "Lock them all behind you."

The activity below them had thinned out and the last bit of celebration was drawing to a close. The bars that were closing for the night had ejected their last straggler and driven the closing time barflies out into the street. A random hoot or whoop invaded the otherwise finally quiet space.

Carefully sliding his ring from his hand into his pocket, he watched her lace-covered backside swaying as he crossed the threshold, then turned and secured all of the locks. "I wouldn't have invited me in," he playfully chastised. Then cleared his throat, "Not that I'm going to do anything bad." He was awkward; it was kind of cute.

"Oh, in that case, never mind, you can go," she drawled as she pulled a large swig directly from the bottle then placed it carefully on the table. With very little modesty she sprawled across the chaise at the end of the sofa, lying on her stomach. She was reaching for something under the sectional. Her feet swayed in the air and her butt wiggled a bit. "Aha!" she exclaimed as she found her phone.

Without even glancing at it, she tossed it aside and walked towards him. He was sitting nervously on the other end of the sofa. His face resting on his palm, resting on his elbow, resting on the arm of the over plush furniture. As he was gazing at her and smiling, he realized how unsettling that might appear and reached for the bottle on the coffee table.

"So," his voice betrayed him, he cleared his throat and tried again. "So, what are we doing?"

Pointing to the indention on his ring finger, she chastised, "Looks like you already had some ideas."

Embarrassed, he blushed and turned for a moment. Gathering his drunken thoughts, he whispered enticingly, "Come here." She obliged and walked up to him, straddling him, face to face. "I know your name, but I haven't..."

She pressed her fingers to his lips, "I don't care," she whispered back as thickly. Then leaned forward and whispered with sultry tones in his ear, "You're leaving after this."

He didn't argue. And he didn't wait for further invitation. As he nervously touched her, she pawed at his shirt, slipping each button slowly out. His mind wandered. *Was he really about to do this? Was he about to cross a line he couldn't come back from?*

He had had no intention of actually coming inside. He had honestly intended to return her driver's license and leave. But when she turned away from him at the open door, the sight of her round backside and the black lace lured him in. As her mouth found his over and over again, he forgot about any reservations.

Her hands were so soft, her body was even softer. It had been so long since he had held something that wasn't rigid and cold. They moved like poetry. Her song was tender, made up of whimpers and moans. At some point they made their way to the bed before both passed out, still partially drunk and completely spent.

Perspective

Buried beneath a stack of old scratchy musty blankets, Queenie tried to preserve what little warmth she could muster. The chiminea slowly smoked in the corner. The last embers of the fire had just sputtered out and the mouth held a glowing accumulation of ashes. It wasn't the safest way to warm the loft, she knew that. But she couldn't afford a fancy central heater. This would have to do.

Shifting restlessly over and over again, she tried to escape the dream she had so often. Contemplating re-igniting the fire, she rose and shuffled towards the small pile of wood she still had beside the portable fire place.

Dawn seemed to be close, but the blackness of the night had eclipsed all but halos of the streetlamps, illuminating tiny circular pockets on the ground. At this hour, nothing but shadows and darkness existed. Queenie shivered as she thought about the darkness.

Abandoning her task at the fireplace, she strode across the tiny room to retrieve a smudge of sage and some incense. She was aware that her looks were a discredit to her. When she was young and considered beautiful, it had been so much easier to get a body to listen. She lit the tiny candles around the altar and said a prayer.

Since she was already up it didn't make any sense to go back to bed. Not when the dawn was so close. She'd seen the man follow that girl, but she wasn't in the business of interfering with people's sin. The darkness in that girl was much more likely to eat *him* whole rather than the other way around.

Scraping together leftover coffee grounds from the past few pots, she was able to manage enough to make at least one cup of fuel. She fumbled for a butt in the large sand filled vase. Finding one that was less than half burned was a windfall to start the morning. As she sat in her filthy chair, smoking her cigar and sipping her half-burnt brew she began to hum.

Only parts of the old church hymn had stuck with her. Every so often she would pause, unable to remember the melody. In perfect time, she picked up at the parts she knew. The song prepared her for the coming day. Saturdays were the worst of the days. What one did under cover of night during the week was perfectly acceptable in the light of day on Saturday.

She had a lot of work to do today. It was time to take up her perch.

...

Quietly, Eddie slipped out of bed and stumbled in the dark to find his clothes. He didn't want to wake his gracious host. The trail from his socks to his shirt progressed one article at a time. His conscience came in swarms of voices creating a nauseating wave as he battled the hangover that was coming on. The clock was blinking 4:40.

At least he didn't have to explain where he had been all night. Rosalind was in Montreal for the Virology Conference and was likely just waking up. He tiptoed across the apartment in his socks, snagging Hana's key. He was able to lock the door and then slid the key back under the door hard enough so that it would be visible.

He didn't stop to put his shoes on until he got to the bottom of the stairwell. While his wife was off curing cancer or whatever and networking with some of the most brilliant scientific minds in the world, he was out...he didn't know *what* he was out doing but he knew where he had ended up. It probably could have been any damsel in distress. Oh, but wasn't he lucky it had been Hana?

Chasing the thought away, he walked down the empty sidewalk towards his car. Although it was dark, he could see his breath on the air, catching glistening rays from the gas lamps. The Quarter was very ominous this close to dawn. When the sky was the darkest and the streets were the quietest. Aside from the tapping of his loafers, it was silent. Even sin needed its sleep.

As he stepped up on the curb, just one more block to his car, he was startled when a cane shot out from the darkness. The dark voice that followed it made the hairs on the back of his neck stand up. "Now you been cursed by tha darkness." It was the old Hoodoo lady. He chuckled and attempted to step forward. "Who's telling jokes?" she chastised.

With a gentle and polite demeanor, Eddie requested, "Excuse me, please."

"Ahh, *you* got manners!" she giggled. "No one ever listens to the old lady til it's too late." The laugh came out more as a hack as she coughed her morning ritual. "But I seen something. Something in that girl."

Slightly annoyed but still amused he quipped, "I did too."

"Ooowee *and* you got spirit!" She stepped out of the way and gave a half curtsy, half bob. "I expect I'll be seeing you again real soon."

Shrugging her off before he reached his car, he clicked the *Start* from his pocket. Leaving his phone in the car hadn't been the best idea but he didn't care. There were no missed calls. Catching wisps of a soft fragrance, he breathed in deeply. He smelled like her. He was completely lost in last night and before he realized it, he had turned on his street. Somehow, he had managed to get through the gate and not even notice.

While a little gauche for his taste, Rosalind had to have the sprawling Garden District estate. It seemed like a colossal waste of space for two people. And with her gone so much, he rattled around the six-bedroom monstrosity by himself. He poured a scotch, neat, and carried it off to the den.

Staring at a glowing laptop screen, he nursed the drink. Best hangover cure there was. A wave of panic washed over him as he looked down at his left hand. He could still see the indention from where his ring should be. Jumping out of his chair and almost comically shoving his hands down both
pockets he realized that he had dropped it somewhere along the way. "Just fucking great," he hissed.

...

Drooling on her pillow, Hana rolled over to see if her mystery man was still sleeping but the bed was empty. Her head was pounding and her mouth felt like she had licked an ashtray at the bar. The tiny coffee maker in the kitchen area had been working off and on. She hadn't cared enough about it to complain, but today she needed coffee. She cheered quietly when the brew light came on.

She was surprised by her disappointment of waking up alone. But in all fairness, he did what he was asked to do. While she was replaying the events of last night over and over again in her head, she caught the glimmer of the kitchen light reflection on the floor in front of the door. He even locked the door behind himself.

The sun had begun to make its appearance, sending tendrils of warmth and light across the Quarter. The cheap curtains didn't pull together all the way and the rays scattered throughout the room. As it trickled across the floor, another hidden treasure was revealed.

"Shit!" she exclaimed quietly as she retrieved the silver band from the floor. Turning it over and over again in her fingers, she wondered if he was already missing it. Or had he even noticed? It was a nice ring, titanium most likely, encrusted with tiny diamond solitaires in two angled stripes. The inscription inside caught her eye.

One love. One life. 1998 – Bélisaire.

Twenty-one years. She caught herself wondering if she was an anomaly in his life or if he just couldn't help himself. Either way, she wasn't judging. Last night had been the first time in a long time she had felt alive. Even if it was just for a while. He should get his ring back.

Because she had so callously tossed her phone aside when her mystery man arrived, the charge had been depleted. She had to wait until she had enough battery life to start looking up Bélisaire. While she was waiting, she quickly showered and got ready for the day. The coffee maker hadn't produced any of the good stuff and it was likely she was going to have to go down to the cafe on the corner and get a cup.

There were two Bélisaire surnames in the white pages online. Doctor and Pat.

The clock blinked 6:27.

...

Eddie jumped just a little when the phone on his desk rang. Nobody called that number. He glanced down at the time display on his computer. It was 6:33. Wrong number? Who would be calling? "What?" he barked as he put the phone to his ear. It was a little gruffer than he meant.

"Doctor Bélisaire?" the soft feminine voice on the other end of the line questioned.

Why would someone be calling this number for Rosalind? "She's out of town." He paused and then added, "I could have her call you."

"No," the woman laughed.

He caught the fragrance of the subtle sweet perfume that still hung around him. Was it her? "Hana?"

For a brief moment, he thought she had hung up. He heard her take a sharp breath. "You could have just come back. You know where I am." Her tone was playful. But he wasn't sure what she was talking about. Understanding that he was lost she clarified, "I wouldn't even have tried to find you ...but it's your wedding ring."

It wasn't a tragedy. He really didn't even care that he had lost it. It was a lie. It had been for a very long time now. But still, he needed to get it back. "Why didn't I think about that?" His head was still pounding but he managed to laugh. "How inconvenient would breakfast be?" He shouldn't have asked, and he knew it.

"If you're not Doctor, what do I call you?" She almost sounded annoyed about having to learn his name.

"Eddie." He caught his non-presentable reflection in the mirror and added, "Give me an hour. There's a little cafe one corner over. The food is greasy, but it's great for a hangover."

Was she actually excited she was going to see him again? No. The highs from last night hadn't completely worn off. She could still smell him. The faint aftershave or cologne he had been wearing had hung about the apartment. It was sweet. Mustering as much apathy as she could she agreed, "I was going there to get some coffee anyway. Whatever you want to do."

It took her about twenty minutes to completely dress and pick up a few things. Her oversized, overstuffed hand bag had been discarded in the corner. The contents had been dumped again. A sickening wave of heat and chills washed over her. She frantically dug into the bottom of the bag until she located the pendant. Just a tiny vial of ashes. She ran her thumb over the smooth surface.

As the relief came, she tossed the long cord over her head and tucked the bottle into her shirt. The Quarter had a different feel in the morning. The early dew made everything shiny. Even the shabbiest of exteriors seemed to glisten in dawn's light. As Hana stepped out into the day, she winced as the sunshine assaulted her behind her eyes. Before crossing the street, she rifled through her bag and found her sunglasses.

The crosswalk lines on the ground had long faded and only tiny strips of the white paint remained. There weren't any crossing lights anyway, so zoning the area didn't seem to matter. A handful of shop owners had already entered their stores, but the street was completely empty. Void of any life. That is why she was so startled when she passed the old woman's store and heard the strained whisper, "I see you."

Not this again. Hana sighed and tried to muster a smile. She had absolutely no patience right now, but she didn't want to be completely rude. She was relieved when the old woman didn't try to stop her. "Have a nice morning," she called back as she passed. The most important thing to her right now was coffee.

It seemed like an eternity between the time she took a seat and the time she was greeted in the completely empty dining room. Based on the amount of noise coming from the kitchen, it would seem the restaurant had been packed. Stacks of plates clinking together, tubs of silverware being poured out, pans being dropped, every single one of those things echoed through her head and made her teeth rattle.

"You waiting on someone, or you ready to order?" the young, seemingly disinterested waitress said gruffly. Mistaking her hesitance to answer immediately as a misunderstanding she added, "You just want to start with some coffee?"

"Yes, please," Hana replied overly polite.

As she twirled the ring between her forefinger and thumb, she was lost in thoughts she couldn't put aside. The sudden appearance of the coupe outside the window brought butterflies to her stomach. The car was sleek, black and had curves that she had never seen before. It was obviously a much more expensive car than she had ever owned, she mused as she watched Eddie fumbling with the parking meter.

It wasn't quite 7:30, but he wasn't sure how long he would be here. He carefully loaded the quarters in until the timer read 2 hours. It was probably overkill, but he was hungry and didn't know how long they'd be there. His stomach growled as he reached to open the storefront door.

The temperature had climbed quite a bit since the sun had made its debut for the day, but the wave of heat that rushed past him when he entered reminded him that it was still chilly. His hands were cold. The moment he saw her, a warmth spread through him quickly. She was just as stunning to him sober as she had been when he was drunk. He smiled.

In about a week the Quarter would be packed for Mardi Gras. Tourists from all over the world would be celebrating their sin. Even people without religion loved to celebrate the holiday. The only acceptable time of the year where taking a leave of absence from your morals was encouraged. But for now, it was quiet. He wasn't in the mood for noise. This was perfect.

Sitting across from her in the booth, his eyes darted around the room over and over again. As he leaned forward her perfume wafted past him. Fighting the urge to suggest they go back to her apartment, he cleared his throat. "Thank you for calling me." He didn't know what else to say.

Other than ordering food neither of them spoke until after the waitress had set down the greasy collage of eggs, meats, hash browns and a bowl of watery, pasty grits. The lump of butter floating in the top indicated that the grits hadn't been hot enough. It looked disgusting. She almost gagged.

"I know you won't believe this..." he stalled. It took him a moment to gather his words, or maybe find his voice, before he continued, "I've never done that before." Realizing that it sounded like a line, he stumbled to clarify, "I wasn't out hunting last night."

Finally feeling the effects of the coffee, she couldn't help herself. A slight chuckle, slight snort escaped. "You're the one that knocked on *my* door," she teased. Other patrons had started to pile into the cafe, and the ambient noise continued to slowly increase. Sliding his ring across the table she admitted, "I don't make it a practice of picking up strangers, no matter how attractive they are." She blushed after the words escaped her lips.

The entire breakfast was an awkward pause. He realized that. He shouldn't be here. But the food, although mediocre at best, was making him feel better. He noticed she hadn't touched anything. "I'll get out of your hair as soon as..."

Across the cafe, salt shakers and sugar jars rattled in unison. Suddenly a loud boom screamed across the Quarter. The sound was almost deafening. Heavy waves that felt like gravity pushing down crushed the air around them. Sharp knives seemed to plow their way through her head and she moaned. As soon as the sound had dissipated, Eddie was out the front door. Watching his reaction from the window, it confirmed that something horrible had happened.

Abandoning the greasy meal, her handbag and his ring on the table, Hana darted out the door as well to see what he was looking at. The scene was almost surreal. Wood, ash and debris littered the air and the ground. Chunks of cinders and ash floated on the breeze, almost as though defying gravity. Turning the corner towards her apartment she gasped. The entire front of the building had been blown out. The central location pointed right to her room. Unable to move, to breathe or even think she stood blankly staring at what used to be a legal office.

The few patrons that had already begun occupying the establishments filed out onto the sidewalks, each looking up and gawking. Flying planks of wood had carried remnants of the fire almost to the meter where Eddie had parked, narrowly missing his car. Spying a large pile of debris in front of the old woman's shop, Hana darted towards the corner. Eddie realized what she was thinking and ran after her.

Fortunately, she was not sitting in her chair. Unable to see the roof from where they were, he pulled on the shop door, expecting it to be locked. He was surprised when it swung open freely. As they entered the damp dirty store, they were both assaulted by the acrid smell of mold and mildew. The shop area was fairly sparse. Just a tiny round table covered with an antique faded velvet drape, a few chairs scattered throughout the room, a small stand with various trinkets and talisman and a tiny little glass showcase with unusual stones, several worn pouches of cards and what looked like animal teeth.

The showcase was immaculate. The contrast to the dingy dirty store was almost comical. The old woman was obviously very proud of what it contained. A slight smell of burning wood crept down the stairs and Eddie sneezed. Understanding at the same time that the explosion could have caused the roof to catch fire, they both hurried up the stairs.

There was no landing. The stairs opened out into the room. Most of the sunlight was eclipsed by the blackout curtains, except for the places where the fabric had worn thin or pieces were missing. It created a hazy, eerie atmosphere. The smell of body odor, incense, tobacco and wood fire mingled together. It was nauseating.

The old woman was sitting with her back to the smoldering mouth of the terra cotta fireplace, facing the stairs. It was as though she hadn't heard the explosion.

Unsolicited Secrets

The shrill of sirens echoed louder and louder as the emergency crews were making their way to the scene. Madness had begun on the streets below them. The soft strobe of blue and red lights seeped into the room. They were likely to be caught up in some kind of investigation and for just a minute, Eddie contemplated bolting. "Shit," he mumbled.

"Indeed!" the old woman chuckled. He leaned in to whisper to Hana. Before he could speak, Queenie protested, "You got no secrets man, I know what you been up to."

Straitening up like a student that had be reprimanded, he took a deep breath and told Hana, "Go get our stuff." Pulling money from his wallet, he added, "And pay for breakfast. Please."

Without saying a word, she snatched the cash and darted back down the stairs. The smell of mildew was making her sick. As she stepped out of the store, she took a huge breath only to be suffocated by the taste of fire and the smell of smoke. She coughed and stumbled, then regained her balance. The sidewalk from the little magick store to the cafe suddenly seemed twice as long.

Relieved and a little surprised to find their things untouched in the booth, she understood that no one was paying attention to them. If the circumstances had been different, the situation could have provided some cover of anonymity. Being that it was her apartment prevented that. A feeling of absolute panic washed over her. What caused the explosion?

She gave all of the money to the waitress, who had long since forgotten she was working. As the waitress thanked her, she absently shoved the cash into her apron. Hana mused as to whether or not it would make it into the register. She didn't really care.

Checking the time on Eddie's meter, she saw there was well over an hour left.

Dodging the growing crowd, she made her way back to the shop and up the dingy stairs. Neither Eddie or Queenie had spoken a word in the few minutes Hana had been away. The look on his face begged to leave, but the concern in his eyes for the welfare of other people was endearing. As he surveyed the filthy tiny area, he felt sorry for the old woman.

"No need to be thinking all that now." Queenie stared across the tip of her cigar, peering almost through him. "I do alright. I don't need any of the pity." There is no way she could read his mind. But she could read his body language, his face. Like any good salesperson.

Shifting her attention to Hana she softly wheezed, "Why don't we go on downstairs. Let me read for ya?" It was a mix of a question and a statement. "My treat!" She seemed overly excited to work for free.

Recognizing the opportunity, Eddie stepped forward and pulled two twenty-dollar bills from his wallet. She didn't want charity, but at least he could pay her for her services. He knew her reputation. She was always incredibly vague with her readings. Very carnival type fortune telling. Even the locals who believed in this insanity thought she was a hack. "How about both of us?"

"Are you kidding?" Hana didn't try to hide her total disbelief.

Without missing a beat Queenie jumped up, plucked one of the bills from his hand and pushed past them to the stairs. "There's just the one." Her round figure barely fit through the tiny space and as she made it to the bottom of the stairs, she appeared to spread. The old filthy bath robe she was wearing was at least two sizes too large and it hung comically from her frame.

She didn't wait for them to get downstairs. She was already contemplating which bag of cards to pull out. Hana thought to herself that if this old woman pulled out a crystal ball, she would not be able to stop laughing. No crystal ball was presented. Queenie took a seat at the table and patted her hands down on the surface. "Y'all gonna sit down? Awful rude to just be hanging 'round doorways."

"Name's Queenie, by the way," she introduced herself. As if they had been waiting with bated breath to know. Although it felt like it had been hours since the explosion, in reality, only ten minutes had passed. It was likely the fire department hadn't gotten the flames down yet. Hana wasn't sure which was worse, the air in here or the air out there.

As they both took a seat across from her, neither knew what to expect. Queenie methodically lit two candles and a stick of incense. She waved the burning stick in the air and quietly chanted something unintelligible. Placing the stick in a holder, she clapped her hands. As she slipped the cards from the dingy pouch Eddie noticed that they looked brand new. It seemed to him the same sentiment as setting out the good china for special guests. Whether that was it, or she was just trying to be flashy, he wasn't sure.

Once she was convinced that they had been shuffled properly and both Hana and Eddie had touched the deck, she laid out an asymmetrical grid of seven cards. Turning the first, almost immediately she laughed a hearty laugh, "Ten of Swords." When it was evident that the message hadn't been conveyed Queenie shook her head and said, "Catastrophe. I'm guessing we can go on and skip ahead."

They both remained completely silent. The roaring of running water, idling fire engines and all of the other busy sounds trickled through the dim interior. As Queenie turned over the second card, she shook her head again. "Would you look at that. Three of Swords." She leaned in and dropped her voice down to a strained whisper, "Girl, tragedy must follow you around."

"But it's alright. Queenie is going to find the silver lining." She turned the third card and fourth card in unison. One card appeared to have a Knight on it and the other said Death. Jumping up, the magick woman almost turned the table over. "It's you," she pointed accusingly towards Hana. "You got to go. Now."

Was she really ejecting her from the shop? "Are you serious?" She'd had enough of the drama and enough of the smell anyway. She got up and walked towards the door, Eddie followed. They were both confused.

From where she stood the old woman called out, "Tu vas finir le monde. Tu vas finir le monde." For emphasis, she slowly spat out, "You gonna end the world."

...

In the fifteen minutes since the explosion, crews had already outlined the most dangerous areas with caution tape. A lot of it. Small flames still lapped out from the loft. Eddie didn't even know what to say. He had no idea how long she'd been staying in that apartment. Did she have a life there? Had she lost everything? Should he help her? Aware he was going to drive himself crazy with all of the questions, he asked, "What can I do?"

Fumbling with the cord around her neck she clutched at the glass bottle. It all felt like more sinking. Everything was still moving in slow motion for her. At least she didn't have anything important there. Everything she needed was in her bag and around her neck. "I have no idea." She was a little surprised by the fact that he hadn't jumped into that expensive car of his and squealed off.

By the time the interviewing officer reached them, other task force representatives were corralling and herding everyone away from that side of the street. A convergence of body odor, strong cologne and bad breath had come upon them. "Is the occupant of the apartment here?"

Sighing, Hana made eye contact and replied, "Yes. That's me."

All of the questions he asked were pretty easy. It was apparent that the police department was familiar with the office, with the attorney, with the lofts. Without paying much attention, she answered everything as quickly as she could. She couldn't even remember what she had already answered. She was just ready to get away from the crowd.

Not sure where she was going to go, she didn't realize that she and Eddie were walking towards his car. Neither of them said anything. Her mind was racing. What did she do now? It was likely that there were no hotels available, not this close to a holiday. Maybe she should just go home? No. There was absolutely nothing there for her.

Finding herself wishing she'd eaten, Hana tried to quiet the rumble in her stomach. She looked up to see if Eddie had heard. If he had, he didn't react. When he stepped off the curb and opened the passenger door, she was a little taken aback. Was he intending on taking her somewhere? That would actually be helpful. "Where are we going?" She didn't step off the curb.

"Where do you need to go?" He smiled. He genuinely was willing to take her anywhere. A hotel, a friend's house, a family member's house, his house. He stopped himself before the thought materialized into words. He added timidly, "Do you *have* anywhere to go?"

There were only two kinds of money in Orleans Parrish. There was the old money and the new money. A social wedge divided the two. The old money folk were proud of their heritage and their old things. They would tell you stories about a time they hadn't even lived through as though it were their own accomplishment. The family *name* meant everything. And they would look down their nose at anyone that didn't possess the heritage they did.

New money was viewed as wasteful. Flashy cars, fine jewelry, expensive shoes and tailored suits. Those things embodied Eddie. He was definitely new money. She could handle that. At least he wasn't a snob.

She still wasn't sure if getting into his car was a good idea. But what was he going to do that he hadn't already done, or had the opportunity to do? The time on the parking meter read out twenty-three minutes. The Saturday crowds were arriving, creating more havoc and more noise. Without answering him, she got in. The interior smelled brand new, fine leather. It was immaculate. She placed her purse in her lap carefully, so as not to scuff the seats.

Gently he closed the door and scurried around the back of the car. It seemed they had finally extinguished the fire and had begun cleaning up the mess. The heavy thick smoke still hovered just above head. He felt as though they were escaping a war zone. Pushing errant memories aside he climbed into the driver's seat. "Where to?"

"Where does one go to end the world?" she quipped sarcastically.

A look of empathy crossed his eyes. "Aww, go easy. She's an old woman who obviously believes her own lines after all these years." Starting the car, he put it into reverse and, while he was looking behind the car, he added, "I'd imagine she's lonely."

Hana couldn't muster the empathy. What she saw was an old woman who obviously had lost her senses long ago. She shouldn't be by herself. She should be somewhere that she could be looked after. She wasn't blaming Queenie for her situation, but she didn't get the impression that there was anyone else *to* blame. "Are you?" she whispered as he navigated out of the Quarter.

Without taking his eyes from the road he asked, "What?"

"Lonely," she repeated. There had been a longer pause between the conversation than she realized. "Is that what last night was?" She wasn't accusing, she wasn't judging. She was just curious. He could tell by her demeanor. He didn't know how to answer her.

As the quaint shops of the Quarter faded behind them, they drove towards the freeway. The roads were wider, and everything felt more open. She could breathe better. She could think better. She still had no idea what to do. He kept driving.

Glancing over at her as she inspected the dirty city in the daylight from her window, he was stunned at why such a beautiful woman would be slumming in NOLA. He could tell when he looked in her eyes that she had some baggage. Likely some demons. Who didn't? She seemed completely unfazed by the revelations of doom. Even a non-believer was still moved over predictions of evil and death.

"My wife will be gone until next Sunday." He was about to offer something he shouldn't. He knew it. She knew it. They both knew it was a terrible idea. He did so anyway, with a boyish waiver in his voice, "Might be nice to have a little company. Until you know what you want to do." With only a slight breath he asked heavily, "Was that your home?"

What should she reveal? What should she say? She simply chose, "No." That sounded so cold, so sharp. But there weren't many ways to deliver *no* and it not feel that way. Still, the word left a bitter taste on her tongue. "I'm just..." Too many things could follow this. "Waiting to die" sounded too harsh so she simply squeaked, "visiting."

She didn't actually accept his invitation, but she didn't decline. He wasn't sure what she really wanted. It was likely she didn't either. There was no way she could be thinking clearly. Was he about to take advantage of that? There were five other rooms in the house. It didn't have to be anything more than that.

Hana was actually relieved when he quit talking. The noise in her head was already drowning everything out. Having to focus on conversation was tiring. The traffic was light and by the time they made it into the private subdivision the clock on the dash read 9:32.

There was a slight curve between the entrance of the drive and the break in trees, and when they rounded the corner, she couldn't help but gasp. This wasn't a house. This was a mansion. She blushed as she tried to hide her childlike awe. Before she could stop it, she blurted out, "What do you *do?*"

Up to this point, she had seemed unimpressed. Well, except that whole thing last night. She was pretty impressed with that. As he climbed out, he pushed that thought out of his head and jogged again around the back of the vehicle. Before he made his way to the passenger side, she had already opened the door and was climbing out. He looked disappointed.

The front lawn covered more space than an entire block of the shops in the Quarter. She realized that might have been an exaggeration, but only by a little. Every speck of grass was a vibrant green, cut to a perfect height. The walks and places where the lawn met anything were sharply edged. The flower beds on each side of the walk up to the house were balanced by type and color of flower. Even the decorative trees that lined the drive were completely symmetrical. Everything was perfect.

The walkway from the drive to the front steps appeared to be halfway paved and halfway lined with cobblestone. The inlays of the tiny stones created beautiful patterns flowing towards the door. He paced her, watching her take everything in. Enjoying the slight reprieve from the madness that preceded her visit was welcome. For just a brief moment he got lost in her, remembered what they were doing, and led her through the front door.

He hadn't set the alarm or even locked the door. Although none of that was particularly necessary in this area. But still he paused before going in, assessing any possibility that someone might have entered the house. It was training from a life he had completely left behind but couldn't shake.

Too tired to take in much else, she followed him quietly through the foyer into an open space. The area was for entertaining and was set up almost like a fancy night club. The kitchen was a junction of this room and a beautifully decorated sun style room off the other side. The whole house was built for entertaining. Who did they entertain?

...

Queenie sat in the chair next to the overturned table for at least an hour after she chased the devil out. Burning sage at each end of the room as well as multiple different fragrances of incense. Her goal had been to drive out the evil that had invaded her space. She felt bad for running that poor girl out. She realized that she'd had no idea.

Nevertheless, she continued her task of purging the intrusion. The scene outside her doors was still that of chaos and upheaval but she needed the calm. She was sitting in a circle of ashes that she had scraped from the trays that held the sticks as they burned. There was so much more coming. She wished she could see it more clearly.

From time to time the chimes on the front door would ring. But no one ever fully opened the door. It was likely someone in the wrong place. No one ever came in. She very rarely ever went out anymore. She was going to have to soon. She knew that.

Scraping together her various teas and potions she boiled some water on her tiny gas burner and poured it over the leaves. It was an offering to Saint Michael in return for imbuing the grigri with protection. Her prayer was short and as she finished, she chanted twice. One time for each talisman. She dropped several tiny stones and a couple of teeth in and swirled them into the mixture. Pouring the hot liquid out over a cloth, she carefully placed two of the teeth and one small stone in each pouch. Carefully, she sewed each one closed then tied dark yarn around each creating a necklace of sorts.

She left them in the circle and went about extinguishing all flames and smoldering objects. The morning had already contained way too much excitement for an old woman. After painstakingly wrapping a small brown paper package, she left it by the overturned table. Her body ached. It took all the energy she could muster to drag herself up the stairs and to her bed. She was asleep as soon as her head hit the pillow.

Worlds Collide

Wandering around the open downstairs, Hana tried to catch a glimpse of Eddie's life. The immaculate furniture and decor seemed so very sterile. There were beautiful objet d'art strewn throughout on pedestals or shelves. No sense of who lived there. No personality. They didn't even have family pictures on the wall. Instead there were matted photos of scenery or other mediums of art hung throughout the house. Not even a wedding photo.

They were both covered in soot and ash. "I could really use a shower," she stated matter-of-factly. The grit and grime had seeped through her pores causing her to itch and sweat. All she could taste was ash. "And some toothpaste." She scooped a toothbrush case from the bag she had not put down. "Never leave home without it!"

He was still gazing at her. He couldn't stop. Even with the gray smudges on her cheeks and the positively filthy layer of black sediment that covered her clothes, she was beautiful. "Rosalind has an entire closet of clothes she's never worn. I'll find you something." Then, directing her to the back of the house, he pointed out the stairway. Absently he added, "First door on your right when you get to the landing. Everything you need should be there."

Hana didn't say thank you. She didn't know if she needed to. He was a nice guy. That was unexpected. She had no idea why she'd come home with him. But where was she going to go? She could figure it out *after* a shower. By the time she reached the landing and turned to the right she heard footsteps banging up the stairs.

As she opened the door, she caught a glimpse of a polished light wooden floor, a white circular rug with pink lace and the corner of a princess bed, complete with canopy. The sweet smell of cotton candy wafted out. Before the door was opened completely, Eddie reached over her and pulled it shut. "I'm so sorry. Not this one. I meant left. I'm sorry." He guided her to the other door and repeated his sorry over and over again.

Finding a treasure of soaps, body washes and hair products, Hana picked what she would need and undressed to shower. The three-way mirror beside the garden style bath tub seemed a little strange, but she was able to view herself from every angle and noticed the ash and soot had collected under her clothes. She needed a good scrub.

Opting to soak in the huge bathtub, she located some oil beads and bubble bath in the linen closet. Turning almost no cold water on, she opened the hot valve all the way and dumped the floral scented additives into the mix. It was *hot,* almost unbearably so, but only almost. She stretched out and lay perfectly still for a while but as the water cooled just a bit, she began scrubbing at the greasy mess that had accumulated on her skin and in her hair.

The noises in her head began to roar. That was a little girl's room. That's all it could have been. The look on Eddie's face when he shut the door said that was more likely a shrine than a bedroom. She knew a little something about that. There is no way a child lived in this house. Judging by the lack of dust or any other signs of life, no one actually *lived* in this house. It didn't take a rocket scientist or a doctor to realize that there was absolutely no love in this home.

...

Browsing through the insane amount of clothes that Rosalind had collected, Eddie tried to clear his head. He must have looked like a madman the way he reacted. All of this had been a terrible idea. From the moment he saw her, everything he did had been a bad decision. Hana was a few inches shorter than Rosalind, and at least one dress size smaller. Collecting up the smallest sun dresses and outfits he could find, he carried the arm full of clothes to the guest room.

He contemplated the room at the other side of the stairs, shook his head and turned to the door behind him. She had been in the bath for almost an hour. Lightly tapping on the door, he called through, "You okay in there?"

"Yes, thank you," the answer came from the other side quickly.

The fragrance from her bath bubbled up from under the door and swirled in his senses. It was inviting. But he hadn't been invited. "I put some things out for you in the room across the hall. The door is open. I think it's all going to be too big."

"I'm sure I'll manage," she assured him. Adding, "Thank you," as an afterthought.

After cleaning himself up, he made his way back downstairs and to the den off the back of the kitchen. The den was the only room that contained a television. Fumbling around for the remote, he bumped the ornate bar stand where his abandoned scotch was still sitting. The narrow table rocked and tumbled the glass off before he could react. The table didn't topple, but the glass shattered into a thousand pieces spraying shards across the room. "Just perfect." He turned the TV on and went out back to get what he needed to clean the glass up.

It was crystal. Antique highball glasses to go with that ridiculous globe bar. That thing had always been an eyesore and had claimed the lives of many glasses over the years. This set had been a wedding gift. He didn't care for it. But it seemed to tickle Rosalind. Somehow it had ended up in his study. The ice bucket inside actually worked, incredibly. That's why he kept it.

After selecting a simple t-shirt and pair of shorts, Hana quickly dressed. He had been right that the clothes were too big, but the shorts had a draw string and she cinched it just a bit. She found some makeup under the sink that had never been opened. The good doctor probably had totally forgotten it was there. *Like she seemingly had forgotten everything in this house. That isn't fair,* she chastised herself, *you have no idea what is going on.*

Brushing her teeth, she was unable to get the taste of fire out of her mouth. She repeated the process three times before she finally gave up on getting rid of the acrid flavor. Once she felt presentable, she made her way to the stairs. The soft sound of television news wafted up the steps.

Hana followed the sound of the television down the stairs and to the back hallway. She saw the flickering light through the clear divider. Before she walked into the room, she saw the broken glass and liquid on the floor. Stepping back, her heel contacted an errant jagged piece. "Damn it!" she sat down on the cold tile floor and yanked it from her foot. For a little cut, there was a lot of blood.

From the corner of her eye, she caught the flicker of the television again. The volume was up enough that she could clearly make out what was being said, but she didn't realize that until she focused on the sound. Eddie had come back into the hallway holding a broom and a mop with a small bucket. It was almost comical.

"In a breaking story we're only just now getting any information on, a currently unfolding tragic event. We're going to go live with our correspondent in Quebec. Richard, can you hear me?"

"I can, thanks Liza." There was a slight lag in transmission and the audio and video didn't match up. "From what we can piece together right now, the madness you're seeing behind me is The Queen Elizabeth Hotel here in Montreal." The camera panned just a few inches away from the reporter and focused on the entrance to the hotel. "Investigators are on the scene and are still unsure what caused the fire that broke out in one of the rooms. Two guests were trapped and have been confirmed dead."

No matter how bad things had gotten, Rosalind was his wife. Of course, he loved her. A sickening feeling washed over him, twisting his stomach in knots. He dropped the mop bucket spilling the cleaner he had already put in it. Retrieving his cell phone from his desk he frantically dialed her number. He breathed out an exaggerated sigh of relief when she answered.

"Hey, I guess you're watching the news?" indicating that otherwise he had no business calling her.

The sudden defeat in his eyes caught Hana. She couldn't hear who was on the other end, but she was guessing it was his wife. She was out of town; apparently, she was in Montreal. He croaked, "I just wanted to make sure..."

"I'm fine," she snapped. "And now I've got to deal with this drama." Everything to her was an inconvenience. "They've suspended the conference until the investigators are done doing whatever it is they do. I'll be staying here until then." She disconnected the call.

He was relieved. First and foremost, that she was okay. Secondly, she wasn't coming home next week. The pain of regret hit him as he realized he was happy about that. The newscasters droned on and on for several minutes. He had completely quit focusing on what they were saying and continued with his task of cleaning up the mess. Now he didn't have just glass, he had this pine scented pool and Hana's blood.

Hana had not stopped listening to the low drone of the television.

"Wait, Liza we're just getting word. Most of the guests registered in this hotel are here for this year's Virology Conference. If you don't know, Virology is the study of viruses. These scientists are here to share what they have learned about manipulating these viruses to ultimately cure disease. Some very promising research has come out of this area recently. Apparently, some of the most brilliant scientific minds are here together right now. "

The smallest hairs on the back of her neck stood up as Hana turned her full attention to the television. The camera switched again to the local desk. "Thanks Richard." She then added in that ridiculous news fashion, "Are all of the scientists accounted for?"

A creeping groan of fear escaped her, and Eddie turned his attention to the report.

With his hand cupping the earbud to cancel out any background noise, you could tell that the reporter was hearing the question *after* she finished asking. Nodding while he listened, he replied, "At this point there is still one of the registered scientists that is *not* accounted for..." Fumbling to find the information on the card that someone from off camera handed him he sputtered out, "A Dr. Patel. Noah Patel."

Unable to breathe, Hana's vision was reduced to a tiny circle of light. The perky blonde at the local desk continued to ask questions. "Any information as to what started the blaze?"

After the regular pause he replied, "At this time we are unable to confirm. There are several different accounts of what happened. But it seems as though the fire may have been deliberate. That's all I have for now, Liza. Back to you."

A dull roar started a ringing in her ears. She couldn't move. She had completely forgotten that Noah was in Montreal. She hadn't actually *known* he was there, but it made sense. He had become obsessed. Swallowed by the whale. Reaching up, she cupped her necklace. Holding onto it like a lifeline.

As he watched the color drain from her face and her eyes grow wide in horror, it came together for him. Hana Patel. Was Noah her husband? Her father? Her brother? He was afraid to ask, afraid to feed whatever fear she was experiencing. Instead he snatched two paper towels from the roll and sat down next to her. Her foot hadn't stopped bleeding.

She didn't speak, she didn't breathe, she didn't move. Quietly he took her hand and ran his finger up and down her arm. He hadn't noticed the tiny tan line on her finger before. The divorcee tan. The ring hadn't been gone for very long either. "Can you call him?" he finally muttered.

"What the fuck?" she spit out when it dawned on her that her husband and his wife were in the same place. Her phone was dead because she hadn't charged it fully, so she reached for his. He didn't protest as she slid it from his hand. Breathing deeply, she slowly dialed the number. As she listened to the ringing, the tones in her ears grew louder. She was literally fighting the noises in her head to hear the phone. The room started to spin as the automated voice answered, "Please leave a message for...". Before it dictated the number back to her, she hung up.

It was twelve minutes after noon.

...

Rosalind peered at her reflection in the vanity mirror. When had she gotten so old? The too-tight bun in her hair produced thick bands of gray and silver. The lines on her face were carved deeper than the Grand Canyon. She knew that Eddie resented her. Hell, she resented herself. She didn't tell him that she hadn't been staying in her room at The Queen Elizabeth. Not that he really cared.

Because of the high-profile nature of the investigation, the Sûreté du Québec had already started their investigation. They had proven it was arson quickly. The absolute nerve they had to imply that *she* was officially a suspect. In all fairness what they had said was that no one was, at this point, above suspicion. But what that boiled down to was that she was a suspect.

She found herself wondering if Eddie even missed her anymore when she was gone. He never called. But that might have been her fault. No, it *was* her fault. But still. Why did they both insist on living a charade any longer?

As she finished making up her face, she stared at her sallow reflection again. Did she even know how to smile anymore? She then glanced towards the beautiful curves of porcelain white skin on the king-sized bed across the room. The last two days had been a hazy mix of fine champagne, caviar and Olivia. That made her smile, but it cracked the corner of her mouth where the too-thick foundation had been applied.

Olivia had been a distraction. A fairly amazing one, but a distraction nonetheless. The last time she had seen her was when she was in Georgia six months ago. As soon as she learned that Olivia would be attending the conference here, she reached out to her. Contemplating leaving without saying anything, she crossed the room and sat gingerly on the bed.

The room was nice. It was nothing like the one she had reserved. This one was quite a bit more modern. More of motel feel than a five-star hotel. But still nice. The short carpet was a perfect shade of tan and brown. It looked like it was shampooed frequently. The stark white sheets were actually soft and smelled clean. The view was beautiful. Everything in Montreal was beautiful. Olivia was beautiful.

Her thick mane of sandy blonde hair, the upturned nose, the "pools of blue" eyes. And her lips. They were like soft sweet candy. She learned that when they got wasted a little over a year ago in Munich and ended up waking up together the next morning. She brushed her hand slowly down the small of Olivia's back and placed her palm flat on her butt. This stirred Olivia from sleep and she stretched and smiled. The British lilt in her voice was so seductive. "You look very pretty. Where are you going?"

...

The mess in the Quarter was cleaned up at record speed. Firefighters were still scouring the building to be certain there were no smoldering remains before allowing crews to board up. By the time the flames were fully extinguished a total of three buildings had been affected. They had been very lucky the fire hadn't spread beyond that. Water damage claimed an additional two of the shops, but they had already brought in drying fans and extractors.

Neighbors, friends, acquaintances and even complete strangers stepped in to help. Over the years she had seen a lot of crazy things happen in the Quarter, but when it came down to it the people of New Orleans pulled together when things went south. When they were all working side by side, there was no social station, no color, no religion, no gender. Just compassion for their fellow man. Too bad it only happened in times of tragedy she mused. At least no one had been seriously injured. Yet.

Even city officials made it to the scene to discuss options to help re-open any businesses that were able to before the busiest celebration of the year reached them. Queenie watched the commotion quietly from her perch. Because the chaos had spread all over the Quarter, rescue crews were bringing in bottled water, coffee and other offerings for volunteers or victims. She was so grateful when one of the young volunteers brought her a nice hot cup of the black, steaming nectar. She sat sipping on it and slowly rocking.

Queenie overheard some of the firefighters talking and learned that the explosion had been caused by a random series of events beginning with a broken coffee maker, a bad cord, faulty wiring and shoddy preventative maintenance. The fire had ignited a gas line leading to the water heater, creating the chaos that now inhabited the streets.

That handsome young man had left the other twenty-dollar bill on the table when he left, leaving Queenie feeling rich. She had hobbled down the sidewalk to the convenience store and selected her favorite treats. A Mounds Bar, a large bag of Funyuns, two packages of cheap flavored cigarillos and a 40-ounce beer. She even had change left over. It was definitely a blessed day for Queenie even if the rest of the Quarter was going to hell.

Twenty-Four Hours

Elmer wobbled out among the plots, the canvas bag tied to his hip. He'd been there all morning and was almost done. As he inspected each area, he would stoop and bend to pick up any errant trash that had blown in. Truth was, most of the trash was carried into the cemetery these days and discarded. But he liked to believe it had all blown in. Otherwise, it was as if they were just disrespecting the dead.

Everything in NOLA was a tourist attraction. Even the cemetery. Lafayette 1 was the most popular by far not just with the death hags and tourists, but for some reason even Hollywood was caught in its spell. No telling how many countless film crews he had seen over his forty years keeping the grounds. If you asked him, and nobody did, the dead should be left alone. Instead, the mausoleums, tombs, and graves had become an amusement park for the disrespectful.

At least the death hags picked up after themselves. As macabre as the hobby seemed to him, they truly respected the deceased. It was those trendy twenty-somethings that came in and wrecked the place up. At least all the stones had survived through the night again. From time to time he'd find one all busted up. The sun was already beating down and even though the morning had started chilly, he was sweating.

He paused only to drink his water or wipe his brow. Get the job done as fast as you can. That had always been his motto. The call of the air-conditioned shack he occupied was getting louder. He was ready to be done for the day. But no matter how big of a hurry he was in, he did his job thoroughly. Crossing to the last area of plots, he sighed in relief: the end was in sight.

Nothing to him was sadder than the grave of a child. He couldn't read the word parts, but the date parts always stuck out to him. The newest grave was also the end of his route. Although he'd come upon this one every day for the last three months, he shook his head sorrowfully to see the dates 2015-2018. Every time he saw it, he almost wept.

The wind was picking up and in the distance the sky was growing darker. It appeared a squall had surged over the bay. Whether it would reach this far inland, he couldn't say. As the wind shifted a strange odor overwhelmed him. It was a combination of rotting flesh and sulfur. Although it had been three months, the ground hadn't fully seated back and much of it still contained loose dirt which appeared to be bubbling. "That ain't right," he muttered.

Ants? he wondered. *Was there a colony running beneath this ground?* He reached out with his hand to touch the parts that appeared to be moving and pressed his finger into the soil. Instantly a putrid yellow foam began to seep out from the ground. Elmer jumped slightly, causing him to topple forward and hit his head on the grave stone as he fell face first into the ooze. The blow to his head knocked him unconscious.

...

Saturdays were pretty busy in the ER at University Medical. Usually self-inflicted accidents caused by drinking and recreational drug use or bar fights. That didn't start until after five or six in the evening. It was only one o'clock when Morgan got the short staff text. It seemed three of the duty nurses had called in sick. Things were pretty quiet when he arrived. At least he could get some downtime before the rush began.

Kate was relieved when Morgan arrived. She had so many patients to attend, that she needed someone available for any incoming. It seemed highly unlikely that all three of the absentees were truly sick, but they worked the same shifts and could have picked up the same bug. Either way she definitely needed help.

"You are a lifesaver!" She hugged him clumsily, picked up several of the patient records from the desk and almost sprinted down the hall.

Although he was behind the doors to the emergency area, Morgan could see the empty waiting room through the wide window at triage. Scanning the daily record, he was surprised that there hadn't been an influx of activity this morning. Just a few cases of possible smoke inhalation. He had heard the explosion from his apartment. Saw the smoke. By some stroke of luck, it appeared that no one had been injured.

Almost completely lost in the quiet, he jumped a bit when the screech of the siren approached outside. Kate had already reached the back door and was ushering the EMTs towards an empty room. Within just moments two of the doctors had also appeared.

"It's Elmer," she shouted to Morgan as they passed. They all knew the old man. He had been down at the cemetery for as long as anyone could remember. Worked himself almost to death from time to time. Mild heat stroke, cardiac issues and other things had brought him in to visit often. As the gurney passed the station, he realized this was not one of those times.

The mangled bloody face wasn't the worst part. It was the crust of what looked like amber snot caked around his mouth and nose. "What happened?" he called out as they progressed down the hall at a hurried pace.

"Don't know yet," she shot back as they turned the corner out of his sight.

...

Stretched out on the leather couch, Hana nursed her foot. It had finally stopped bleeding, but she figured she'd stay off of it. Eddie was more than willing and almost happy to cater to whatever she needed. He really was one of the good ones. At least he was acting like one of the good ones. For now. She couldn't stop thinking of Noah.

She'd tried to call several times but now it was going to voicemail before it rang. It was either turned off or depleted. Either way it seemed like an ominous sign. Noah had been one of the good ones too, but after Ebby... She halted her train of thought and shook her head. He was just different now. She was too.

"Does it hurt?" Eddie asked as he handed her a drink.

Of course it fucking hurts, she thought. Then fussed at herself internally for being so difficult. He seemed genuine and she should be grateful. Especially because he didn't seem like he had any intention of prying. "A little." She forced a smile.

This time yesterday, Hana had been completely alone in the world. As she sat beneath the Tree Of Life, she had contemplated the unthinkable. She was aware of the irony but was unmoved. Instead she'd ended up sitting at a bar, drinking whatever they'd hand her as fast as she could. It was pretty much the same as dying, but without the mess.

While Ebby was being treated at the Children's Hospital, Butterfly Park had become his favorite place. That's why it made sense. That's why she chose that place. She emptied the contents of the urn and watched as the ashes floated with the wind, eastward on the Mississippi.

After discarding the useless vase in a trash receptacle, she managed to find her way to the tree. Had she not instructed the Uber driver to come back and get her at a designated time, she may have still been sitting under the tree. But when he arrived, she reluctantly left the park behind her and proceeded to drown herself at the bar. Where she met Eddie. And now she wasn't *completely* alone. At least not for now.

"So..." she attempted awkwardly to break the silence that had settled, "What *do* you do?" Referring back to her earlier question. She shifted back and forth several times, trying to separate herself from the leather where her skin was sticking.

Misinterpreting her movements as discomfort, Eddie jumped and scooped her off the sofa in one fluid motion. His intentions had been true. He was just going to carry her upstairs where she would be more comfortable. The cut on her foot wasn't *that* bad but it had taken so long to stop bleeding. He didn't want that to start up again. He already felt so bad that she'd hurt herself.

As they reached the top of the stairs, he paused. Instead of carrying her to the guest room across from the bath, he went straight and continued to the master bedroom. As she realized where they were heading his lips found hers again. She didn't hesitate to return the passion that was bubbling up. Pausing again as they reached the bed he whispered, "You can say no."

"Why would I do that?" she drawled back.

...

The interview process was finally over, and Rosalind fumbled for her phone as she entered the car. "Hey, feel like tapas?"

The lilt of Olivia's voice replied, "Not really hungry, but I could use a drink."

"That was the idea," she chuckled. "I'm in the Netlift now, I'll call you when we're outside."

She was aware that most of the time her demeanor made her seem unapproachable. She was okay with that. After his initial, "Bonjour Hi!" the driver didn't try to chit chat, which was perfectly fine with her. Today had been an absolute waste of time to determine that she wasn't a suspect in this case. Three hours. For the most part, she had an alibi, except for the short time Olivia had been shopping. She just hated involving Olivia. Not so much for Olivia's sake as for her own reputation. Not that that even mattered anymore.

Recognizing her cues, Olivia didn't ask about the investigation. Instead they rode quietly to the restaurant. It didn't matter where you went in the city, it was always bustling. Things were even worse tonight, with people crowding into the city to see what they could of the investigation. Rubber neckers and tourists. That's all they were. They were at least able to get a table, but it wasn't as quiet as she had hoped. Even that would be okay when the wine hit her soul.

It didn't take very long to get served and Rosalind was grateful for that after realizing how noisy it was going to be. She was ready to drink a couple of glasses of wine and go back to Olivia's room. She had enough of the day.

Setting aside the tiny little dishes of quail, olives and other various things, Rosalind raised her glass. Olivia followed suit and raised hers. "What are we toasting?"

"You," she smiled and clinked her glass to Olivia's.

...

At about three o'clock all hell broke loose. The quiet waiting room had turned into a three ringed circus. Fortunately, it was shift change. They were well staffed for the moment and attempting to get through it all quickly so that some of the doctors could go home. Morgan made his way back to the nurses' station in the ER. "What the hell is going on here?" Charts and clipboards were piled up all over the counters.

"I have no idea," another of the nurses answered, "They just started pouring in." Shaking her head, she added, "This is what happens when an entire city doesn't get their flu shot."

Several patients from all over Orleans Parish filled the waiting room as the doctors rushed back and forth between triage and examination rooms. Uncovered mouths sent a fine mist of germs spraying across the room connecting to others spewing vomit into tiny bags. The smell of sour vomit and sick crawled up his sinuses and Morgan quickly snatched his sterile cap from his head and covered his mouth and nose.

This was his first year, but already he understood that this wasn't normal for flu season. They had recently battled an influenza outbreak. This wasn't the flu. This was something different.

The other RNs were ushering patients to examination rooms, but since there were so many people pouring in, they had to start doubling up on occupancy. The task they were working carefully on was to place similar symptoms together. It didn't take long before hospital staff donned masks. They finally made it mandatory for everyone that entered the hospital to put one on. Just in case. They had no idea what they were dealing with.

Young, old and everything in between seemed to be affected. A rumble among the staff had suggested that something in that explosion this morning must be at work. Some kind of chemical or something. No one knew what to make of it, but everyone had a theory.

The commotion from the examination rooms caught everyone's attention. The sound of metal trays and stands being turned over violently followed by several screams. The waiting room occupants rushed the triage window, trying to get a peek at what might be happening. The sound of shattering glass preceded a short scream. Kate was flying through the air as though she had been thrown backwards by a blast.

Plowing his way up the hall was one of the patients they had recently moved out of triage into examination. As he came towards the nurses' station, he flailed his arms, knocking over portable EKGs and other machinery. Each time something hit the ground it created a rattling sound that echoed through the halls.

Several doctors, nurses and other hospital staff attempted to console the raging patient. As he got closer, Morgan could see what appeared to be the same sticky residue on the tips of this man's fingers that he had seen on Elmer's face. The substance seemed to be eating his fingers. Just before the man reached him, a noxious odor shot up his nose.

Morgan was unable to react as the burly patient reached out and snatched him from behind the desk. With what seemed like an exaggerated strength, he threw Morgan across the room. As his head hit the wall, he blacked out.

...

It was almost six when Hana woke up. At first, she was disoriented. It took her a few moments to become fully conscious before she remembered where she was. The light snore next to her answered the next question. They were both exhausted; today had been horrible. She didn't even remember falling asleep. Come to think of it, she didn't remember much of anything after he had gently tossed her on the bed.

The bed was incredible. It was a mixture of the softest down filling, the best memory foam and what seemed like clouds. Even the comforter and pillows were almost ethereal. She was used to nice things, but this was another class of nice altogether. This was a class above even Nobel money. It wasn't lost on her that twice he'd avoided her question. She giggled at the thought of him saying, "If I tell you, I'd have to kill you."

Tiptoeing so as not to put any weight on her heel, she surveyed the room. It was huge. There was a sitting area to one side that opened into a walk-in closet and a massive master bath to the other. In the sitting room were two shelves, full of mementos. The one that caught her attention was the Lasker Award. The funny little angel without the head was pretty unmistakable.

Rosalind had won a Lasker. She actually remembered Noah referring to a Rosalind. "A chip on her shoulder the size of the moon," he had said. "But more brilliant than anyone I've ever met." Even then, it was obvious to her that he had been jealous of Rosalind. It made more sense now.

When he was younger, Noah had been all about the awards. He said that if he could just get the Lasker, the Nobel would surely be right behind. They could have used the Nobel money. Maybe things would have been different. That didn't matter now. Guilt washed over her as she remembered that he was missing. Checking her phone, she saw she had missed a call. She didn't recognize the number. The area code read 514—that was Montreal. A sinking feeling hit her, and she began to cry.

Eddie heard her soft sobs as he stirred. He jolted up from the bed and reached for his pants. She was on the settee at the closet. He didn't take the time to button or zip them before he reached her. "What's wrong?" Taking her hand, he winced. One of his weaknesses were tears. Genuine tears, not the crocodile kind, but Hana was truly upset.

"I can't," she said as she handed him her phone. He realized that she had it set up to call voicemail but had not connected the call. Understanding, he took the phone from her and pressed *Call*. The voice on the other line identified himself as an investigator for the Sûreté. The somber tone and the request to call him back as soon as she could didn't sound good. Eddie found the number in her missed calls list and hit the *Redial* button.

"This is Édouard Bélisaire," he announced softly as the person on the other end answered. "I'm calling on behalf of Hana Patel."

The investigator took a sharp breath and proceeded to inform Eddie that they had found the body of a man that fit Dr. Noah Patel's description just twenty minutes prior to calling. He was found near the Old Port of Montreal. He kept talking, but Eddie couldn't focus. How could he possibly relay this information to Hana? She seemed so fragile right now.

Reading his face, Hana sobbed harder. She understood.

...

There weren't as many people out tonight as there should have been. Queenie noticed that by about eight o'clock. Sure, part of the street was closed off, but that never stopped the party before. She never knew anyone to be deterred by fire either. Something strange was happening and she could feel it.

Retreating into the shop she quietly retrieved the grigri she had prepared. The glowing embers of incense partially circled the rickety table, still overturned. She needed to pull out the big guns. No disrespect to the saints, but they were going to need a lot more than prayer.

The Enemy

Shortly after they arrived at the hotel, Rosalind received a call from one of the dozens of people investigating the situation. She shuddered as she was informed that the arson case had been escalated to murder.

Olivia was sitting cross legged on the bed, surrounded by scattered notebooks and staring into the glowing laptop screen. They hadn't had much conversation since the restaurant. Realizing that Rosalind was more quiet than usual she set her work aside. "Do you want to talk about it, love?"

"What is there to talk about?" she replied, completely emotionless.

A mild panic crossed Olivia's eyes. "Are we in any danger?" As brilliant as she was, Olivia was so innocent and naive.

The odd desire to protect Olivia threw Rosalind a little. She wasn't used to being in that position. She genuinely cared for her. "I don't know," she lied, then changed her mind. "I mean, they have suggested this could have been connected." The truth was they hadn't just suggested it. As a matter of fact, what they had said was because the fire had started in his room, it was possible that he had been a target. If that turned out to be the case it was more than likely that they had reason for concern.

Although she hadn't cared for the man, Dr. Patel was a brilliant mind. He was actually responsible for discovering an easier way to manipulate viruses. In fact, it was his research that spearheaded an entirely new way to disarm them. His work had often been compared to Southam or Pasteur and was considered to be the biggest discovery since Stanley and Lauffer first discovered how to separate proteins from nucleic acid. He was unpleasant, detestable and arrogant. His personality was often sandpaper to her. But he hadn't deserved to die. He wasn't *that* annoying.

As a matter of fact, the buzz was that he had solved the RH Factor problem for the research he was working on. At least for every blood type except O. If he had, that could bring them light years into the future from where they were. She was actually looking forward to hearing him speak. Well, not so much hearing him speak. But at least what he had to say.

Olivia moved all of her things to the desk and then stretched out long ways across the bed. Patting the mattress, she softly invited, "Come on."

...

It was well after eight o'clock when the forgotten rumble in her stomach from breakfast finally resurfaced. She was starving. It was odd, seeing the endless cupboards and refrigerator in a house like this completely empty. They weren't *completely* empty but unless you counted wine, beer and condiments as a meal, there was nothing in the house to eat.

He wasn't sure whether to be embarrassed or sad. He didn't take care of himself. He hadn't eaten anything at home in months. What was the point? He just felt awful he didn't have anything to offer her. He suggested takeout, but they couldn't decide between pizza and Chinese, so he ordered both. *Why not?*

The sofa in the den pulled out. He had actually slept on it more times than he could count. Eddie decided they'd have a picnic style dinner and watch something stupid on television. He hadn't done that in years. Break all the rules at once. Dinner in bed while watching TV. Rosalind would have never agreed to something so ridiculous. Hana, on the other hand, seemed to enjoy the idea. By the time he had their little camping area set up, the church bell-like door chime sounded. The food had arrived.

"You don't have to do this," she said as they both sat cross legged on the pull out. Cartons of rice, pepper steak and vegetables as well as the pizza box took up more than half of the space.

"Feed you?" he joked as he dug into one of the cartons with a set of chop sticks.

Looking around the room she sighed, "All of it."

Without missing a beat, he replied, "In that case, give me that" as he playfully reached for the rice she was holding.

She chuckled nervously and was about to say something else but then changed her mind and began eating. She was *starving*. It seemed like it had been days since the explosion, when in all reality it had been just over twelve hours ago. Musing, she realized that she still knew absolutely nothing about the man she had spent the entire day with. In all fairness, he didn't know anything about her either.

As though reading her mind, he said, "Corporate law." Then he added quickly, "Used to be at least."

A real conversation. Was she ready for this? Before she could shake that thought she engaged. "Why used to?" she asked just after she had shoved another bite of food in her mouth. She knew she probably looked like a pig, but she was so hungry. She should be mourning, but she was already mourned out.

The television was whispering in the background. They weren't actually watching, it was more for background noise. The undetectable hum that the TV created when it was on actually helped him relax. That bottle of scotch in his bar would help too. Without asking, he poured two glasses.

He was stalling. He knew he was. She seemed to recognize it too. She was looking at him wide eyed, waiting for more. "Served a couple of tours. Had the brilliant idea of going into military law. Was going to be a JAG, but after I got my degree, I got an offer from a private firm." He gulped the glass of scotch and got up to pour another. "They offered me five times what I could make as a JAG. It was a no-brainer for me."

"We represented some of the biggest Fortune 500 companies all over the country. In only two years they had offered me a partnership." He sat back down next to her and put the bottle between them. "A couple of years ago, we had a case. A little boy." He sighed for emphasis, not sure he wanted to continue, but he did. "The doctors couldn't quite get a handle on it. It just spread so fast. Didn't respond to any of the treatments at all."

"I represented the insurance company, but the case had me all messed up." Her eyes widened a little, a quick look of pain crossed her eyes. She didn't speak so he continued. "They decided that his treatment was getting too expensive and they were looking for loopholes to get out of it."

She gasped slightly and reached for the little bottle around her neck. A sinking, sick feeling washed over her. *No, no, no.* she thought to herself. If he saw the look of dread on her face, he didn't react. Instead he continued telling his story. "After I found it, I resigned," he added woefully. "An experimental procedure was used... " Before he finished, she sprung up from the bed creating a rocking motion that sent the containers of food crashing to the floor.

Surprised by the sudden movement, Eddie attempted to catch whatever he could before it spilled everywhere. He was unsuccessful. He hadn't really been paying attention to her while he was talking. As he focused his attention to her, he saw a wild panic in her eyes. The bottle around her neck was clutched tightly in her fist.

"Fuck," he hissed out as he realized what was happening. He didn't have to strain too much to remember the boy's name. It was Ebrim Patel. "Hana..."

"You have got to be kidding me!" she nearly screamed and ran out of the den and through the back hall behind the stairs. The French doors to the sun room led out to the back and she burst through them like a football team on homecoming night. She couldn't breathe, she couldn't think. Her ears were ringing and she heaved several times without vomiting. Hammond, Young, Brown and Bélisaire. *Bélisaire.*

Behind the house was a well-lit garden. It was as perfectly manicured as the front. Everything was symmetrical. Everything was perfect except the empty Olympic sized swimming pool. It had not been attended to well. Pieces of plaster were peeling off and tiles littered the bottom. There were places where chunks of cement were broken or completely missing. It appeared the pool had been empty for a long time.

...

Chaos had preceded him as Joaquin entered the parking lot at University Medical. Ambulances and other official hospital transport had littered the entire drive in back and they were rolling patients through the waiting room. Before entering the hospital, he had already equipped himself with a sterile mask, booties and other things to prevent contamination. It was overkill, but just in case.

A hysterical representative of the hospital had called the CDC to report the sudden outbreak they were experiencing. It was required by law to report if a certain percentage of a population was affected. This had blown past the required number hours ago. Something was definitely up.

They'd seen mutated strains of the flu, staph and strep viruses that did not respond to traditional treatments. He was sure this had to be one of those cases. He walked around the back of the structure, wanting to avoid the waiting room area. If he were to have walked through the front door, the sight of him might have caused panic. It was his understanding that there was already too much of that. He wasn't here to cause a stir, he was just here to see if this required the CDC's involvement. But he also wasn't taking any chances.

Before he reached the sliding doors, he could already hear the commotion inside. The receiving doors were open. As he crossed them, he realized why. The odor wafted out in waves. It smelled like dead flesh and sick. A tiny, middle aged woman in a nurse's uniform ran to greet him. "Mr. Rivas?"

"Please, Joaquin." He didn't extend his hand to shake hers. He was sure she understood. "You must be Kate."

Turning, she led him around the hall to a waiting area that had been reserved for staff. They had finally calmed the situation down, but it wasn't easy. "I am. Thank you for coming so fast."

The truth was, nurses weren't supposed to call the CDC. He knew that, and she did too. But given the bizarre circumstances, nobody seemed to care. "It sounded like it was a lot worse on the phone." He tried to sound matter of fact, but the slight condescending tone poked out.

"You have no idea," she sighed and flopped down in a chair. "You should have been here when the cops were. I've never seen anything like it. He threw me through the window." She shivered, recounting the situation. At least she hadn't been injured and was able to shake it off.

She was obviously distraught. It seemed as he looked around the room that everyone was. Doctors and nurses trying to catch a breath after a big disaster or terrible accident was normal for an emergency room staff, but these people looked terrified. "Speed has similar effects." He tried to sound supportive. "Rage, madness and super-human like strength. You sure he wasn't just..."

"No!" she almost shouted. "This is NOLA, I've seen that. I've seen that a thousand times." She looked around at everyone who was now staring directly at her because of her outburst. "This was not anything like that." She sat there shaking her head. It was obvious she was in shock.

He gently put his hand on hers. "It's okay Kate. I believe you. I'm just here to see if we need to get the CDC involved, or someone else." She nodded her head exaggeratedly. "You said something about an unknown substance?" He tried to corral her into getting to the point.

Reaching for the cold bag, she produced three sealed biohazard containers. Each had a strip of masking tape across the top. Each had a name written in black felt tip. She held up the one in her left hand which read *Borre, Elmer* and recited, "This was found on a patient around one o'clock P.M. today. The best we can piece together, he fell, hit his head and landed in this." The second dish said *Site Sample* and she explained, "This was collected from the site where they found Elmer."

As she held up the third one, she shuddered. It read *Cane, Bo.* "This is from the guy that wrecked the place up." She shoved them all towards him, obviously ready to be done with them. They had been properly prepared and sealed, but he put them in a bio hazard bag and closed it tight.

"Had Mr. Cane been to the site where Mr. Borre was found?" he asked.

She shook her head. "Didn't get a chance to ask him." Pointing the direction of the broken window she shuddered again, "You're welcome to try, but he's still sedated."

As they walked together back out towards the ER, he stopped to survey. The destruction was fairly superficial if not incredibly expensive. Many of the machines most commonly used were strewn about, most of them were destroyed or just smashed. Glass partitions and windows had been shattered. The glass had since been cleaned up but the gaping holes remained.

A couple of sizable chunks of plaster were missing from some of the walls. Before they reached the station again, Joaquin turned and looked back at Kate. "So, you're telling me that one man did all of this?

"That's right," she confirmed.

"So what about the other patients?" he pried a bit. "Do you think that this was connected to them as well?"

"Every single person we saw tonight that wasn't an accident or an injury had the same symptoms. Vomiting, difficulty breathing, coughing, rash and I swear they all smelled like their mouths were rotting," she shot defensively. Then waving her arms in the air for show she added, "Smell that...that is rotten breath."

"I'm not doubting you. Just wondering why it would have affected him this way and not any of the other patients," he explained.

"So many of the patients got treated or seen in triage and released. Or arrested. Several of the patients that were brought back here were getting agitated," she recounted. "After Mr. Cane went crazy, Dr. Schwartz said that anyone exhibiting signs of possible violence should be sedated..." She waited for the look of horror she was expecting Mr. Rivas to give her. But it didn't come.

Instead he nodded his head. "For their own protection too," she said, defending the doctor.

He smiled. "I've known James for a while. If he asked you to sedate patients, he had a good reason." Raising the bag just a bit he finished, "Got to get these to the lab. Call us if anything else happens. In the meantime, suggest to the off-duty staff that they stay the night and don't discharge anyone."

He left before she could relay to him that they hadn't actually admitted anyone, not officially. Although cleaning crews had already managed to get things back into some kind of order, all Kate could see was chaos. Something was happening. She needed to go check on Morgan.

Before he drove off, Joaquin made a call to the office. "I have some samples of the substance they were talking about. I'm bringing them to you now." Before hanging up he added, "This whole situation is definitely weird, but I'm not sure if we should be sounding the alarm just yet."

...

The bar fights were rowdier, louder and more violent tonight. She'd been expecting that. She wasn't sure why she had made two grigri but she was sure it meant they were coming back to see Queenie. She just wanted to be ready. She had long since retreated to the safety of the loft, barring and locking the doors up tight. She didn't need any unexpected visitors.

She was convinced she had thoroughly driven the devil out. For tonight. The fact remained that the end was coming. It wasn't the cards that had gotten her so upset. No, but that surely didn't help matters. But these dreams she'd been having. Couldn't remember much, just the death. But not just that. As she looked around her dismal room, she sighed. This isn't where she'd meant to end up. But here she was.

Seemed like many of the bars were closing up shop early. They'd had it with the broken glasses and bar stools for the night. Granted, things usually did start getting out of hand this close to Mardi Gras. You had your tourists coming in early that don't want to deal with the extra crowds, some folk on Spring Break and even the locals working to get their last bit of partying in before they decided to avoid the area completely for a week.

Several of the shops up and down the street had been victimized by vandalism and a little looting. Small things here and there. Just enough to add insult to injury. Not unexpected, but not normal. No, nothing about tonight was normal at all. Even the air looked different. The peaceful currents of energy that flowed so carefully into each other had become broken and jagged. Queenie wondered if anyone else felt it too. This was only the beginning.

She gnawed a little on some of the Funyuns she'd had earlier. She'd gone and gotten another 40-ounce too. Just the thing she needed to keep her warm. It had grown chilly again but after the events of this morning she didn't feel like lighting a fire was the best idea. The blankets would do just fine. The world was going to be a different place tomorrow.

Always Darkest

Today had been a *long* day. It started with the explosion this morning and just kept coming. Iris took off her glasses and rubbed her eyes. The reports were making her cross eyed. She had been working as a detective in New Orleans for five years. There were eight precincts that all fell under her. Tonight, she had heard from all of them. Nothing she hadn't seen before. A few bar fights, some vandalism and other rage type disturbances. What had her baffled was the scene at University Medical.

To make matters worse, one of the nurses had actually called the CDC. Now they were already calling asking questions she couldn't answer just yet. The consensus from them had been that they weren't needed at this time, but talk about your panic situations. All of this didn't bode well for the next couple of weeks. She hated Mardi Gras.

The hospital had rushed the toxicology report on Cane. Everyone was actually surprised when the results came back clean. There had been no narcotics or other drugs found in his system. That bugged her. If it wasn't drugs, what had caused such a violent outburst?

"You still here?" one of the uniformed officers asked as he passed by.

She glanced at the huge clock on the wall. It was after midnight. It was already Sunday. Waving her hands over the overwhelming stack of papers she had collected throughout the day she sighed, "Let the good times roll."

"Need any help?" He was still walking slowly away. It was obvious he was ready to get out of there.

Sitting straight in her chair and stretching she replied, "I may just finish this up in the morning."

Satisfied that meant he didn't have to stay, the officer hurried his pace and disappeared around the corner. At least he was *willing* to stay. The tap of his shoes was all she could hear. As they grew fainter and finally faded, she yawned.

Fortunately, they had solved the explosion pretty quickly. It was definitely an accident, and only minimal injuries had been reported. She held up the sticky note with the occupant's name and phone number, it had been a miracle that the woman had gone to breakfast already. She needed to call her in the morning. Just had a couple of things they needed to know to wrap this one up. Mostly for the insurance, but it was important that she was thorough. She was always thorough.

There were still calls coming in from all over the Parish. Breaking and entering, domestic violence, unprovoked fights and other regular Saturday night business. Fortunately, with most of the businesses shutting down a little early tonight, those slowed down but it still seemed like a lot more than usual. The fire departments were overwhelmed as well. But except for the sheer volume, it was nothing unusual.

Finally deciding she'd had enough for the day, Iris shuffled everything together, stacked them and shoved them into the drawer in the desk. Reclaiming her glasses, she looked again at the clock on the wall. It was after one in the morning. How did so much time pass since the last time she looked at the clock? It was time to go home.

As she made her way out to her car, she noticed that several of the parking lot lights had been busted out. Likely kids throwing rocks or someone with a BB gun. It cast an eerie dark shadow across the area. The darkness didn't usually make her nervous, but tonight everything had a macabre sheen to it. She was exhausted.

By the time she reached her car, she had succumbed to three coughing fits. She could feel the croup bubble up from her lungs. "Just great," she muttered as she wiped the spittle from her lip. She then reminded herself, "I cannot deal with the flu right now."

...

The flood lights that illuminated the back-garden area had long since turned off. Hana realized they were on a motion sensor. Although she thought it was odd that Eddie hadn't come after her, she was relieved. She couldn't stay holed up in his backyard forever, but she had no idea what to do. She should have stayed home. She almost had. But it had been time, she had to finish. For Ebby. It was time to go home, but she couldn't bring herself to think about that yet.

Eddie sat quietly on the sofa bed. It was littered with rice and other parts of their discarded dinner. *They're not people. That's the only way you can get through this.* The sage advice he'd received from the senior partner after he started working on the case. Eddie never could quite see these people as faceless, and that's why he had quit. And now he was looking at one of those faces.

It took him about half an hour to muster up the courage or even the physical strength to go look for her. He just wished she hadn't gone out back. As he approached the sun room doors, he remembered and felt the pain in his arms and down his back and in his heart. He almost didn't join her. Breathing deeply, he pushed aside the nausea that was overwhelming him. "Hana."

As he stepped through the door the motion sensor caught him and flooded the yard with a soft white light. She was sitting on the porch swing slowly swinging back and forth. Without looking up at him she said, "What do you want me to say? I don't blame you." She didn't sound convincing. Obviously eager to change the subject she deflected, "What's up with the pool?" As soon as she asked, he looked like an overfilled balloon that had deflated.

Hours seemed to pass for him as he slowly made his way to the swing. He sat beside her but scooted as far to the edge as he could. He was sure she didn't want him touching her. Not now. "Not that it means anything, but I understand."

With no emotion she replied, "How can you possibly..." but stopped when she remembered the room upstairs. She was tired of being angry, tired of fighting it. "You were doing your job." The tone in her voice wasn't forgiveness. She stared off towards the eyesore.

Peering out at the shattered concrete and plaster he breathed deeply. *What was he doing? Was he giving her the short version? Was he telling her a story?* The truth is, if Rosalind hadn't been Rosalind, she'd be in jail. It wasn't that it was her fault, not completely. The worst part was that her life went on like normal. Realizing that she was waiting for something he finally said, "Five solid hours with a sledge hammer."

"What are you talking about?" She was confused.

Without looking at her, he reminded her what they were talking about. "The pool."

Reverently, she put aside her anger, understanding exactly what he was saying. Her heart sank. She looked over towards the empty crevice and saw the hammer lying just beside the ladder leading out of the pool. It was in pieces. The handle had been broken in 2 places and the head had been completely separated from the wood. "What happened?"

"It was three months ago. I don't even remember what we were fighting about." He sat back, it was obvious every breath he took was like re-living it over and over again. "It was late. Just a little after midnight. I was gone for maybe two, three hours tops. Had a couple of beers and came home." He sat up again, increasingly uncomfortable.

A pleasant fragrance of toasted sugar wafted past her. That's what the room had smelled like: cotton candy. Had he gone in there before he came out here? She didn't ask. He kept talking. "Rosalind was out cold. Her way of dealing with conflict is pretty much taking a Xanax and having a glass of wine," he snorted.

A lifetime seemed to pass through his eyes, although it had only been a few seconds since he quit talking. "It's okay," she urged him to stop.

"Dellie was our little miracle." He strayed, but not far. "We didn't think she was going to make it through her first couple of months.

She was born with very little immune system. So bringing her home was the single most amazing thing that ever happened to me." He looked down but didn't stop. Instead he navigated himself back to the topic. "So here I am, wandering around wondering why I was even still here. I was just going to peek in on her and remind myself why. But she wasn't in her bed. I didn't really panic until I noticed she wasn't in our bed either. She was *three years old.*"

His voice cracked, and she realized there were tears forming in his eyes. "Really, I get it. You don't have to keep..."

"Thank you." He wiped his face with the back of his hand and stood up. "Please come in. I'll take you anywhere you want to go in the morning."

She stood and reached for his hand. Remembering how hard the loss had been for her, she softened. She didn't want to go back to Tiki. She was a nervous ball of emotion. She was in no position to be making actual decisions tonight. Quietly she led him through the house and up the stairs. He didn't speak or let go of her hand.

...

The CDC had more than one function. Because Hollywood was fascinated with the terror, that's all they showed so people thought that was all they did. The truth was, Joaquin spent more time on environmental study than viruses. Aside from a couple of bad flu cases and the whole thing with Ebola a few years ago, his job was mostly just recognizing environmental hazards that could be health threats. And there were plenty of those.

Fortunately for him, this also meant that they had the ability to test anything he brought in at any time of day. This was no exception. He was greeted by a short but excitable lab technician. The dark halo of hair he still had left on his head was littered with gray strands. "What did you bring us?" he spouted as he reached his hand out.

Lifting the bag and passing it off to the stout man was a relief. It wasn't that he was afraid to have it in his possession. Truth was, he just didn't want to hang onto anything that resembled bodily fluids. No matter how many times he had to do this it creeped him out. "I have no idea. Thought you might have some guesses."

Joaquin explained everything he could about the incident at the hospital as they carefully opened the bag and removed the prepared containers. "Curious," the technician mused. He placed the containers on a sterile table, put on a pair of gloves and motioned for Joaquin to leave. "I can call you if you want."

"I could use a cup of coffee. I'll stick around for a bit." After that Joaquin stepped back and let them work. At least these guys made a good cup of coffee, that was a nice surprise. He wandered over to the break area to hang out a bit. It was late, but he was all worked up. He was always worked up. As he tipped the cup and took a big gulp, he recognized that the coffee wasn't helping.

The sterile smell of the surrounding rooms mixed with the fresh aroma of coffee created a strange odor as it wafted in. *At least it wasn't more bad breath,* Joaquin thought silently. He was lost in his head making mental notes of everything he needed to do when the short man found him. "That was fast," he said surprised.

It was obvious that something had confused the lab technician. "Are you sure you brought me the right samples?" He tried not to sound condescending but didn't quite land it.

Trying not to be offended Joaquin replied, "I brought you what they gave me."

"It's just that..." the man was obviously trying to figure out what to say. "This is just water."

...

Queenie tossed and turned until well after three o'clock. The dreams were more and more vivid. Although it was flames in her dreams, she knew that in reality there was something different coming. The fire was just a symbol. Chuckling to herself she thought, *I can't even dream right no more.* Finally deciding it was best to just get up, she stumbled into her house shoes and fumbled for a smoke. Getting a little jump on the dawn would be a good idea anyway.

This was the darkest time of the night. Before the sun started making its debut. She wondered if she was going to see those two today. More than likely they were going to have questions. Yeah, lots of questions.

She had heard various bumps in the night but didn't investigate. She wasn't schooled, but she knew better than to go sticking her neck out. Besides, she had bigger things to worry about. The dawn wasn't going to be kind she'd figured. Times like this she wished she had a television. But she didn't need the news folk to tell her about things she already knew.

She was able to make a full pot of coffee this morning. She'd probably need more. As the fragrance from the brew reached her, she was already feeling more alert. The usual ray of artificial light from the street lamp below didn't find its way through the curtains. In all of the commotion last night, someone must have broken it out. Or maybe it had been the explosion.

Either way, she couldn't see and lit some candles. As the dancing flames projected shadows on the wall, she sat back and read the story they were telling. The shadows cast by various items around the cluttered room seemed to paint a mural on the wall. Because this old place was drafty, the light of the candles was moving constantly. Yes, today was the day. She was almost certain of it. As she sipped at the hot steaming black liquid, she decided it was time to venture out. But maybe she'd wait until first light.

...

Kate had been at the hospital for almost twenty-four hours. She was exhausted. They all were. Fortunately, by one o'clock in the morning everything had calmed down. If people were sick, they weren't coming here. Morgan hadn't regained consciousness. He took a hard hit with that head to the wall. Nothing broken. She just hoped he hadn't been too badly injured.

Crews had cleaned up the mess in record time. Sort of. There were fresh sheets of plywood stacked neatly outside, waiting for morning to board up what they could. The broken machinery and other things that had littered the hallways had already been deposited in the dumpster. At least what couldn't be salvaged.

The gaping holes in the wall weren't a big deal. But it didn't look good. They were probably going to have to do something about that tomorrow too. Kate was relieved that the administrators would handle all of that.

There were more people than necessary bustling around. But since they didn't know what had caused the surge in patients, everyone was on edge. No matter how many times she played the conversation in her head she wasn't convinced that Mr. Rivas believed that it was connected. He didn't seem to take it all that seriously.

It was about three-thirty by the time she found an empty room on the second floor. There were more than enough people on duty now. She wanted some quiet. She needed sleep.

No one had noticed the homeless man that pushed his basket up to the front of the hospital. Usually at this time of the night there were people leaving or coming in. He had probably come to see if he could beg a dollar or two before he went to sleep. As the automatic doors opened, he pushed his cart inside.

He was mumbling something indistinct and continued pushing his belongings towards the front desk. Before he could make his way beyond the door separating the waiting room from the ER, two orderlies appeared in his way.

"You need some help?" the first one spoke with genuine concern.

As he continued to mumble, the shuffling man raised his voice to just above a whisper in mid-sentence, "...sword, and with hunger, and with death, and with the beasts of the Earth."

The other orderly stepped towards the man gently attempting to stop him from ambling forward any more. There was no aggression in his stance. The feeble, smelly old man pushed forward. Gently placing his hands on the basket, attempting to stop the old man without actually touching him, he felt a slight rhythmic vibration on the metal grid.

Still mumbling, the man tried to push forward again. Raising his voice slightly again, mid-sentence he spat out, "...and his name that sat on him was Death, and Hell followed with him"

The other orderly made a quick call to security and the uniformed officer was there within moments.

By the time the officer had arrived the old haggard man had become agitated. He yelled out, "And I looked, and behold a pale horse and his name that sat on him was Death, and Hell followed with him."

Struggling violently to push past the obstacles that were thwarting his entry into the emergency room, he rammed the basket into the security officer several times. The repeated impact caused the contents of the basket to shift, revealing an LED readout. As the guard peered inside, he realized it was a timer counting down. There was only one second left.

On A Pale Horse

Sunday morning came crashing through the almost, but not quite closed curtains. The rays screamed at Rosalind, setting off fireworks in her head. The light was punctuated by the crashing thunder in her ears. She was getting too old to drink like that, but the world just kept coming at her. Olivia stirred and turned over but didn't wake up. She left her sleeping.

The shower didn't get nearly hot enough, but the pressure was amazing. She stood letting the water hit her face for several minutes. The clean smell of the soap and shampoo cleared her head a bit. A Bloody Mary would work better. As she finished and began to dress, she relished the fact that nobody was bothering her right now. These conferences always stressed her out because everyone wanted to be social. No one wanted to be social today.

Regret crept through her. Everyone thought she was cold, unfeeling and didn't care. That wasn't true. She just knew better. Her entire career, she had to constantly prove herself. Although many brilliant women had littered scientific history, it was still considered a man's job. She was always, really smart *for a girl,* had amazing ideas *for a girl.* It was even worse when she had been pregnant. As the thought crept into her head, she pushed it back. She didn't need that drama bubbling up.

She was in no hurry to go home. Truth was, she was already looking at apartments in Montreal. That's why the delay in the conference wasn't a huge inconvenience for her. She hadn't even told Olivia she was thinking of staying. She wasn't sure she wanted to tell her. She wasn't sure what she wanted, but she knew she needed a change. She was sinking.

By the time she'd finished dressing, Olivia was up and looking out the window. A commotion out front seemed to have her attention. Almost whispering, Olivia managed, "Good morning," and winced as the vibrations in her head rattled through her jaw. "Fucking hell," she winced again.

"I told you..." Rosalind started to chastise her for drinking so much, then changed her mind. "I'll get you something for your head." She had hoped to slip out while Olivia was still sleeping, but that wouldn't be possible now. Digging through her travel bag she found the bottle of aspirin and tossed it to her. She just wanted a little time to herself.

"What do you think this is all about?" Olivia called her attention to the window. Several marked cars and uniformed officers were parked haphazardly around the parking lot. Something very official was going on. Closing the curtains all the way she tried to change the mood. "It's Sunday, love. Let's just get some breakfast and mimosas," she nearly sang the words. Olivia's answer to everything. Food and drinks. Mostly drinks.

Before she had a chance to answer a loud, frantic rapping sounded at the door. They knocked so many times that by the time Rosalind crossed the room to answer, they were still knocking. "What is so important that..." she began as she opened the door.

Standing outside were several uniformed SVPM officers. "Rosalind Bélisaire?" the officer close to her spoke.

"What NOW?" she hissed back, realizing that had been a mistake as he presented a pair of handcuffs.

"We need you to come with us." His accent was a thick mix of French and English. But what he was saying was extremely clear.

A hot wave of nausea shot through her as she tried to grasp what they could possibly be thinking. "You're joking right?"

The stoic expression on the officer's face did not change. Instead he indicated for her to turn and locked the hand cuffs on her slowly. "Let's not make this unpleasant." She wasn't sure if the cuffs hurt worse or her pride as she realized that she was being arrested. *Unpleasant?*

"What on earth for?" Her voice shook.

Corralling her out the door and down the hall he answered, "The murder of Dr. Noah Patel."

"Murder?" The word tasted horrible on Rosalind's tongue as she spit it out. "Someone killed him?" She had given them everything they asked for. She had been exactly where she had told them she'd been, for every moment. She didn't *kill* anyone. How could they possibly suspect her? As he rattled off her rights or whatever he was saying her mind raced.

Almost unable to breathe, Rosalind forced out a terrified squeak to Olivia. "Call *somebody,*" she pleaded.

...

Iris arrived at University Medical shortly after dawn. Her head was pounding, but the daytime flu medicine she had taken was finally taking affect. The first responders and fire rescue had cleared the scene as safe. Sort of. Many of the patients were being moved between buildings and the parade of wheelchairs and gurneys flowed through the side doors. The damage wasn't as bad as it could have been, but why would he have done this?

Many of the homeless had spent time in and out of the city jail, simply for trespassing violations or other misdemeanors. Nate wasn't aggressive. As a matter of fact, he wasn't even a drinker or drug user. He had never seemed unstable. Just down on his luck. And missing a few screws. That certainly wasn't a crime. Something else had to be going on. Didn't it?

The blast had been relatively small but all four of them had been killed instantly. There was a lot of glass debris, pieces of twisted metal and wood but at least the design of the hospital kept the damage from affecting any patient rooms. Aside from the two security guards and Nate, there were no other casualties.

The commotion towards the back of the building caught her attention and Iris navigated around the tape to join Dr. Schwartz and Kate,who seemed to be arguing. Kate was speaking frantically when she approached. "I'm telling you, I did. He was there when I started my shift. He's not there now. There is no way he could have gotten up and walked out."

It was obvious the doctor did not believe whatever she was saying, and he was going through a patient's chart in his hands. The folder was labeled *Cane, Bo*. "Nobody is accusing you of anything. Things have been insane since last night. Are you sure you didn't miss something?"

"What's going on?" Iris gently butted in.

With almost a pleading look in her eyes Kate shot out, "Bo is gone." Adding frantically, "But his clothes were laid out in the middle of the bed. And the bed was soaked. Completely soaked. Unless he found some clothes, he is wandering around naked somewhere. He can't be that hard to find."

Before she had a chance to react, another nurse approached them in a panic. "Dr. Schwartz, we have a problem." Acknowledging that she had interrupted their conversation, the nurse nodded and continued, "We can't find Elmer Borre."

Without waiting for the doctor to react Iris questioned, "What do you mean you can't find him?"

The young woman looked back and forth between the doctor and the detective. He nodded for her to continue. "Go ahead," he encouraged her.

Taking her cue, she hurriedly said, "It's like he pissed the bed. The *entire* bed, took off his gown and left."

...

"They *cannot* be serious," Eddie barked into the phone just after answering. He began to pace frantically back and forth across the tiled hallway. The tap of his shoes even sounded panicked. Hana could hear him from where she was sitting. Whoever called obviously had bad news. That seemed to be the going theme.

As he struggled to comprehend what was happening, the tiny voice on the other end replied, "I don't know what happened. I can't even wrap my head around this." Her soft breathing continued, but it appeared she had finished her thought. He disconnected the call and sat quietly for a moment. What was happening?

Hanging his head, he glanced up towards Hana. Things had gone from surreal to devastating. She was watching something on her phone. Likely avoiding any conversation. What could he possibly say to her anyway? Especially now.

In disbelief she looked up at Eddie when he approached her, "Someone blew up the hospital." A wave of empathy crossed her heart as she imagined another parent angry at the system. It hadn't been the case here, but it would have been poetic. That thought was pushed aside as she swiped for the next story. The headline not only caught her eye, but Eddie saw it over her shoulder. "Dr. Rosalind Bélisaire arrested for the murder of Dr. Noah Patel."

She didn't know what to say. She didn't look up. The Bélisaire family was one constant cataclysm. Had they actually managed to take her whole family from her? She felt like she was sitting in enemy territory and she had no clear way out.

He could see it in her eyes. She was terrified. She had every right to be. He was looking for words. "Rosalind is a *lot* of things." He shook his head sorrowfully, "But there is no way she killed your..." Stuttering slightly he finished his thought. "There is no way she killed him." He looked sincere. Deep inside him, his conscious was screaming the whole time. He had, by no means, forgiven Rosalind for anything. He mumbled, "She's not a murderer."

Remembering his promise from last night, he attempted to change the subject. "Where do you want to go?" What was he supposed to do? Was he supposed to abandon Hana and head to Montreal? What good would it do?

"Don't you think you should be booking a flight?" Hana tapped the screen of her phone several times bringing up the Uber app. "I can get a ride."

"Hana..." There were no words he could say that would change what was unfolding. She must be terrified, angry and alone. He should just let her go. Let her get in the Uber and leave. She'd be way better off. Why did he want to beg her to stay?

As the app opened, she let out a frustrated sigh. *No cars available.*

"You can take me to the bus station," she spoke emotionless. Shoving her charging cable in her purse, she stood. As she browsed the Greyhound site, she almost moaned. "Are you *kidding* me?" All of the bus routes had been delayed or canceled for the day. What was going on?

"Hana." She was frantic, a glazed sort of panic had washed over her. She had the look of a terrified deer being caught on a dark night by oncoming lights. He didn't know what to say. He was surprised at how much it bothered him that she was looking at him that way. "Let me..."

"Let you what?" She was rabid, like a caged animal that had just found its way out of a trap. "What could you possibly do *to* me that you haven't done already?" Bolting from the den, she almost slipped on the slick marble but righted herself as she made it to the front. Opening the heavy carved wooden monstrosity, she gasped. The acrid smell of fire assaulted her senses, causing her eyes to water and her throat to constrict. "What the hell is going on?"

From over the trees, in every direction were pockets of black smoke billowing over what seemed to be structure fires. A Coast Guard helicopter passed in the distance. A cluster of 3 military jets flew overhead drowning out her voice for a moment. In the distance sirens blared. It was as though all of New Orleans were burning. They were in the back of a gated community, but the chaos seemed to be spiraling inward even here as she noticed the house down the road was ablaze.

She almost lunged out the door as her phone began to shriek in her hand. By the time Eddie reached her in the foyer, his phone had begun to sound as well. It was a Civil Emergency Alert. Orleans Parish had issued a voluntary shelter in place. There was no explanation. From off in the distance the sound of a rifle firing was taken over by a repeating weapon. Reaching over her head, Eddie pulled the door until it latched.

Fumbling with his phone he looked through his contacts for his friend at NOPD. Detective Warner. The phone rang twice and went to voicemail. "Come on Iris." He ended the call before the message tone sounded and dialed again.

Answering this time, Iris sputtered, "I don't have time right now, Eddie." She spoke before he could say anything. "Things are a little crazy."

"What's going on?" he tried to ask as quickly as possible, thinking she might hang up.

Sighing she responded, "I wish I knew." Wheezing and fighting a cough she added as an afterthought, "Just stay home." It was a definitive instruction. Sirens and noise bled through the background.

Without waiting for him to speak again, she ended the call.

...

The sounds of breaking glass and gunfire began just as the sun was making its appearance. Not that either of those sounds separately wasn't a normal part of the seedy side of New Orleans, but it was the constant crescendo of noises that reminded Queenie, the crazy had begun.

She spent the first hour of the day back, back and forth across her one room loft. She found a small canvas bag and began putting in what few things she owned. If she was going to survive this, she was going to have to get out of here. They should be here today. She saw it in the fire. She had seen so many things in the fire.

Peering down at the street below her, she noticed that a news van had pulled up on the corner. They were fumbling around the back of the van, getting their cameras and broadcast gear ready. The cute blonde girl was way overdressed for a war zone. Queenie tried not to chuckle as she foreshadowed the woman running for her life in those stilts she called shoes. She'd be barefoot soon. Chastising herself silently, she regained her solemn mood. Nothing funny about what was coming.

The mayhem breeding since last night was only the beginning. The exterior of the building shook a bit as the sound of shattering windows beneath her materialized. They wouldn't find anything of any interest. Although she knew the staircase wasn't *really* invisible, she had been chanting her prayer. Obviously disinterested in what was inside, the vandal left. She didn't have anything worth looting anyway.

It wasn't the madness that scared her the most. That wasn't going to last long. It was the deaths that were sure to follow. She still couldn't see some of the finer details, but she knew it had started. Her whole life she had been preparing for this moment. She'd seen it over and over again in her dreams. What she hadn't seen was the kind of darkness that just one girl could carry with her. But it wasn't her fault.

Death didn't always come running up on you in a civilized manner. No, as a matter of fact it was more likely he was going to get you when you weren't looking. But she was looking. And he was still coming. Commotion from outside caught her attention again and she opened the decaying curtains. As the burst of light shone in, it caught the dust and smoke particles in the air and created an image before her.

A stallion standing on his hind legs, no rider in sight. As she breathed out, the horse appeared to gallop away. The shadows danced on the wall for a short time with no form and she lost interest. From down the street, another small explosion sounded. She jumped a little but reminded herself this was going to go on for a while. As it was with the end of the world. Not everyone had gotten the memo yet.

Extinguishing all of the candles at the altar and making sure there were no coals remaining, Queenie retrieved her meager belongings and hobbled slowly down the steps. She collected the few good luck charms as she silently bid the broken-down building goodbye. She was going to miss this place most of all but moving on wasn't new to her. It had just been a while.

She considered cleaning up the mess, setting the table back upright. She thought about lighting the candles and retreating into prayer. She almost didn't want to leave the protection she was sure she had created over the years. But it was time.

As she sat on the sidewalk rocking back and forth in her chair, she waited. Toying with the grigri around her neck, she watched the news people running towards the most recent boom. Quietly she recited from the book of Habakkuk, "Before him goes pestilence, and plague comes after him."

Lunacy

"I see you've done some rearranging since last night." Joaquin greeted Dr. Schwartz with a handshake.

The doctor looked weary, but he managed a chuckle. "I can't even begin to explain what is happening." The main entrance to the hospital had been completely boarded up. The side entries were open, and someone had even made some hand drawn signs pointing to the alternate entrances. There was a line forming at one of the doors. "And this..." he motioned towards the line, "Nonstop all morning."

"Any ideas?" Joaquin looked around him at the continuing chaos and realized that the nurses must have gotten something mixed up last night. He didn't want to sound accusatory, but he needed to find out what they might be dealing with.

"Doesn't really fit the flu," the doctor replied quickly, "but it's definitely contagious. Most of our staff is here, either working or sick." The hospital had continued handing out masks to everyone that came through the doors. It had obviously done no good. "No more ragers. Well, except for that." He pointed towards the plywood walls.

"Was Nate in as a patient?" He was dancing around what he really wanted to ask, but he wasn't sure how to bring it up. You don't just go accusing people of screwing up. But with everything going on at the hospital, it was the most likely answer.

"Hell, I don't know," he answered quickly, and surprisingly honestly. "I'm not even sure everyone was recorded." He realized how incompetent that made the hospital sound, but if there was something going on it needed to get solved immediately.

Seeing the admission of chaos as an opening, Joaquin asked, "So, with all the confusion I think we may have taken the wrong package last night."

While Dr. Schwartz had been slightly distracted for most of the conversation, he turned his full attention to Joaquin. "Why would you say that?" His head was pulsing. He felt flush. The noise around him completely vanished. He could smell his own breath in the mask. What else had they screwed up?

"Apparently, the prepared samples we got were just water." Looking around again at the mess, and the crowd he said, "How are the patients? We may need to get another sample."

...

"So, are we all going to die?" Hana joked, but it didn't land. The look on Eddie's face was heart breaking. He looked like he was about to crumble.

Circumstances had forced them to occupy the same space for a short time. No matter how hard she tried to be, she wasn't mad at him. Whatever was going on in Montreal had everything to do with Noah and nothing to do with Eddie. Hell, if Rosalind had killed Noah, she probably had a good reason. She was almost ashamed at the last thought. Almost.

They didn't speak as she followed him back to the den to turn on the television. Local news was on every channel. They all seemed to be narrating the same scene all over the Parish. Disturbances leading to violence. Violence leading to fire and who knew what else. It was like the entire city had gone crazy. Flipping through the channels, Eddie stopped at another news story, live from Bourbon Street.

The woman on the scene was already in the middle of her story. "And with Mardi Gras just a little over a week away, for the first time in history it's looking like the Quarter may be completely shut down." The camera panned the corner and showed the bar where they had met. From somewhere off sides a small explosion sounded. The camera lurched and then panned into the drama unfolding behind them. The reporter ran to get in front of the lens again, she was carrying her shoes in her hand.

From the angle, it appeared that the entire Quarter was burning to the ground. Hana whispered weakly, "What's happening?"

He had often wondered why something like this hadn't happened before. So much anger just waiting to blow. And with so many people in such a concentrated area, it was bound to multiply. Someone had obviously lit the fire and the whole stand was about to go.

The rocking motion in the background caught their eyes at the same time. It was Queenie, sitting on her rocking chair as though it were an ordinary day. The old bat had taken up her ever-vigilant post. She had changed her clothes and was wearing what must have been her Sunday best. Beside her feet were her cane and a dirty canvas sack.

Hana watched him as he wrestled with something in his head. "You want to go rescue her, don't you?" He *was* one of the nice guys. He just got caught up in all of this, whatever this all was. "You're making this 'hating you' thing pretty difficult."

He blushed and dropped his head. "She can't stay there. I don't think anyone is coming for her," he admitted. "I kind of think she's waiting for us." He argued inside himself. She should hate him. He hated him. "Does that sound ridiculous?"

She tried to stop it before it surfaced. A cross between a laugh and an all-out cackle escaped as she thought of the sight of the three of them driving around New Orleans in his sports car. Once the laughter broke, she couldn't stop herself and continued to almost wheeze uncontrollably for several minutes. With tears streaming down her face, she waved her hands a few times to indicate that she was okay. Eddie was completely confused but had to stop himself twice from joining in the laughter. It was contagious.

As she was able to finally catch her breath he whispered, "So, you don't hate me?"

She didn't. She wanted to. But she didn't. That wasn't the part that bugged her. What bothered her the most is how, despite everything that was going on, she wanted him. Pushing that thought aside she replied, "I am trying to." Then, reaching for her bag and standing, she turned and walked towards the front door. "Are we going then?"

Digging through what looked like a catch-all drawer, he pulled out a set of keys. As they stepped outside, she realized there was a van parked in the colossal drive that she hadn't noticed when they arrived yesterday. The way he approached it seemed timid, almost afraid. Although he had already started the van from the house, the doors were still locked, and he rushed around to get the passenger door for her first. He froze for a moment as he looked behind the seat and saw the car seat.

Her heart ached for him as he visibly tried to toss off the thoughts by shaking his head back and forth. "It's been a while since I drove the..."

"I get it." She touched his hand and climbed in. He closed her door then opened the back slide and removed the seat with fervent speed. After setting it on the drive, he closed the door and walked around to the front again. He drove off, carefully avoiding having to look at the discarded safety device. Attempting to address the white elephant she managed to speak. "So, rescue Queenie...then what?"

He had no idea.

...

Things had gone from bad to worse to way worse overnight. Plowing through officer reports was a horrible way to start the day. Her head was pounding. The same story played out all over the Parish. He/She just went nuts, shot the place up, started the fire, went crazy with the axe. The axe wasn't even the most bizarre case. But what it boiled down to was that something bad was rising. And they did not have it under control.

"You look like shit, Warner." The somewhat playful jest pulled her back to the station and what was going on around her. Realizing he was offering her a cup of coffee, she sighed and reached up to receive it.

"Thanks," she said, unclear if she was thanking him for the coffee or the "compliment". But she did need the coffee.

Pulling up a chair he sat opposite from her at the desk. Because of the thin sheet of metal on the back, he had to sit sideways to lean in. It wasn't odd for her to take his office over when she needed to concentrate. This was one of those times. He was okay with sharing his desk with her. "You look like you could use some help."

"Seriously?" Taking off her glasses she rubbed her eyes. "I can handle a little paperwork." She was surprised at how defensively that had come out. "Sorry, I'm just tired." The suppressant had begun to wear off and she was fighting the urge to cough. Clearing her throat forcefully she said, "Does all of this seem a bit much to you?"

Sergeant Denning was a career cop. Been at the same place for over twenty years. Approaching his mid-fifties, the department had encouraged him to retire. Promised him a nice pension, but he just couldn't do it. "It's been a bit much already for years. This is absolute insanity."

Pushing the stack of files that she had already gone through towards him she relented, "Yes please, what am I missing?" As a trailing thought she added, "What the hell am I even looking for?" Were all of these cases related? Were they all just bizarre coincidence?

They both sat reading in silence. Neither was sure for exactly how long. The drone of the clock caught her in her nerves. Tick, tick, tick, tick, tick. She was trying to shut it out and focus on making sense of these incident reports as Sgt. Denning began to click the back of his pen. The thin metal thunk wasn't as fast as the clock, and it created a dissonant rhythm that slowly grated at her.

A dull roar began in the back of her head. Was it voices? Was she hearing voices? She was. As the noise of a disturbance from somewhere around the corner reached her, she realized someone must have made their way around the posted officers and was on a tirade down the hall. Relieved the noise wasn't in her head, she let out a sigh followed by a fit of coughs she couldn't control.

As the commotion moved its way closer to the end of the hall, she heard a single gunshot. Instinctively, Iris was at attention with her weapon drawn. From where she was standing, she could not see around the corner of the hallway. Whatever was happening was just out of her view. The Sergeant was still seated, visibly confused by her behavior. "What's going on, Iris?" he asked calmly.

The look in her eyes was almost wild. As the sounds of a struggle increased, she became more agitated. "I can't see from here," she whispered, then hacked. The putrid smelling phlegm landed on her hand.

Oddly, the Sergeant remained seated. "What do you hear?" He almost looked confused. He seemed to be straining to catch up with her, wherever she was.

"You have got to be kidding me! You can't hear that?" she half whispered. Slowly, she stepped just out of the door towards the hallway. The voices were so loud. It was as though each were trying to be heard over the other. But the swirling chaos it created made the scene completely indecipherable. Retreating to the radio back at the desk, she pressed the button. "What's happening out there?"

There was a slight hiss on the channel before a voice answered, "What do you mean?" The voice was immediately drowned out by the sound of rapid fire.

"A little help?" She looked back at Sgt. Denning who had finally stood up.

"Iris," he cautiously approached her with a frightened look in his eyes. Extending his hand slowly he whispered, "There's nothing out there. Give me that," indicating that he wanted her gun. A bead of perspiration rolled down the side of his face from his brow. Without taking his eyes off of her he called down the hall, "Need some help in my office."

Before he was finished calling out two uniformed officers came sprinting around the corner. Iris spun wildly, facing the Sergeant, reacting to his call for help. From behind her she heard one of the officers yell, "Put the gun down."

Not certain who they were talking to, she turned again to face the noise. Her knees began to shake and threatened to collapse. Coughing, she squeezed the trigger on her weapon by mistake. Each of the officers managed to get one shot off before the detective collapsed to the floor.

...

Morgan woke up disoriented and confused. His head was throbbing. His left side hurt. He remembered being tossed into the wall. He didn't remember anything after that. The door to the room was open slightly and the daily goings on of the hospital sounded from the hall. The last thing he remembered before blacking out was watching Kate fly through the air. *Kate!* He shot up too quickly and regretted it immediately as the pain washed over him. Reaching down the side of the bed, he located the remote and pressed the *Nurse* button.

Flipping it over in his hand he fumbled for the *TV* button as well. As the picture glowed brighter, he saw the scene in the French Quarter.

He tapped the button *Up* and the next channel was re-broadcasting a story from earlier in the morning. They were standing outside the hospital. *THIS* hospital. The volume was down and as he pressed the button to raise it, the caption caught his eye. "Suspected suicide bombing at University Medical."

"What the hell?" he called out to no one. Realizing that no one had responded to the beacon, he attempted to stand but was caught off guard again at how dizzy he had become. That must have been a hard hit. How was that even possible? He pressed the *Nurse* button again, twice.

"Morgan, I am so glad you're awake." Kate came ushering through the door as soon as she saw the light from his room. "How are you *feeling?*" Her emphasis on the word "feeling" was strange. He was unable to see most of her face, as she was wearing a mask.

"What's going on?" He scanned the room wildly; his vision was still slightly blurred and she seemed to weave back and forth in front of him. She was so beautiful. He was still so groggy from sleep.

Checking the instruments and taking all of the normal vitals she casually answered, "Oh you know, the usual. Superhuman strength, disappearing patients and earth-shattering explosions."

"How long was I out?" He realized that it sounded like such a cliché as he said it.

"It's just Sunday morning," she answered. Satisfied everything was the way it should be she sat down in the chair next to the bed. It was obvious she was exhausted. "Just stay in bed. Trust me," she sighed warily as the pager system indicated she was needed at the nurses' station. "I'll be back in a little bit."

Turning his attention back to the television he understood what Kate meant. It was as though the entire city had gone crazy overnight. They were reporting stories from all over the area that all sounded the same. There was speculation being shared on the airwaves. Was a deadly virus sweeping the city? Could there be something in the water? Could there be something in the air? While the anchor was speaking a voice broke in, interrupting her.

"We're just being informed that there has been a shooting at the NOPD office on South Broad." They switched cameras to someone sitting at a desk elsewhere. "We don't have anyone on the scene yet, but from what we understand there has been one casualty." Looking off to the side at someone obviously directing him he continued, "Detective Iris Warner." Nodding he looked back at the camera and smiled. "We'll have more as it develops. Sorry for the interruption, Liza, back to you."

"Just unbelievable." Liza faked her news smile and continued with her previous topic. "Reports from all over the city are still coming in. Mayhem and madness. Stay tuned to be sure you're up to the minute on all of the chaos." She sounded like she was delivering a sales pitch for the station. Keep them panicked and cut to commercial.

As the TV clown droned on in the background about his newest coronary on a bun, Morgan felt himself becoming drowsy. Maybe staying in bed was a good idea for now. Although the pain had subsided, his head was still spinning. Tasting the almost metallic odor that escaped his breath, he realized that Kate must have given him another dose of Demerol.

Trying to keep his eyes open, he caught the scuffle outside his door. Shadows were dancing as people were moving back and forth down the hall. There was a loud noise from somewhere in the distance. It sounded like something big crashing to the floor. His senses were muted by the quick action of the narcotic. It sounded like something from far away. But he felt vibrations.

As he tried desperately to focus on anything, Morgan realized he had lost the battle as everything faded into darkness. Sleep had completely enveloped him again.

Fault Lines

The sun crested to its highest point in the sky and the shadows shifted. Whatever promise the day may have held for a great many people in NOLA had long been extinguished. The normal crowds exiting their worship did not find their way into the Quarter today. She imagined that the normal crowds hadn't found their way to worship at all.

Queenie rocked patiently as she waited. Not even the street performers had made it out today. There was an eerie silence across the Quarter that she hadn't heard in a very long time. Sure, there was a hustle. All sorts of chaos up and down the roads. But that wasn't the silent part. It was the spirit of the Quarter—it was as though it had up and left.

Still enjoying the spoils of her windfall from Saturday morning, she pulled out a fresh cigarillo and sipped on a paper cup full of lukewarm coffee she had picked up just before the corner store got robbed. No one was hurt. Thief got spooked by something and took off without the spoils. But it was enough that the shop owner decided to close the gate and call it off for the day. Just as well, since most of the roads and intersections were impassable all around.

All except the road out front, which worked out just right for her. She wouldn't have to walk. The sweet scent of tobacco and the faint aroma of coffee that lingered on her breath crept up her sinuses. It was a lot nicer than the fire she'd been tasting for the past little while.

About a lifetime or two ago, she used to sing at the bar across the way. It was all trendy now, but in its day, it was a beautiful space. Dark, smoky and full of subtle sexuality. Of course, she always came in the back, but the line of men coming in the front was for her. They doted on her like a movie star. She had gotten spoiled. More so than any decent woman should be. She always believed that was why she started seeing. It was her penance.

At first the parlor tricks were fun. They got old fast, for her and for her no longer adoring public. But that's where she'd come to. The crowbar to the throat hadn't helped her career either. But that was so long ago. And none of it mattered anyway.

The news folk had made their way back up to her side of the road, focused on something behind her. She hadn't even cared enough to turn around and see what it was. Just more of the same. She almost chuckled out loud when she saw the little blonde carrying her shoes in one hand and that microphone in the other, but she was able to stop herself.

She thought to herself, *Whatever those two were waiting on, they*

sure were taking a long time. "I'll wait," she announced to the breeze and began quietly singing the only Sunday School hymn she could remember all the way through. "Glory, glory, Hallelujah...His truth is marching on."

...

As the officers ushered Rosalind through the entrance of the Provincial Jail, the circus was waiting. A crowd had gathered outside, creating a sweltering feeling even though it was freezing. Her hands had pretty much fallen asleep behind her back and her fingertips were so cold they hurt. Random call outs from media and the other riffraff that had gathered kept her looking around. Realizing that she didn't really want to be recognized, she hung her head instead.

There was a hallway and a turn. And then endless rooms with people running back and forth. It smelled like body odor and stale beer. The man she assumed was a representative of the Consulate seemed to be arguing with the officers. She was instructed to stand here, turn that way, put her hand here, it all bled together. With more than one person speaking at a time she couldn't decipher all of the instructions they were throwing at her, she was trying not to cry. What was happening?

Her shoulders felt strained, as though they'd been pulled out of socket and her wrists were sore where they had tightened the restraints. Somehow, she made it through the grueling processing and instead of taking her to a jail cell, they took her to a small room with a table and three chairs. It was comically familiar, like every terrible police movie she'd ever seen. At least they removed the hand cuffs. Someone even brought her a bitter cup of black coffee. At least it was warm.

Looking around, she realized there was no clock on the wall. She could have been here for ten minutes or two hours. She had no idea. It felt like two hours. Certainly, someone was going to realize their mistake soon. Realize that they had the wrong person. *That must be why things were taking so long,* she lied to herself.

Had someone actually killed him? What had he been in to? Rosalind imagined that the list of people that wanted him to die was probably quite long. He was rude, unapologetic, crass, completely uncultured and conceited. He rubbed everyone the wrong way. But still, how could someone have killed him?

Although it wasn't as cold as outside, the room was still uncomfortably below average temperature. She hadn't had a chance to put on anything warm. They took everything they could when she arrived anyway. Jewelry, shoes, accessories and even the little scarf tied in her hair. Still damp from the shower, it hung in a matted mess around her face. She could still smell her conditioner.

The man in the navy suit from the Consulate finally joined her. "I'm sorry to keep you waiting." Sitting down across from her, he crossed his hands on the table. "So, what happened?"

"You tell me?" she groaned. It wasn't that she didn't want to cooperate, but she didn't know what he wanted her to say. "Do they think I actually killed that man?" Her distaste for Dr. Patel was obvious by the way her words slipped out. She realized that was probably not a good thing.

"I'm not your attorney. You don't need to tell me anything," he said matter-of-factly. "But, due to the nature of this whole..." It seemed he was looking for the best words. Finding them he continued, "...this whole distasteful incident, it might benefit you to tell me everything."

Distasteful? That's what it was these days to murder someone? Distasteful? Her nose and mouth curled into a slight snarl. "I didn't do this."

Leaning in he confided, "That doesn't matter." As he sat up straight again, he added, "At this time, they're offering you legal representation. I'd at least hear them out."

"I have my own attorney," she said staunchly. She understood that he wouldn't believe anything she was going to say. It was obvious he thought she was guilty. It was also obvious that he didn't care. He was definitely not here for her best interests. He was here to represent his country, not her.

"No, you don't," he snapped then reminded her, "You're not in Kansas anymore." Although he didn't grin, he should have. She could hear it in his voice.

Sipping at the bitter liquid, which had gotten cold at record speed, she bunched up her face in distaste. "I didn't fucking do it." She hoped that her annoyance had been relayed this time.

"I told you, that doesn't matter. Here's the thing...," it was apparent he was trying to figure out the best way to deliver his message, "...if you don't want to stay here in Canada for a very long time, you're going to need to talk to me. We are working as hard as we can to get this transferred to our courts." He suggested that like it made her feel better. She was still being charged for something she didn't do.

"They don't care about you or Dr. Patel. Two Americans. If it were just that we'd already be flying you home and charging you there. The **PROBLEM** here is that The Queen Elizabeth was torched. Other guests were injured. People died." Adding almost as punctuation, "Do you understand?"

She didn't speak. She didn't look up from the cup. What was she supposed to do? They thought she was responsible for the fire too.

This was getting out of hand. Fortunately, Olivia had contacted all the right people. At least she assumed it had been Olivia. It was likely she had also called Eddie. Whether he would help or not, she didn't know. At this point it didn't even matter. Maybe she'd be better off disappearing in a Canadian prison.

Truth be told, she deserved this. She knew that. She deserved much worse. This was Karma's way of catching up to her. Shaking that thought she steeled herself. "What do you want me to do?"

...

Sergeant Denning had finally managed to get the media parade out of the station and down to the walk. While they were being distracted, the body of Iris Warner slipped out the back in an unmarked coroner's van. The vultures completely missed it driving off.

Slowly making his way down the hall back towards his office, he paused. Whatever Iris had thought was happening, she thought was happening here. He slowly turned the corner. The faint smell of gun powder still lingered. They hadn't completely cleaned up and the blood stains screamed at him. What did she think she was hearing? What did she think was going on? It was obvious she'd been hallucinating. That was the only explanation.

He had worked with her for years. She was the most level-headed person he'd ever known. But she'd lost it. She had seen something happening, right in front of her, that wasn't happening at all. The same story that had been narrated over and over again in the reports they were reviewing. Everything happened so fast, so sudden. He was still having trouble processing the whole situation.

It was unclear which of the officers actually hit Iris, at least for now. But no charges would be filed, no suspensions issued. Both clearly acted within the law. She had fired at them. It didn't mean they weren't both a mess, but they were still on the clock. Everyone that could was working. That couldn't last for long. Things had gotten completely out of hand.

Annoyed by the ringing phone on his desk, he almost turned and walked out of the office. Instead he picked it up. "What?" He couldn't handle any more questions today.

"Is this Sgt. Denning?" The deep voice sounded official. Without actually waiting for him to answer he continued, "This is Joaquin Rivas. Epidemiologist at the CDC."

"What's going on?" He didn't know what else to say. It was highly unlikely that someone from the CDC was calling to give him information. It was much more likely he was calling to ask questions.

A heavy sigh preceded his response. "I have no idea." He cleared his throat and continued. "What happened there?" Joaquin had already contacted the appropriate chain of command. There was something very bad happening and now he was convinced that whatever was going on at the hospital was connected to this. But now because the CDC had decided to investigate, he was done. He wasn't going to get any more information from this point on.

"I can't..." he started to say but was interrupted.

"I know." Joaquin rephrased his question, "Did the detective seem like she was coming down with anything? Or maybe a little out of her mind?"

This was a tricky line that he was being asked to cross. He wasn't going to do it. He knew this man just wanted answers. Everyone wanted answers. "Right along with half of the damn city." Surely the CDC didn't think that this, whatever this was, was connected to the sudden riotous outbursts across the Parish. Did they?

...

As they curved around to exit the subdivision, it seemed that the madness had made it all the way through. At some point in the night someone had completely removed the gates, quite forcibly. Traffic lights at nearly every intersection were flashing red. The ones that were still hanging. There wasn't much traffic on the streets at the moment anyway. Aside from a few discarded cars here and there, everyone seemed to be running around smashing things. Eddie didn't stop at any of the lights.

The chaos seemed to have started with the explosion yesterday at Hana's apartment and spiraled out into the city. A foul odor like onion breath floated on the stagnant air. Gagging, Hana choked out, "What is happening?" She realized she sounded like a broken record. She also realized he didn't know either.

"I'm having second thoughts," he admitted. What were they doing? Where were they going? He had no decisive plan. Suddenly, he was off to rescue strangers. *Why?* Although stunned by the destruction around him, he didn't make any effort to stop or turn around.

She nodded. "So, we go back to your house and..." Trailing off, she realized she'd made her point and they were on the same page. For a moment they were silent.

The Garden District wasn't far from the French Quarter, but he drove slowly taking in all of the details around him. No one else seemed to be paying attention to their course. It took them well over half an hour to reach their destination. As they turned into the Quarter, the only open road was straight down Bourbon Street. It appeared to have been cleared for emergency vehicles. The rest of the roads were blocked by debris or vehicles. A couple of overturned police cars occupied one of the side streets.

Because the activity was spreading across the city, this part had already been forgotten. As the news crews left it almost seemed abandoned. After passing several intersections they could see the shop sign. Without getting out, Eddie activated the sliding door. "'Bout time." Queenie was already standing at the curb and chuckled as she climbed in the second row. Reaching over and gently placing her hand on Hana's shoulder she solemnly whispered, "I told you you was gonna end the world."

Hana glared at Eddie, but what if the old coot was right? What if this was her fault? What if she did cause this? How could that even be possible? Shaking her head, she reminded herself that it wasn't. How could she have started this? But things didn't go crazy until the apartment had exploded.

Without apology, Queenie settled herself in the seat and watched as the door closed slowly. Smiling at Eddie she clapped her hands. "Where we going?"

END ACT 1

ACT TWO — EPIDEMIC

Up the River

Jim clocked in at 13:17 on the time clock. Shift started at one o'clock, but he was covering for someone. He would have been here on time, but for some reason the whole damn city decided to riot last night. Everything was a mess. Half the traffic lights were out from his house to the port. It wasn't like they really *needed* him, but the containers weren't going to check themselves in. His inspection was just a formality.

The smell of the brackish air mixed with foul odors coming from all around was nauseating. The wind had shifted three times since he'd been out here. It wasn't heavy winds, but it was a noticeable change. It seemed like the fish-kill had come at an odd time this year. Usually didn't happen until the waters got warmer. The smell was overwhelming.

In the fourteen years that he'd been inspecting cargo at the port, not once had anything come through that wasn't supposed to. There might be things missing, but there was never anything scandalous. The cargo had been offloaded from the shipping vessel to the barge before he got there. At least the stevedores came in today. It seemed like everyone else had called in sick. Fortunately, the report was thorough. It would make it easier to count what was on the barge before they sent it up the Mississippi.

Coffee. Tons of coffee. Literally. Walking up and down the aisles created by the smaller containers, he began counting. He knew he was supposed to count each individual item, but he skimmed each just to make sure they all looked like they were there. *It was just coffee for fucks sake.* He had felt horrible since he woke up this morning. He had even considered declining, but he'd crossed into overtime a couple of days ago—he could use the extra money.

The pilot was waiting for him to give the final okay to leave. That guy got paid way more than him. You'd think he could count his own cargo. But then he'd be out of a job. Sundays were usually a breeze, not much going on. Today was no exception, but it was eerily quiet. By the time he'd made his way back to the cockpit the display on the clock said 15:15. It had taken him two hours to count the shipment and he hadn't seen anyone except Dan as he was leaving.

"Looks like everything is here." Jim handed the checklist to Lloyd. "Do you have a crew today?"

Stifling a cough, he gruffly snatched the forms. "Yea, got a couple of hands on their way. We're just heading up to Baton Rouge. We'll do fine with a skeleton crew." It wasn't just his breath on the cold air, but a large amount of spittle escaped and crossed the small compartment. A foul odor accompanied it. "I should have stayed in bed this morning," he admitted, obviously irritated he had to be there.

"You and me both." Jim wiped the disgusting glob off of his hand but didn't say anything. "Any plans for the holiday?" He was only making small talk because he didn't want to clock out just yet. And Lloyd wasn't in a hurry. He was waiting for his crew.

"Nah, not much for sinning these days." He was an older man, very portly and had a red bulbous nose. Quite possibly from years of whiskey. Patting his stomach, he added joyfully, "Except the whole glutton thing. I don't see myself giving that up." Almost as though his mind switched gears he leaned forward. "You didn't catch the news this morning?"

Shaking his head, Jim looked over his shoulder. No one had arrived yet. "Naw, I slept until they called me about noon."

"Coming aboard," someone called from just out of sight. The muffled conversation grew louder and was clearer as the two men got closer. "Yea, she was there all night. Said that people just kept coming in. After the explosion, she just left."

"Explosion?" Jim turned his head towards the two young men that had just arrived.

The other man answered, "Yea, not just the hospital but all over the place. I saw on the news this morning that the whole French Quarter was on fire." He was young. And longshoremen always exaggerated.

"Yup," Lloyd nodded his head vigorously, referring to the conversation they were having when the men arrived. "That's what I was talking about. Doesn't look like there's going to be much of a celebration next week."

The small but adequate crew had assembled, and it was time for Jim to clock out. Wheezing, he made his way back to the dock, climbed down the launch dock and pulled it back so that it was free of the rail. Looking back and forth he thought how odd it was that the port was so quiet. But that happened every so often. What was most odd is that there weren't any signs of life in the office. This flu must be a doozy.

Hitting the time clock at exactly 15:45, Jim realized he was exhausted. Hanging his head as he walked through the hallway towards the parking lot, the large pool of water soaked into the carpet caught his attention. Peeking into his supervisor's office he saw another large pool of water.

"What the hell happened here?" he yawned. He was sure he'd get an ear full about it all tomorrow. He was going home.

...

After the police had cleared out, Olivia stayed behind in the room. She quickly called both the Embassy and Eddie. It didn't sound like Eddie had any intention of helping. He was a waste of space. Worthless. It was a wonder that Rosalind had been with him for so long. She'd heard some of the horror stories. And then he tried to blame everything on her after Delphine died. *Where had he been?*

But she knew he wouldn't help before she called him. So far, nothing had worked out as she had planned. And now Rosalind getting arrested. There was no way she started that fire, but someone said they had seen her there. She wasn't there, and that was part of the problem too. Every scientist had checked into their rooms before the fire, except Rosalind. There were also two hours when they hadn't been together, Olivia had been out shopping and Rosalind told her to tell the truth. She was just doing what she was told. Like she always did. She should have just lied and said they were together the whole time.

Rosalind was absolutely predictable. After figuring out the password, Olivia was able to get into Rosalind's laptop. There were so many files. So many folders. She had no real system. Her desktop was littered with spreadsheets, documents and short cuts. It drove her nuts. After a couple of minutes, she was able to find the folder she'd been looking for.

Startled when her phone rang, she looked at the display. *Unknown.* "What?" she chirped, annoyed that she was being disturbed.

"Did you find it?" The voice on the line sounded eager, antsy.

"This would have been a lot easier if you had just waited, like I said." The folder was crammed with useless crap. How in the world did Rosalind keep track of her own thoughts?

"I didn't torch the hotel," he responded.

"Whatever," she replied almost apathetically and added, "Give me a little while. I'm looking." Without saying goodbye, she disconnected the call.

Sitting back, she reflected. She really liked Rosalind. She *really* did. But there were prizes to be won. There was so much more at stake here than just a fling. No matter how much she was enjoying it. Even though Rosalind treated her like a child. Everyone did.

No one expected her to be brilliant. They just expected her to be cute and grab them some coffee. She had better ideas than any of the disgusting men that degraded her every time she turned around. But

Rosalind was so much more brilliant. And she looked the part.

Shaking off the melancholy washing over her, she continued looking through the folder. Opening file after file. Eventually, she would find the right ones.

...

The clock above the television was blinking. 12:00. It appeared that there had been a power outage while he was asleep. It took a few moments to shake off the groggy effects of the pain medicine. As though coming through a fog, Morgan was finally able to focus on the room around him. The lights were still off in the room and it seemed the sun had long since made its way to the other side of the building, but the door was fully open, and enough light spilled in that he could see everything clearly.

A faint scent of burning wood wafted through the room and tickled his nose. He sat up quickly and was relieved when his head didn't spin. His ribs felt bruised up his chest and down his back, but the pain wasn't as bad as it had been when he saw Kate.

The television was not on, but it sounded like there was static coming from the speaker. It took him just a second to realize that the sound was coming from another room. Why was it up so loud? He struggled for a moment to get off the side of the bed and stand. The pressure from his feet shot up through his back causing him to groan in pain, forcing him to sit back down on the side of the bed. Fumbling for his phone, he noticed it was only a little before five o'clock.

The aroma of meat loaf or some kind of chicken dish should be filling the halls and rooms by now, but instead all he could smell was fire. Smoldering somewhere. He reached for the controls to the bed and pressed the *Nurse* button several times. He knew that didn't make it blink different. He was still a little confused.

Scanning the room, he recognized that nothing looked out of place. But it sure felt like it. Maybe it was just the lingering effects of the drug, maybe it was because of the knot on the back of his head. But something felt off.

Managing to pull himself out of the bed and reach the walker in the corner of the room, he leaned as much of his weight as he could into it and pushed himself out to the door. The hallway just outside his room was empty. It looked as though the sprinkler system had gone off. He waded through pools of water towards the nurses' station. A section of the lights was flashing a little further down the hall, threatening to go out, but they kept coming back on.

The smell of smoldering fire was a bit stronger out here, but there was nothing that looked out of place. Catching his breath, he was finally able to stand straight and abandon the shiny metal walker. "Hey, who's on duty?" he called down the hall. Every step he took rattled back through his hips and into his ribs. Twice his bare feet slipped in water.

"Yoly?" he called as he walked out. "Kate?" A movement caught his eye and he turned to see another patient wandering out of a room. "Do you have any idea what's going on?"

The woman looked back and forth wildly and shook her head. "I was going to ask you." As she shrunk back behind the doorway of her room she managed to add, "But it's something bad."

They were in the tower farthest from the entrance, so the damage from the explosion didn't reach this building. Morgan remembered Kate saying something about an explosion that he slept right through. Maybe that was where the smell was coming from. Passing several rooms, he noted that several of the beds were empty and some were soaked. The sprinklers must have gone crazy. He poked his head into the door closest to the elevator. The man was sitting up, but he looked completely confused.

"You're the nurse that was here Friday," he called out.

"Yeah, had a little accident," Morgan said, then he asked, "Do you know what's going on?"

"This place was full this morning. The nurse that was here earlier said everything was under control. But I've been trying to get someone for at least 30 minutes." He tried to sit up but grunted in pain, "Guess I'm staying here." He coughed and wheezed. "Must have slept right through the sprinklers." He waved his hand towards the empty bed on the other side of the room. "Don't know why that didn't go off too," he said, pointing above him at the sprinkler head. The empty bed was soaking wet. Morgan didn't see a fire device above it.

"Was it Kate?" Morgan leaned against the door to take some of the pressure off of his legs and back.

Shaking his head, he recalled, "Nah, it was Yolo or something like that."

"Yoly." He wasn't correcting the man just confirming.

"Yea, that's it." He nodded a little too fast and regretted it, "Damn, my head."

Morgan stumbled into the room and grabbed the clipboard by the white erase board. *Elkins, Randy.* He remembered them admitting him on Friday night. Three cars in front of Harrah's Casino collided due to a faulty intersection light. "You want something for pain? It looks like you're overdue."

Vigorously waving his head from side to side he blurted out, "Hell no!" It was obvious he was in pain, but he undoubtedly wanted to be alert. "I'll deal with it. When you figure out what's up, let me know?" It came out as more of a timid question than a demand.

As the elevator descended to the first floor, Morgan's ears popped. It was only two floors, but it always felt like he was moving at super speed. The car stopped and created a bouncing motion which sent waves of pain through his back. As the doors opened, he let out a grunt.

He could hear sounds from all directions. Voices, lots of different voices having different conversations. Much like it should sound. Taking the closest hallway to the entry area he finally saw movement, quite a bit of it. It played out in the shadows on the shiny floor in front of him. Turning the corner, he was greeted by the view of several patients wandering around, looking for someone that could tell them what was going on.

Kate was sitting in the middle of the nurses' station. She was watching a live story on Facebook on the computer monitor in front of her. The person narrating was an amateur, this was obviously taken from his phone. "Look at this. What the hell is going on?" He panned around a bit wildly, not stopping long enough for anything to really come into full focus. But there was enough.

Smoke was rising from all angles. There were masses that looked like fire as he panned. In the foreground were several cars that had apparently smashed into each other, then been abandoned. The man continued panning and narrating with a simple, "Oh my God."

"Kate," Morgan said sharply.

"It's insanity." She didn't turn to look at him but sat shaking her head.

"Where is everyone?" He was beginning to have trouble containing the panic that had seized his stomach just after he stood up. "What happened?"

"People just started...," she trailed off. It was just as hard to say out loud as it was to actually grasp the concept. "They just started disappearing." Pointing at the monitor she added excitedly, "See, and this. Like Mr. Cane. They just started going crazy."

A few people walked back and forth around them. Patients and staff alike. No one knew what to do. There were still people everywhere. Just not as many. He realized he needed to get dressed. His locker was on this floor. As he stumbled away from the station he said over his shoulder, "I'll be right back."

Without taking her eyes from the screen in front of her she replied absently, "I'm not going out *there,*" and pointed towards the plywood covering the entrance. It was as if she had completely forgotten where she was, or that there were still patients on the floor.

By the time he reached the lockers, the time on his phone read 5:28.

The cable news station played twenty-four hours a day in the rest area. It was broadcast from New York or something and the stories were usually poking at politics and all-out battles over social issues. Catching the tail end of the latest scandal in Washington, the camera cut to a much more solemn scene.

"We're getting reports from our sister station in New Orleans that are, quite frankly, confusing." The older man sitting behind the news desk crossed his hands and recited from the teleprompter in front of him, "We don't have confirmation from authorities at this time. But as you can see from some of the images here, we have what appears to be mass rioting." Obviously ad-libbing the next part, "Rioting? This looks like Afghanistan." Clearing his throat, he continued reading the prompter.

"What we *do* know at this time is there has been a wave of some kind of sickness and the hospitals are overwhelmed." It was apparent by his eyes that he was reading the screen in front of him. But he quit speaking. A look of confusion crossed his face and he closed, "It seems that there are many people being reported missing. We'll bring you more on this as it develops." Before the last syllable of his sentence sounded, the camera cut to a commercial.

Agonizing over the jeans and shirt he was climbing into, Morgan tried to hurry. Whatever was happening seemed to only be affecting New Orleans. For now. He wasn't convinced it wasn't all connected. It all started when they brought Mr. Borre in.

Something was incredibly wrong.

Dissension

By the time Sgt. Denning left the station, the phones had been ringing off the hook. Missing persons reports were coming in from all over the city. As tired as he was of answering "rapture" phone calls, he only left because there had been some confusion at the coroner's office. Someone had misplaced Detective Warner's remains. *Misplaced.* How incompetent did you have to be to lose a body? But this was what he was dealing with.

Clicking the remote on his car alarm, he paused and lit a cigarette. The whole city was on fire. Not just the explosions from yesterday, but everything was burning to the ground. The fire department was overwhelmed and there was no way they were getting it under control tonight. The acrid smell of burning electronics and smoldering wood assaulted him, creating a tickle in the back of his throat. He coughed to clear it. "Fuck me," he whispered to himself.

Looking around, he tossed the cigarette into the parking lot and climbed into his car. The soft tones of his phone sounded from somewhere under his jacket. He rooted through his coat pocket and retrieved it just in time to miss the call. He paired the phone to his car and pulled out as he dialed the number back. It rang twice then went to voicemail as he navigated out onto the road.

"This is Joaquin Rivas, leave a message." It was short and to the point.

A little aggravated, he waited until the tones. "This is Denning. If you know anything, I'll buy you a cup of coffee." He ended the call from the buttons on his steering wheel. Things had gotten out of hand before anyone even knew something was happening. He expected things were about to get a lot worse.

At least the coroner's office wasn't too far. It only took him a few minutes to get there. He had to drive around a few abandoned cars. He half expected to be assaulted by a pack of zombies craving human flesh as he hobbled from the parking lot to the door. There were no such attacks. But isn't this how those zombie movies always started?

The scene inside wasn't any less chaotic. Only a few people running around trying to make sense of the strange things that had been happening. The girl at the front desk greeted him with a frantic "Hello." He recognized her but couldn't remember her name. She was fairly new. "Ben is waiting for you. I'm so sorry about Iris." Her eyes widened a bit as she looked around her at the chaos and asked, "What is going on?"

"Your guess is as good as mine," he growled.

Making his way to the back he was greeted by Ben Rowlings, the Parish coroner. "It gets worse," he said as they walked down the hallway to the back. "It's not just Detective Warner."

"What?" He wasn't following the thought. Certainly he didn't mean they'd lost *other* bodies too.

As if understanding what was going through his mind, Ben quickly added, "Before you start giving me shit, no one *lost* anything. I was here. She was here," he pointed to the small door at the bottom of the cooler unit. He then pointed to the one next to hers. "And *he* was here," indicating another missing corpse.

"So how many are you *missing?*" He emphasized the word like it was bitter on his tongue.

Sighing deeply Ben ran his hands across his almost panicked face. "Four here, three more down at the morgue at the hospital." Looking back and forth he added, "And the hospital has lost *dozens* of patients."

"Dozens?" There was no way. Someone was smoking something. "I get misplacing a body, but how do you lose *dozens* of living patients?"

"See, that's the thing…" Ben turned around and opened the doors that should have contained pending autopsies. Instead all 4 trays were full of water.

...

"Chaos all across New Orleans this evening as local police and federal officials attempt to find answers," the soothing female voice carried over the airwaves. "Good evening, thanks for tuning in." A gracious formality, seeing as how the entire city was already watching. Had been for hours. The small crowd gathered at the sports bar had long since abandoned their pool games and spats, focusing only on the words being shared throughout the viewing area.

"As most of you already know, the madness that seemed to have started with an explosion in the French Quarter has spread across the Parish." She paused for just a moment as though being directed from off screen. Turning to face another camera she continued, "All of the emergency rooms and hospitals have been seeing patients with mysterious symptoms. While loosely resembling the flu, this does not seem to be an influenza outbreak."

Breaking in over her audio from somewhere out of view was a male voice, "We have no confirmation at this time as to whether this may or may not actually be a flu virus." Then added hastily, "Sorry to interrupt, Liza."

"No problem Rich." She faked a smile and continued reading the prompter before her, "At this time authorities are requesting that everyone that is able, to remain home." Liza blinked and turned again to face the first camera. One of several tired theatrics they still performed. Switching gears to the next headline. "The scene at the police station earlier today has had a bizarre and almost terrifying twist. We have just confirmed that at some point this afternoon, the body of Detective Warner has been reported as missing." Turning side to side Liza looked confused. "Missing? Do we actually have confirmation of this?"

The same voice that boomed in before quietly agreed. "Yes, Liza, at this time we have confirmed that several reports of missing remains have been made all over the city."

Shaking her head slowly she seemed to stray from the words in front of her. "Do we have any idea what's happening?"

Not too far from the sports bar, a small restaurant had opened their doors and kitchen to anyone that needed a hot meal. Things were crazy, neighbors mattered. Ask anyone in the city. They'd agree. Thing is, they'd expected more people to come in. Free meals are a draw, even during the end of the world.

The few people that had gathered in the dining room all sat at the same table with their attention to the all-news cable station. "Fires and explosions rock the city of New Orleans." The aging anchor cleared his throat and continued, "First reports of a small blast early yesterday morning were followed by a flood of similar situations. At this time the police and fire departments are overwhelmed with calls and are asking for volunteers to help with the remaining flames."

The image behind him changed and his demeanor seemed to be flipped by a switch. "We're getting reports of a spreading virus, chaos and missing persons all over the area." Nodding he finished, "We're not sure at this time how much, if any, of these things are connected." Listening to someone he asked, "Do we have any live footage?" After a pause he said, "Guess not. In other news..." As the caster began to drone on with the story of a dog show seven hundred miles away, the small group sat completely dumbfounded.

Across town, University Medical had become a circus. People wandered the halls. Doctors, nurses and patients alike. All confused. All seemingly waiting for an explanation. Gathered in the main waiting area on the second floor, at least a dozen dazed faces focused on the broadcast.

The usually perky adorable blonde reporter appeared distraught and confused. She had dressed for the occasion this time and wasn't wearing heels. "On location here at the city morgue where a bizarre scene is unfolding." She turned to face the steps to the entrance, where several officers and other city officials had begun pouring in and out. "As if the shooting at the station wasn't enough, it seems the body of recently deceased Detective Iris Warner has completely vanished. And it appears that this story is repeating itself across the Parish."

The shift from audio was easily detectable. The mic that the reporter was using was not filtered and the noises of a city burning to the ground leaked through. As the voice boomed in, the camera did not break from their representative on the scene. "Are you saying that you have confirmed that there is more than one person's remains that have been lost?"

Nodding she excitedly confirmed, "Yes, yes. At this time the coroner's office is confirming the disappearance of several persons' remains that have not been autopsied yet." Visibly shuddering she added, "How could that happen?"

...

Joaquin received Sgt. Denning's message, but he didn't know anything. He had been calling to see if there were any updates. Sitting at his desk, he sighed and browsed the local television station on the laptop in front of him. The sensational headlines made his head swim. Had he not witnessed the "crazy" of the past couple of days, he would have called bullshit.

"Mysterious illness may be linked to madness and disappearances." Scanning through the article he realized it was an editorial piece and wasn't backed up with any fact. However, he was starting to believe that there had to be a connection. Whatever it was, it was about to get way worse.

He dialed the Sergeant back and was relieved when he answered on the second ring. "Rivas! Still want to talk?"

"Can you tell me *anything?*" Joaquin pleaded.

"I think now might be a good time to compare notes," he answered quickly, then added, "Meet me up at the station."

...

A little over 1,600 miles away, the tiny television droned in the background. "In world news today, behind me is a scene in the Southern United States. The city of New Orleans in Louisiana." The screen flickered an image of what looked like something from an Armageddon-type movie. Discarded vehicles, fires, sirens and frantic people vying for a moment onscreen. "Although it seems to be centralized within the New Orleans area, other reports are coming in from neighboring areas as far as Texas of similar events. Though nothing as chaotic as what you are looking at."

Rosalind sat up, trying to lean closer to hear what they were reporting about on the news. She hadn't seen a judge, a lawyer or anything yet, so they still had her in an informal holding area. "Can you turn that up a little?" She expected to be ignored. Instead, the burly officer retrieved the remote and raised the volume to a level she could hear. It was obvious he wanted to hear what was happening too.

"Currently the local media and law enforcement in the area haven't told us much. Most of the footage you are seeing was sent to us by citizens and people in the area. Speculation is wild at the moment, but we will report back when we have confirmed our sources." Although his accent was thick, every word he said seemed punctuated.

"What the hell is going on?" she almost whispered.

The officer turned to her and his reply was surprisingly warm, "Do you know anyone there?"

Although she hadn't intended to start a dialog, she welcomed the attention. "I live there." Thinking, she asked sheepishly, "Would it be possible to call my husband?"

Normally that wouldn't have been permitted. She knew that. She was surprised again when he handed her his cell phone. "Make it fast so I don't get in trouble."

There was an exaggerated pause before the call connected. Every worst-case scenario hit her as the phone went unanswered after the first ring. By the time the second ring sounded her mind wandered to "what ifs". The third ring was interrupted. It sounded like someone had answered, but the interference or static or whatever it was she was hearing had made the voice on the other end unintelligible. "Eddie," she barked in the phone hoarsely.

The voice on the other end seemed to answer but the tones were delivered in static and noise rather than a human voice. The call ended. Redialing the call took even longer to finally connect. The dead air as she waited was ominous. Instead of connecting to a ring this time, she was greeted by the tones of a land line that had been left off the hook for too long. But this was sounding much faster. More than likely tower failure.

At least he'd answered. Or she thought he'd answered. It was more static and interference than voice. He never let his phone out of his sight. It had to have been him. Didn't it? "What is going on?" Wide eyed, she passed the phone back to the gracious guard.

"It looks quite the same as any news I see from the South." Realizing what he had said could have been incredibly offensive, he added, "With respect to you, Madame."

Sighing, she corroborated his statement. "No, no you're right. It's always a mess down there. But doesn't this seem...strange?"

...

Truth was, there was no plan. He was a sucker for a damsel in distress. Didn't matter who she was. And he just couldn't see leaving an old woman alone in the middle of what resembled an active combat zone. He found amusement in the not so gracious acceptance of his weakness by Hana. She was obviously annoyed but willing to let him do his thing. They drove up and down the roads, wandering almost aimlessly for a couple of hours. He took in the sudden destruction that surrounded them.

He was torn between just finding a nice hotel for Queenie or taking her to his house. But the way things had looked earlier today in his neighborhood, they wouldn't be any safer there.

In the far distance, a commercial airplane appeared to be falling from the sky. The blinking lights descended faster than they should have. The airport was in the other direction, so it wouldn't have been landing. As the plane hit the ground and the explosion sent plumes of fire and black smoke into the air, Eddie gasped. "I don't know about either of you, but I think *maybe* we should just get out of town for the night."

"Won't stop what's comin." Up to this point Queenie had been fairly silent. She sat in the back with her eyes shut. She had been humming the same sweet tune for over an hour, but it was so soft that it didn't bother either of them. The melody was kind of pretty and she carried it low and perfectly in key. It was almost as though she were serenading the end of the world. "Ain't a place you can hide from the pale rider." She cleared her throat and pulled out a cigarillo, "May I?"

"Whatever." He rolled her window down slightly and the acrid fumes from the air overwhelmed them all. Rolling the window up, he said, "Just use this," and handed her an empty coffee mug that had been sitting in the cup holder for months.

"Pale rider?" Hana scoffed.

Drawing heavily on the tightly wrapped sweet tobacco she leaned forward slightly, addressing Hana. "He gonna follow us wherever we go," she whispered.

"Death." Eddie explained abruptly.

"What?" Hana seemed confused.

Without turning his attention from the road, he elaborated, "The paler rider is Death."

"Mhmmm," Queenie agreed. "He's coming for all of us." She waved her arms above her head, causing an ash to tumble down her dress. "Mr. Eddie, you been to war. You've seen stuff like this before, right?"

He was startled at first that she knew his name, much less his military career. Had Hana said anything during the drive? Probably. "How do you mean?" She started humming again. Obviously, she wasn't going to answer. He still hadn't decided where they were going as they entered the freeway heading West. The opposite direction from his house. The idea was to see how far out this went.

Realizing they had entered the westbound freeway, Hana's palms began to sweat. "Where are we going?" A few cars rushed past them at incredible speed. Although he wasn't crawling, Eddie wasn't driving the speed limit either.

"Just getting a look." Twilight had started to creep in. They had been driving around since this afternoon. How had time flown by so quickly? He looked down for a moment to assess the fuel situation, but he still had just under three quarters of a tank. A little bit ahead of them a pair of headlights shone back. Someone was going the wrong way. *How could that have even happened?* The dividers kept the eastbound and westbound traffic separate. Someone had to have turned around.

Swerving to miss the barreling SUV, Eddie ended up skidding across the shoulder as the oncoming Explorer slammed head on with a car behind them. Two more crushing impacts sounded. And all of them jumped as the speakers began to ring. The display on the screen was an out of area number. Montreal. It would take too long to un-pair the devices. Pressing the button on the steering wheel, he answered, "Hello?"

It was Rosalind, "Eddie." She managed to say just before the static invaded. The speakers spat and hissed.

He tried to respond, "Kind of in a situation here. I'm sorry..." The call ended. He hadn't hung up. He was sure she hadn't either. The towers must be struggling. It was likely they were just over taxed at the volume of calls that must be coming and going. He'd call that number back later, when he had a better signal. He was sympathetic of what she must be going through. But the situation at hand seemed more urgent.

Forty-Eight Hours

"*Buy* me a cup of coffee? You really are a cheap bastard, huh?" Joaquin ribbed as he sat down across from Sgt. Denning in the break area at the station. Although they'd never met, it was well known that the Sergeant was a bit on the frugal side. Even caused some issues with his department. But that got all sorted out. It was the strangest news story he'd ever seen.

"That's what they say?" he chuckled and handed Mr. Rivas a cup of stout fresh coffee. "I may have heard that a time or two." Almost immediately, the causal formalities ended as he spat out, "Here's the deal. I've got no idea what's going on. But when I start hearing on the radio that CDC vans are hovering just outside the city, I get a little jumpy."

Nodding, he was deep in contemplation. "Was the Detective sick?" Like a bull realizing the chute had opened he took off from the gate. "What *really* happened today?"

Assessing the scene around him, Denning slowly and casually made his way to the door and closed it. They were the only two in the break area. It took another couple of moments for him to make his way back to the table and take his seat. Although the sound was closed off, the scene was perfectly visible through the glass window that separated them from the cubicles. The whole thing looked ridiculously obvious, but who was looking?

After taking a huge gulp of his coffee, the Sergeant sighed. "Yea, I mean I think so." He rubbed his face with one hand, obviously exhausted and distraught. "She said she was coming down with the flu." Struggling for what to say he took another deep breath. "Maybe she had a fever? I'm pretty sure she was hallucinating."

Joaquin nodded and sipped at the scalding black liquid. "That would have to be a really high fever."

"Whatever. I'm just telling you what I know." He wasn't irritated. Just wanted to hurry up and say what he had to say. "She heard something though. She may have even seen something. Scared the shit out of her." His voice wavered as he finished, "Enough that she pulled her gun." Hoping that he didn't need to go further into detail he closed with, "I guess you've heard by now that she's missing. I have no idea how the hell that got out, but it did."

"Were there any clues at the coroner's office?" He wasn't a scientist. He wasn't a forensics specialist. He had no idea where his own questions were leading. He was in over his head. But he'd been doing this long enough to know that this situation needed to be identified now. Not tomorrow. Not later. Now.

"Is water a clue?" He crossed the line. Up to this point every word he'd said had been within the realm of public information. But this guy seemed to have some ideas. He could use some ideas. He also knew that Iris had been working with Mr. Rivas already. She had indicated that he was the reason she was trying to find some kind of connection.

"Under any other circumstance, no." He leaned in and recounted for the Sergeant the details of the unknown substance that had been present in both Borre and Cane, and how by the time they were able to test it, they were also left with nothing but water. "I thought someone screwed up. Rationally, I still have to believe someone screwed up." He placed the paper cup on the table and cradled his head in both hands.

"You sick?" Denning seemed to be changing the subject. But that wasn't the case. His train of thought had skipped to something else.

Shaking his head, he straightened again. "No. Not at all."

"I'm not either. So, is it even possible that this could be a virus?" It was obvious he was trying to rule out whatever he could.

"There's always immunity, for any virus." Nodding, he added, "This fits the structure of a contagion. But I've never heard of anything like it."

This was not what Sgt. Denning had expected to hear. It was clear. "It's spreading isn't it?"

"Looks like it," Joaquin agreed. He had no idea that there were CDC vans outside the city. He wasn't even sure that was true. But Denning had an amazing record. His service to the department was unchallenged, except the whole cheap supplies thing. But as far as his reputation preceded him, it was that of a stable, level-headed man. He didn't seem prone to panic. Then again, hallucinations? That could be plausible. "Who told you the CDC was standing by?"

Pulling out his phone, he opened a message and turned it around for Mr. Rivas to see. "One of our officers sent me this about forty-five minutes ago." The video was dark, but the surrounding light was enough. He recognized the vehicles. Most of them were marked. They weren't hiding. Just waiting.

What were they waiting for?

"Want to go for a drive?" Sgt. Denning slipped his phone back in his pocket and opened the door.

...

Something was wrong. Very wrong. It didn't take Morgan long to get the message. After struggling to dress, he was able to make his way to the parking lot where his car had been parked for the past couple of days. At some point someone had broken out one of his headlights, but there didn't seem to be any other damage. The parking lot was littered with vehicles that didn't fare so well.

As he drove through town, he realized it wasn't just the parking lots. The whole town was littered with, well just about everything. Off in the distance he was sure he saw the wing of an airplane sticking up from the ground. The scene morphed from surreal to bizarre over and over again. "What the fuck?" he whispered to himself as he dialed his phone.

He was greeted by voicemail. "Mom, hey. I'm coming to visit. I'll be in later tonight. I have my key. I'll be quiet." He disconnected the call and tossed the phone into the passenger seat. His mom was in Lafayette. It was just a couple of hours west. Well, depending on how fast you drove. It was Sunday evening, so traffic through Baton Rouge shouldn't be an issue.

It took him a little bit to navigate through the continual mess of what used to be NOLA to the interstate. He was mesmerized by the smoky plumes that seemed to blend into the clouds. How did things get so out of hand so fast? What had he slept through?

He jumped a little when the phone rang and swerved a bit as he reached for it. "Hello?" He saw it was his mother calling back.

The sound of fear in her voice indicated that she was watching the news. "Are you okay?" Every mother's first question.

"Yeah, I'm fine Mom. Banged up a little but I'm fine." He contemplated whether to tell her anything or wait until he got there. A sick heat washed over him as he thought about the possibility that there had been a contagion. Was he about to take it to her? "Just have a few days off and thought this was a good time to come see you."

"I'll wait up," she said and then there was a buzz of static. It sounded like she was still talking but instead of her voice, it was just interference.

"What was the last part?" he asked her to repeat herself. He wasn't sure if she could hear him. Looking up he saw oncoming headlights. Before he could react, the vehicle smashed into the one in front of him. His reaction time was still slow from the fading narcotic in his system. He didn't get out of the way in time and the Explorer clipped the front end of his car. Spinning, his car then contacted the front end of the car behind him.

The sound of crushing metal and shattering glass echoed in his ears as the emergency air bag smashed into his face with the impact of a ton of bricks. Fumbling for his phone as he fought with the nylon bag in his face, he attempted to continue his conversation.

"Mom?" The call had long since ended.

...

"It has been a long tenuous road, but we are finally seeing our collaborative work come to fruition." It was obvious Rosalind wrote her own speeches. This opening was all her. What she meant to say was that she had done most of the work, but she had some good ideas tossed at her. But she'd never say that. She was so indoctrinated in the "man's world" that she never realized how taken for granted her mind was.

"Without many of your advances, this project could have taken decades." Okay, that part was true. Each little thing had its place. But they were all little trivial things. Somewhere in here, Rosalind must reveal what she found. After reading all seven pages, Olivia grunted and tossed the laptop aside. Nothing. There was absolutely nothing in there. So where were the notes?

The call she'd received just moments before she found the speech was still in her mind. "You really need to try to visit her. Make it look like you care."

"Fuck you," she replied.

"Hey, this was your idea," he reminded her.

"Not *that*." She defended herself quickly, "I never suggested that."

The calls never lasted long. And here she was reading this long-winded pat on the back. Truth was, she did care and maybe going to visit Rosalind would be a good thing. Maybe she could just come clean and ask her. No. No she couldn't do that. Not anymore. The murder of Dr. Patel had closed that door.

Turning on the television, she had come in on the middle of a news story that was taking place in New Orleans, where Rosalind was from. It looked like the entire town had been gutted. They didn't have much information but that wasn't surprising. What was surprising was how very little attention the station had given to the story. They switched to something more local and way less exciting.

The car was already waiting by the time she made it down to the lobby and out the door. She had called ahead and gotten permission from the station to visit. They had informed her it was highly unusual, but the circumstances were unusual as well. She just figured that meant they didn't want a public incident.

What she wasn't sure of was how Rosalind would greet her. She hoped that she was scared enough that some of the details would be forgotten. She didn't like the idea of playing these games. Well, not all of them. She liked some of them. The point was she needed to keep up appearances. Maybe she wouldn't hate her too much.

What she didn't expect was the warm hug and gracious greeting. "Thank you for coming. I know how unpleasant it is."

Olivia glared at the woman standing in front of her. Not in an angry way, just in disbelief. Did she really mean what she was saying? Had she cracked? Who was this understanding human being she was looking at? No, it was more than likely she was being sarcastic. Forcing a sweet smile Olivia said, "It was more unpleasant being where you weren't." She meant it.

The guard didn't seem to want to be there, until Olivia came in. He watched her like a hawk. Rosalind couldn't tell if it was because she was stunning, or they really did suspect foul play. Either way, she had absolutely nothing to hide so she didn't care. For some reason though, Olivia seemed jumpy. It could have just been the ambiance.

Olivia eyed the room repeatedly. Her eyes shifting from side to side. It looked like she could bolt at any minute. Instead she whispered, "There's something going on down in..."

"I saw," Rosalind interrupted her. "You need to get me out of here."

...

"Holy shit." Eddie pulled over carefully on the narrow shoulder and climbed out. Traffic wasn't bad but there were a few cars speeding by. No one else stopped. Fortunately, the freeway was well-lit here, and they were visible. Dialing 911 on his phone he was met with *No Service.* Realizing that it would take time to get help, he made his way to the vehicles.

"Be careful," Hana called out. She also attempted to reach emergency services.

"Won't do you no good right now," Queenie reverently whispered. "Things are all going down as He planned them to."

"He who?" Hana was tired, she'd had enough of the hocus pocus, but she still forced herself to be nice. It wasn't Queenie's fault any of this was happening. It was apparently *her* fault. Although she wasn't sure how she could have started this, she certainly didn't disregard the old woman anymore. In fact, she'd welcome bringing on the end of the world if it meant she was done. She was so tired.

Slowly nodding, she smiled. "God, the Devil, whoever is running the show now." Giggling she added, "At this point it could be either."

Another car whizzed by, creating a rocking motion in the van. Hana dug into her bag and found a cigarette. She lit it and turned around to face the back. She didn't believe in the devil and she certainly didn't believe in God. But she also understood how faith could be useful. If she'd been a woman of faith things might have gone differently after Ebby's death. But she wasn't, and here they were, sitting on the side of Interstate Ten with literally nowhere to go.

From out of the back window she watched Eddie check from vehicle to vehicle. It looked like he was assessing the situation. The crumpled twist of metal and debris on the road caught nearby lights and flickered. She contemplated helping, but he seemed like he knew what he was doing. The steady tick of the hazards seemed to be keeping the beat as he danced back and forth. He pulled the passenger door open and climbed inside of one of the cars. It appeared the driver of the car was conscious and responded to the assistance.

It had been roughly forty-eight hours since they had met. Two days. Since that time the entire city had literally destroyed itself. She realized that even though the old woman might be eccentric, she knew *something,* whether it was just damn good intuition or magick. She shuddered as she realized that meant the worst was still coming.

Fumbling with his seat belt, Morgan was able to release the restraint and sit straight. "What the hell just happened?" He clutched his ribs as someone opened and climbed into his passenger door. Recognizing the concern in the man's eyes he explained, "This is from last night. I'm fine. Slide out, I'm coming."

"We can drive you to the hospital." The rescuer stepped out onto the highway and looked up and down. Aside from the occasional car in the left lane, most of the traffic had ceased. He looked as confused as anyone.

As Morgan climbed over the console and out the passenger door he replied, "Hell no! Just came from there. Trust me we're a lot better off in the middle of the highway." After taking just a couple of steps, he realized that his injuries had been aggravated by the impact and he almost crumbled. The man helped him to the van and the door slid open to receive the new passenger. "I'm Morgan," he introduced himself to everyone at once. Then added a gracious, "Thank you."

Eddie stood on the shoulder for a few moments, trying to decide what to do. They still couldn't get any service where they were, for whatever reason. Climbing in he decided they should continue forward and see how far this went.

After everyone introduced themselves, Queenie looked at the newest passenger and smiled. "You're that boy from the hospital. The really nice one."

He remembered her, odd but really nice. He'd seen her at the end of the summer for heat exhaustion. He couldn't remember much else, but he did recognize her. "That's right. You stayed over a couple of nights if I recall."

"So where are we going?" Eddie was getting tired. He knew it. He couldn't just drive around all night. He still needed to figure out how to help Rosalind. Thinking about his question he asked again, "Morgan, where were *you* going?"

"Away from NOLA." He nursed his side, shifting frequently to relieve the pressure. When he realized the seat laid back, he reclined fully. "Something really bad is happening. It started when they brought Elmer in."

Before he could continue, or explain who Elmer was, Queenie shook her head slowly back and forth. "Brother Borre was a good man. Spent way too much time with the dead." No one noticed that she had used the past tense.

Nodding, realizing that she knew him, Morgan continued. "He was brought in directly from work. He fell, hit his head on a stone." Swiping through images in his phone he pulled up the image that the officer on the scene sent him. They had needed to identify the unusual substance. At least that's what he told him. "This one." He turned the phone around, so Eddie could see.

As all of the color washed from Eddie's face, Hana reached for the phone to see what had caused such a strong reaction. The name on the stone read *Delphine Bélisaire 2015-2018.*

Say Goodnight

As Olivia browsed the many speeches and lectures on the laptop, her mind drifted to the first time she'd seen Rosalind speak.

"In just a few short years we have managed to identify a new way to treat these cancers on the molecular level. Inert viruses are easy to manipulate. Now that we have a better way to remove the stinger, so to speak, it has become even easier."

Even her lectures were so perfectly narrated before she gave them that it sounded like she was running for office. She really should have. Olivia had been following her career for a while, and when she had the opportunity to finally get to know her in Munich, she jumped at the chance. It was the first time that Rosalind had spoken publicly about the new methods being implemented in, not only the field of virology, but other avenues of bio research.

It's also why she won the Lasker. And she hadn't even cared. She tossed the whole thing aside as though it was a bother. She was in it for the science and the discoveries. She didn't care about the prizes.

"By introducing the modified viruses into all of the test scenarios we have had one hundred percent success rate. Each time the cancerous cells have been completely isolated and once they have been choked off, they continue breaking down over time until the only element left is pure H_2O." Pausing for emphasis she added, "We are almost ready for real trials."

From the back of the room, a man stood and almost shouted towards the front of the small auditorium, "What about the immuno research? Two years ago, you said those were almost ready for trials too".

Without changing her expression, Rosalind countered, "This is not an immuno lecture. That one isn't until tomorrow." She shook her head and added, "Hecklers!"

The small crowd erupted into laughter. Rosalind brought them back to her prepared speech with so much ease. "The research isn't just mine. It's a collective of several amazing minds all over the world."

Sighing, Olivia brought herself back to the present. This would have all been so much easier had she not actually developed a fondness for Rosalind. It would be a lot easier if she understood the filing system too. Rosalind had made an astounding breakthrough and was set to share part of it tomorrow. The lectures had been postponed, she still had time to get everything together. If she could find it.

Reorganizing as she went, Olivia finally realized that she had read everything, watched every video and reviewed every spreadsheet. None of the newest research was here. "Seriously Ros?" she sighed and closed the computer up. Maybe she had it on a portable drive?

The phone call interrupted her again. *Unknown.* "What?" She was getting really annoyed with Rex.

"You watching the news?" He sounded a little panicked.

"I'm a little busy right now," she said. Annoyed, but only slightly. She needed a little break from all of the reading. Flipping on the television she turned the volume down most of the way. "What channel?"

"Seriously?" he scoffed. "Just pick one." The call disconnected.

...

"This is the scene tonight in Baton Rouge." The forties-something reporter looked like she'd just been called out of bed. Her hair was a mess and she wasn't wearing any makeup. It was the story that might earn her an Emmy. It was obvious in her eyes that she knew that too. "What started this morning as a routine delivery quickly turned to anything less than routine for this crew."

The wind was blowing, and, in the distance, there were orange flames dancing. "All three crew members that should have disembarked here today are missing." She walked closer to the barge in question. "Officials say that the barge was towed into the port after being found unmanned floating down the Mississippi River."

From off-camera a loud male voice boomed in, "Do we have any idea what might have happened here?"

"Officials have been trying to reach the employee that signed off on the load before it left New Orleans. As far as we know they have not been able to locate him." She slowly walked towards the entrance to the offices as the camera followed. "Shipping lists show that all of the product loaded onto the barge is accounted for. There are currently no signs of foul play or theft suspected."

"Do we know what they were delivering?" the man's voice boomed again.

She nodded, acknowledging his question. "Nothing scandalous, Tom. Just coffee. We'll have more as it develops."

The camera cut back to the studio. Tom was reading something on the teleprompter. "It appears that the flu virus is on the move again. If you have already had your flu shot this season, doctors are advising that you stay home. If you haven't had your shot, please report to any one of the local clinics on the list behind me. Free flu shots will be provided without question at any of these locations." He paused and turned to the list behind him. It was obviously a green screen, but he was going through the motions.

"Authorities are asking anyone that is not seriously ill to refrain from reporting to the hospital to prevent the flu from spreading any further." He looked directly into the camera and smiled. There was a slight pause before the next story began.

"In other news..." the woman's voice sounded just before her face appeared. "Riots across Baton Rouge tonight have officials concerned." She turned to face the man sitting beside her and continued. "What seems to have started in New Orleans is spreading throughout the state. At this time, authorities have no answers as to what has brought on this sudden rash of crime and looting."

As Shari flipped through the channels the story was the same. *Live from Louisiana.* The national and local news stations all seemed to be telling the same story. At least Morgan had called, but they had gotten disconnected before she had a chance to find out where he was. But he said he was on his way home, so she'd stay up and wait.

She'd been alone in the house for the past year after Grant had his heart attack. Morgan didn't seem to make his way home as much as she would have liked, but she was so proud of him. Saving lives. He'd be able to tell her a lot more when he got home.

She could smell smoke wafting in. Although it wasn't unusual to smell fire on the air in February, she was unsure if she was smelling her neighbor's fireplace or something further down the way. Either way she was going to do exactly what the news said and stay indoors. Although it was getting late, she started a pot of coffee. She didn't want to fall asleep before her boy got home.

...

Rosalind was exhausted. The past twelve hours had been a complete blur. One minute she was a world-renowned scientist, the next minute she was the prime suspect in a murder investigation. She had no idea how things had gotten so far out of hand. Obviously, she wasn't guilty but whatever they had seemed to point to her.

The guard had left the television turned up so that she could hear, but she was ready for him to just turn it off. The local news was littered with stories about her, her career and her life. She didn't need the replay. As she was settling into the cot praying for sleep, the sounds of voices began to get louder and louder. There was a crowd gathering just out of her view. Unable to make out all of the voices, she strained to hear what was happening.

"This is coming from way above us." One voice stood out above the others. It sounded like her representative at the Consulate.

Someone replied loudly in French. She didn't know much French, but she understood "CDC". The overpowering scent of men's cologne made its way around the corner before the group did. There was more arguing in French. She should have known way more than she did. But the French in New Orleans was dirty. Her mother had pretty much done everything she could to prevent her from learning the Creole abomination when she was young. Even that knowledge would have been useful right now. She never bothered to learn because it all left a terrible taste in her mouth.

"It doesn't matter." Her representative was speaking again. "This is coming straight from the World Health Organization. You understand? That's a lot more important right now."

The WHO? Why would they get involved in a murder case? Unless this wasn't about that. She thought about the sensationalized news story about the viral outbreak in NOLA. She thought she had seen something that sounded the same but further North. "Hey, what's going on?" she shouted, a little louder than she meant to.

"Dr. Bélisaire." It *was* the same man from earlier today. He came around the corner so that she could see him, and the rest of the group followed him in. "Some kind of virus. Seems to have started down South." He looked completely wrung out. She wondered if that meant he had been working on a way to get her out of here.

"Isn't that your specialty?"

She replied dryly, "That's what the news keeps saying." She shook her head, almost apologetically. "What is it?"

He sighed. "They're not sure. They thought maybe you could take a look, or whatever it is that you'd do." He seemed to be holding information back. There was definitely something he wasn't saying.

"There are *thousands* of scientists between here and NOLA." She was trying to grasp why she was being asked to "look" at anything.

"This one is spreading *fast*," he spat out. "And some of the reports are..." Stammering, he was looking for the right words, "...well, just puzzling." He looked her directly in the eye through the holding cell.

Until this moment everyone else in the room had been quiet. The gruff explosion of French from the short portly man made her jump slightly. "Cela peut attendre jusqu'au matin." [This can wait until morning.] Shaking his finger in her direction he added. "Nous verrons ce que le Premier ministre a à dire." [We will see what the Prime Minister has to say.]

Holding up a small stack of papers in his hand the rep countered, "People are dying."

Whoa. She heard that loud and clear. "What's happening?" Obviously, it was worse than she thought.

"Started yesterday, in the morning I think." It was pretty clear he was running on very little sleep.

She scoffed, "You can't start screaming epidemic after just forty-eight hours. That's ridiculous."

"Elle admet que ça peut attendre!" [She admits it can wait!] he almost screamed. The pungent odor of cologne was coming from him. He stepped forward, almost accusing. She was getting very tired of it all.

"No!" her defender shouted over him. "She did no such thing." Pointing at the locking mechanism on the door of her holding cell he ordered, "Open it."

"What is going on?" Rosalind whispered sheepishly as she climbed into his car. He closed the door and ran quickly around to the other side.

As he got in, he answered, "This isn't exactly how I pictured getting you out of here."

She realized that the scene inside had not been a ruse. Something bad was happening. "This is serious?" she questioned, still trying to grasp what could possibly be going on.

"Normally, I'm not privy to information like this. And to be honest, I don't understand the science parts." He sighed, almost defeated. "What I do understand is that in a matter of just two days an entire city has burned to the ground."

"Viral outbreaks tend to bring out the worst in people," she nodded solemnly. "It's the fear. Things like looting and wanton destruction fit the pattern without being a symptom of the virus. If that is what you're getting at?" Surely they weren't trying to suggest that?

"I don't know," he answered truthfully as he pulled out onto the road. It was raining. Not heavily, but enough to make the dark corners of the night completely disappear from sight.

...

The roads were a mess. The physical activity seemed to suddenly die down, but the disaster remained. As Sgt. Denning drove up and down the roads, Joaquin was taking pictures with his phone. Everything had spiraled out of control way too fast. They both knew it. It was likely no one was going to need his photos for the reports. Everyone saw the same thing. He kept taking captures anyway.

"This is some kind of shit," the Sergeant drawled. "I have never seen anything like this before."

The news app broke in over his camera settings and the headline flashed across the screen. "Mysterious flu taking over Baton Rouge." Then another that said, "Riots spread West into Texas and North into Arkansas." Nothing moved this fast.

Joaquin realized that Denning couldn't see the headlines, but he was sure he'd understand. "If this is a virus, we're in trouble."

The Sergeant nodded. "I think those pictures are on the eastbound side. We're just going to go up here and turn around." He entered the on ramp carefully. They had only been on the freeway for a moment when they saw crumpled metal and what seemed like several abandoned cars littering the road. "What the hell is this?"

As they pulled over onto the right shoulder, they both saw the tail lights of the van parked in front of them. Had they called for assistance? Is that what they were waiting for? He pulled up slowly about a car's length behind the van. The dome light was on. He saw people inside. Sprinting across the lanes to check inside the mangled vehicles, he was startled to see all but one were empty.

A car flew by in the lane next to him. Joaquin felt the car rock just a bit. Because he was shoulder side, he climbed out and made his way up to the van. Peering inside he saw four people. One was the nurse from the hospital that got tossed across the room. He looked like he was in bad shape. Calling as loud as he could to Denning, who was already making his way back to the van, he said, "We have injured over here."

Although his phone was working fine just moments ago, Joaquin couldn't find a signal.

"Won't do you no good, baby," the old woman called out of the window. "This here is a dead zone."

The chill that crawled down Joaquin's spine was more a reaction to the woman's words than the cold air.

"What happened to the other drivers?" Sgt. Denning was standing next to the driver's side window. "That car is the only one occupied." He pointed to the last car in the line behind Morgan's. The front end was crushed and there was a man slumped over the steering wheel.

"That's my car over there," Morgan pointed towards his vehicle. Raising his arm caused a little stress on his ribs and he winced.

The accident had happened nearly twenty minutes ago. The Explorer and the other car were empty? How could that be? No one had gotten out. No one had run. Eddie sounded completely confused. "No, there's one guy in the Explorer and a woman in that car." He pointed to the last car.

"Hate to break it to you," Denning said flatly.

Eddie slightly raised his voice. "No. I saw them. They were both..." he trailed off. He didn't even like saying the word.

Joaquin interjected, looking directly at Morgan, "You're the nurse from University Medical. The one that Bo Cane attacked?" He knew it was him. But it still came out like a question.

Morgan nodded slowly, trying not to stress his injuries. He didn't recognize the man, but he had been unconscious for the whole night. "I missed all the excitement."

"Can we *go?*" Hana almost whined out the words. Trying to sound a little less childish she added, "Aren't you a police officer?" she directed towards Denning.

"We should get all of you to the hospital. Just to be sure. I have some questions." Two cars sped by. Both swerved just before hitting the procession of broken vehicles. The van rocked.

A wave of panic swept over Morgan. "No. No. No. I'm going to my Mom's." Waving his hands wildly he added, "They were just witnesses." It was obvious he was about to panic. He wanted out of NOLA.

"I have a signal," Joaquin called out from the back of the van. He began dialing a number. Muffled sounds of a conversation echoed through the van. But what he was saying was indistinct. He walked to the car behind them on the shoulder, then walked around to the driver's side of the van where the Sergeant was still standing. "Any of you sick?" he directed to the van.

None of them had any symptoms of the flu or anything else. Morgan's injuries were simply that, injuries. As they all shook their heads, he added, "Any of you been around sick?" Then looking at Morgan, he added. "Well, I know the answer to that one." Gently tossing a handful of surgical type masks into the van he said, "Blue side out. But I don't know what good that's going to do. Just drive safe."

Sgt. Denning's expression went from confused to irritated quickly. "What are you doing?"

"We have way bigger problems. This is playing over and over again as far North as Little Rock and all the way into Houston." He shook his head, "And whatever it is, it's moving fast." Almost apologetically he addressed everyone in the van, "Sorry, don't mean to scare any of you."

"No," Eddie answered, "We're all sufficiently scared already."

Joaquin realized that he was saying way too much in front of everyone. The information he'd been given was to be relayed to the Sergeant, not them. He also knew that Morgan understood what was going on better than any of them. He figured it might help them out a little. "WHO is stepping in here. They have a virologist coming in from Montreal or something. They said this looks like one of hers. Whatever that means."

Eddie sat back, rubbing his face. It was obvious he was experiencing the onset of a panic attack. Hana watched his face as he tried to catch his breath. Looking Joaquin directly in the eye she asked, "They didn't happen to say it was Dr. Bélisaire did they?"

Joaquin nodded, "Yes. That's her name."

From the back, Queenie was humming softly. She looked up at the men outside the vehicle. Almost jovially she said, "Oh, I didn't see that one coming."

It was obvious that Eddie was in distress. But he held it together enough to catch the strange thing that the man had said. "What do you mean it looks like one of hers?"

"That's Mr. Eddie's wife," Queenie filled their new friends in. Then directing towards Eddie, she continued the song she was humming, "Dites vos prières et dis bonne nuit." *[Say your prayers and say goodnight]*

The Only Thing Missing

Within three hours of leaving the Provincial station in Montreal, Rosalind was in Washington DC. They had a small plane waiting for her at a tiny landing area. She hated those small planes. Every bump, every strong wind was transferred through the cabin and shook her deeply. At least the larger planes weren't as treacherous. Physics wasn't her thing and to be honest, *all* airplanes scared her a little. What scared her more were the words coming from the man sitting across from her.

It was the Director General of the WHO. She had never met him, but she recognized him immediately. Dr. Amadi Tedesse. Referring to the pools of water in the coroner's report he continued, "We dug in a little deeper, and found the faintest traces of biological proteins. But it was *so* minuscule."

"I don't completely understand." She was being honest. "What are you saying?"

He shook his head several times. Although his accent was thick, he was very articulate. There is no way she misunderstood his words. "At this point, we are investigating the possibility that these *are* the remains of the deceased."

A bolt of lightning struck off in the distance and was punctuated with a loud clap of thunder. The slight bit of turbulence that followed made her stomach turn. She hadn't eaten anything all day, but something wanted to come up. "That's impossible." She swallowed hard, attempting to keep whatever contents that remained in her stomach, in her stomach. "There is no way the cells could possibly break down that fast. It's not even possible."

Even at the cellular level, it took weeks for the proteins to completely break down. All of these reports appeared to have taken just hours for the sick to disappear. *Disappear.* That word disturbed her.

The rest of the flight was quiet. They exited the storm just after entering it and there were clear skies the rest of the way. She still wasn't comforted. Everything looked so dark. Even the lights that were littering the scene below seemed dim. By the time they landed in DC, she had skimmed all the notes. While it seemed to fit, it was all wrong. There was something they were missing. There is no way this virus could have done this. Not on its own. There would had to have been something else introduced. Something that sped up the process?

No, it was ridiculous. There is no way this was what they seemed to think it was. But whatever it was, it was terrifying. To add a little more to the panic that was welling up inside her, they were met by a military transport at the air field. She wondered if anyone knew that she'd been suspected of murder. Did they care? What was going on? "Can I have a phone?" she finally asked after they began to move.

The soldier in the passenger seat handed her a manila envelope. Inside were her belongings that were taken when they booked her in. Her phone had been turned off and the charge was still full. She started to dial Olivia, then changed her mind and called Eddie first. It went directly to voicemail. She didn't leave a message. Emptying the bag in her lap, she almost dropped her wedding ring and snatched it up before it hit the floorboard. The rest of the contents spilled around her.

Leaning over, she absentmindedly picked up the small flash drive from the mess and tucked it into the pocket of her slacks. No one spoke on the ride. The silence assaulted her with memories she'd been fighting so hard to keep at bay. Unable to resist them, her mind wandered.

...

"Rosalind. Eddie. Thanks for coming in," Dr. MacGregor greeted them as they made their way into his office. "How are you feeling?" he directed towards her as he motioned for them to have a seat.

They both looked nervous. He decided to just get to the point.

"We're not seeing the development of lymphocytes that we should be seeing by now."

Looking back and forth at the doctor and his wife's faces, Eddie was trying to grasp the solemnity of the situation. He realized that she understood, but he didn't. "What does that mean?" he asked.

Without expression the doctor explained, "By this time, we should see a lot of development in the liver and spleen but there isn't enough happening." He sat back and sighed, "It's likely she'll be born with very little, if any, immune system."

Rosalind hadn't said a word. Whatever cues he was hoping to get from her didn't come. Leaning forward in anticipation Eddie asked, "But, that's not that uncommon right? I mean, you've seen this before? Aren't there treatments and things we can do?"

"We've still got several weeks. It could just be slow development." The doctor crossed his hands on his desk. It was obvious it was to keep from fidgeting. "It's just important that we know what to expect."

"I understand," Rosalind stood and it was apparent she was done with the conversation. She took two steps as Eddie and the doctor looked at her somewhat confused. "Are you coming?" she asked Eddie without looking back over her shoulder.

He stood and addressed the doctor, "Thanks Doctor." Catching up with Rosalind he gently took her arm and led her out of the office. "Don't you want to hear what our options are? What we need to do?"

"I know what I need to do," she replied staunchly. She walked away quickly as though she had just dropped a timed explosive and she wanted to make a quick getaway. Eddie followed behind her quietly.

She withdrew completely during the last few weeks of her pregnancy. No matter how hard he tried, she wouldn't talk about it. She kept insisting that everything would be fine. He knew that she knew the truth. It would probably have been easier on her had she *not* understood everything. But for her to deny and insist that things would be fine... He was so afraid she was setting herself up for a very damaging fall.

...

What seemed like a lifetime of memories flooded to him and his head was pounding. Delivering Morgan to his mother seemed like the most important task at this point, so they had traveled on to Lafayette. Things were just as bad there. Eddie was glad when they finally arrived at the modest but beautiful Lake Martin home. It was a cross between a beach home and a log cabin, raised a couple of feet from the ground. The backdrop was the gorgeous swampland.

"Did you grow up here?" Hana tried to keep the conversation light as they pulled down the long but well-lit drive.

"Nah." Morgan released the seat belt, finally grateful to have the pressure off of his chest. "They moved here after dad retired." He was quiet for a moment then added, "It's just my mom now."

"I'm sorry to hear that." She lowered her head with respect for a moment then released her own belt. By the time the van had come to a complete stop, her door was already wide open. She was ready to get out. How on Earth did she end up in Lafayette? What was going on?

With the dome light lit, Queenie was able to dig into her canvas bag and she retrieved a tiny, dirty bag tied with a string. She extended her arm towards Morgan and said, "I think this one might be yours."

Without really understanding what she was giving him, he graciously accepted. He knew she was eccentric, but she was kind. She also seemed to know something. Or maybe she didn't. It could have all been for show. But whatever was happening, she wasn't sick either. Not yet at least. A wave of absolute panic washed over him, starting at the lowest part of his stomach. As it spread through him, he almost shouted, "I don't want to get her sick."

Queenie picked up the stack of hospital facial covers that the man had given them. "Blue side out then," she laughed and added, "But you know this."

Hana had been flipping through several news stories as they drove. The internet had been spotty in several places, but it didn't seem to be a continuous outage. "I hate to be "Captain Bring Down" here, but I don't think those masks are going to stop this." Waving her hands wildly over her head she added, "Whatever all of this is."

Eddie walked just behind them, watching. Hana had been a very good sport up to this point. But she was tired, he was tired. There was a lot to process. This place seemed incredibly out of the way and very safe. He should just leave everyone here and figure out where Rosalind was. As he was considering what to do, he saw that he had a missed call. It was from Rosalind.

As they got to the door Queenie breathed deeply and said, "Coffee's on!" Watching Morgan fumble with his key, she giggled again. "I already love this woman."

The door opened before Morgan had a chance to turn the key. Shari almost exploded out onto the porch, wrapping her arms around him. He protested, trying to instill in her all the reasons why it was better to just sit and talk. She was his mother, she didn't care. It was more of a statement than a question when Shari said, "We all staying here tonight? I got a fresh pot of coffee on." Hugging Morgan one more time, they entered the home of this gracious stranger and she added, "Might need a minute to get some clean sheets on the beds."

The aroma of warm cinnamon and apples permeated the entry. As they came through the door Shari turned around, taking them all in. "Take those ridiculous things off," she demanded. "I went out earlier, people are already sick here. If I'm getting it, I'm getting it." She then looked concerned at the strangers in her house. "Are y'all sick? I have medicine." Then added somberly, "For whatever good it will do."

Eddie considered excusing himself to the front porch. He needed to call Rosalind back. He had no idea what he was going to say. As he was contemplating a speech, a text came through. It was her. *In DC. I'll explain later.* He was exhausted. They all were. It would take at least an hour to get from where they were to any hotel. He wasn't going to make it that far.

Shari was already busying herself with the task of clean sheets.

...

Things had gotten so far out of hand. The plan had been to get the data from Ros' files. It wasn't completely selfish, she was going to share. But, Rosalind had *something.* All he was supposed to do was toss the room, grab a couple things. No one was supposed to get hurt, much less *die.* It was as though Rex was just improvising. That's what she got for hiring an idiot.

If Rosalind were to publish her research, she'd just *give* this away. Her charity was one of the things that Olivia liked so much about her. But this was a cure for cancer. This was a lifetime of work. Not just hers, but all of theirs. And not everyone had the capital behind them to be able to afford to give it away. This was supposed to be a windfall for all of them. But now things had become so muddy that she had no idea what to do. And to make matters worse, she still hadn't found what she was looking for.

As the news played in the background, stories of riots and a mysterious bug continued. It had cluttered up almost all of the airwaves nationally. The whole world was already watching. Even though she knew she was waiting on a call, she still jumped just a little when the phone rang. Everything was making her jumpy. "What?" she answered.

"See, it all worked out. Your girlfriend is in DC now," the voice on the other end began speaking as soon as she answered.

"DC?" she asked incredulously.

Breathing heavily on the other end the man said, "Apparently they needed her help with the bug going around." He was incompetent, but at least he knew what was happening.

"Rosalind doesn't do *bugs*," she spat out, as though the thought tasted terrible on her tongue.

"Well whatever, I'm not a brilliant scientist," he fired back.

"You're not a brilliant anything." She was tired of him. Tired of this conversation and ready to go home. Blatantly spouted, "You were supposed to get his computer. That was it. No one was supposed to get hurt."

"Things happen." He was right. He wasn't a scientist. He wasn't a doctor. He hadn't taken an oath to protect life. He was the muscle. But still. "But I didn't do this." He breathed heavily again, likely exhaling smoke from a cigarette, and added, "Tell me you at least found what you were after."

"It's not here," she admitted. "I've gone through everything." Rolling the suitcase out of the room, she headed down to the lobby to check out. "I'll call you when I find something. Don't call me back," she demanded and made her way to the front desk. Apparently, she was heading to DC.

...

Normally, after any accident, the freeway would be littered with tow trucks waiting for the coin toss. That's how it worked, whomever won the toss got the tow. No one had shown up yet and Sgt. Denning called dispatch to radio whomever might be available. After all four vehicles were tagged and loaded, he and Joaquin headed back towards the station. The whole process took over an hour, way longer than normal.

Unable to locate the CDC vans that had been in the photo, they headed back to the station. By the time they made it back, things seemed to have calmed down. Missing Persons was ringing off the hook, but the madness had died down. It was likely many of the people reported missing would be found hiding or confused. That's the way it always happened after riots and whatever this might be.

"What now?" Joaquin was tired. He hadn't slept in a couple of days. It was likely Sgt. Denning hadn't either. They were running on fumes and still had no idea what was happening. The blood stain from yesterday was still visible, if only slightly. It seemed like a year had passed since the detective was shot, but it had only been about thirty-six hours.

The problem was, the events in NOLA were playing out all over now. Not just in Louisiana and Texas, but it was spreading. Joaquin texted a colleague at the CDC, *What's happening?*

As if she had been waiting for the text, a reply came immediately, *Just chill.*

"For fuck sake," he sighed loudly. Turning his attention to the Sergeant, he explained, "I think I just got told to back off."

"That doesn't sound suspicious in the least." Denning poured a cup of coffee from his small pot and offered a cup to Joaquin. They were running on caffeine. "That means we should stick our noses in, right?"

Before either could say anything else, Joaquin's phone rang. He connected the call on speaker, "What do you mean chill?"

The female voice on the other end replied, almost in a whisper, "Those samples were sent to the WHO. They did find something. I can't go into it now. I'll call you later."

Before she had a chance to end the call, he almost shouted, "People are dying, right?"

"Are you sick?" she asked quickly.

"No." He tried to add more but she cut him off.

"Then you're fine. For now." The call disconnected.

"She sounds lovely," Denning joked. The sounds of sirens had become so prevalent over the last couple of days, that it was almost surreal how quiet things had gotten. As suddenly as the madness had begun, it seemed to be dying down. At least in NOLA. "We should both get some sleep."

Joaquin almost laughed, "My apartment burned down this morning."

"Ain't that some shit?" Denning replied sarcastically. Then offered, "I have a couch here, and one at home. You're welcome to either."

He hadn't even considered what he was going to do. "Got family in Baton Rouge," he replied. "Talked to my sister earlier. I guess I'm going to head that way." Almost as an afterthought he added. "You'll call me on anything right?"

"What else could possibly happen?" His voice was dripping with sarcasm.

Joaquin shuddered, the Sergeant was tempting fate.

Balance

Shari and Queenie hit it off as though they were long lost family. They had absolutely nothing in common. But the spirit picks who it picks. It was strange that in a time like this the women would connect over trivial things, but none of their conversation included the happenings of the past few days.

They talked about how cold the winter had been. How dry the summer had been. They talked about the televangelist that had recently been involved in that scandal. They talked about the saints. That was where they settled as the two women moved into the kitchen. "Has anyone eaten today?" None of them had. Shari was definitely in tune with her motherly instinct.

As exhausted as everyone was, no one wanted to go to sleep. Not yet. Watching Shari and Queenie in the kitchen making a midnight meal fit for a king turned out to be the best way for everyone to relax. She had been to the market earlier in the day and everything was fresh. "Broiling a chicken at 12:30 in the morning. Haven't done anything like this since you were a boy," she smiled at Morgan.

For a single widow, she had an awful lot of wine. It was a collection that her late husband had been accumulating his entire life. There were some amazing labels in there. Shari had tasked Eddie to pick a wine because he just looked like a "wine guy". She was right.

"Are you sure you want the *best* one?" He walked out of the tiny closet with a bottle of Cheval Blanc in each hand. As he walked through the kitchen the scene became completely surreal. Who were these people he was about to have dinner in the middle of the night with? How did he get himself here? A burst of laughter erupted, and he had missed what had been said. But Hana's laugh reminded him quickly how he had gotten here. "What?"

Morgan's face was beet red. Trying to restrain the laughter in her voice Hana tried to explain, "She said..." she breathed heavily.

"Oh, don't go repeating that. My word," Shari stopped her. They all laughed again. It was obviously a joke at his expense. He was okay with that. He should have been paying attention anyway.

"They're pretty valuable though..." Eddie started to suggest he pick something else, but she snagged both bottles from him.

Digging for the corkscrew she said, "Can't drink it dead." A solemn silence overtook them all.

...

The open dining area of the house was comfortable and spacious. The five of them sat at the dining table. Probably the first time in a while there had been that many people at the table. It was a reprieve in the middle of chaos. For just a short time it felt like the world was right. Like everything was going to be okay. Queenie looked around the room as everyone talked. If she was going to find balance, this would be the place. The fire was dying a little, but Mr. Eddie had gotten up and handled it before anyone else had a chance. There was a lot of darkness in this room, but a lot of good too.

She watched as the shadows from the fire danced against the far wall. The shadows always told more than the light. The last time any real cleansing came was in 1905. Yellow fever took thousands. Her grandmother told her all the stories about how the papers and the doctors didn't tell anyone. So, everyone got sick. She thought they were going to see it again in 2014 when Ebola came. That was more scare than sick though. Thing is, this one didn't seem natural.

The media sure had hold of this one though. And they were yammering about it all over the news. Queenie had been relieved when Shari suggested they turn off the television. The conversation at the table remained light. Everyone was worried and tired and just plain confused. It seemed like the fellowship was a necessary medicine right now.

Mr. Eddie kept messing with his phone, but that was to be expected.

The rest of his tribe wasn't here. But the rest of them. They were their own tribes. It was probably why they ended up here, now. Whoever up there was running the show right now decided they were going to need each other. Or maybe it was all random. No. She'd seen what was coming.

As the shadows danced back and forth on the wall, she was mesmerized by the glow. She didn't realize she was humming. Not at first.

"I love that song," Shari said softly. "Used to play that record over and over again."

Morgan and Eddie had begun collecting everything from the table. Although he was still hurting, the pain had finally begun to subside a bit. It might just be because he was numb. Everything seemed out of place. They all knew something bad was happening, but they sat here at the dining table like it was Thanksgiving. The warm smell of burning oak lent to the feel.

The Magicicada were chirping. That didn't seem right. It was February. It had only been a few years since these cicadae had emerged last. Wasn't supposed to happen for at least thirteen years. But there they were. Even *they* knew something was on the wind. Maybe they were trying to warn everyone? The locust always seemed to accompany the plagues.

Queenie gently placed her hand on Hana's. "Girl, I guess I owe you some kind of apology," she sighed and chuckled. "Us old women get a little lofty sometimes." Nodding she continued, "Something connected y'all two long before this weekend." She turned to Eddie and spoke a little louder, "The cards weren't telling us what was gonna happen. Just how it happened."

"Happened?" Hana had given up being skeptical. She didn't believe in the cards or the Hoodoo, but she did believe that something was happening. "That makes it all sound final. Like there's nothing anyone can do."

Eddie's phone dinged again. *I didn't do it. You know that right?*

He sighed. Of course he knew. He replied, *I know.*

Her next text said, *I don't know how, but they think this is my fault.*

Unsure of what she meant he replied, *What's your fault?*

The phone was silent for a few moments. The others were lost in a conversation and he hadn't been paying attention to. Again. When it dinged, he jumped a little. He was exhausted. *Whoever it is, someone has done a very good job of making it look like EV-121.*

Her cancer cure? Was she suggesting that they thought her cure had started this? *How is that even possible? You haven't tested it yet, have you?*

Of course not. He could hear the indignant tone in her reply.

Another text came through very quickly, *I can't say anything else.*

...

"Are you okay?" Hana had taken the chair next to Eddie. Queenie and Shari had moved off to the living room to discuss the statues of the saints. Morgan was lying on the sofa watching them. It was almost three in the morning. Eddie's eyes felt red and dry. When he rubbed his face, it was like sandpaper on his skin. But the touch of her hand was as soft as silk.

"No," he admitted quickly. "You?"

"Of course not," she said solemnly. They could hear the crackle of the fire. Somehow, the voices in the background seemed to fade out. "When Ebby died, Noah kind of got lost in whatever it is he was working on. I know how competitive and consuming his work was." Where was she going with this? She sighed and turned so she was facing him and took both of his hands. "The experimental procedure was a virus. After it didn't work Noah just kind of..." she trailed off for a moment but caught her thoughts again, "...he became obsessed with solving it. It became a puzzle for him."

Virus? She said virus. "What virus?" He wasn't sure if she was done or if she was reflecting. But his stomach started to turn, and he felt light-headed. He already knew what she was going to say. The fragrance of the wax melts in the dining room created a sweet nauseating scent that assaulted his sinuses. "I don't suppose you'd remember what it was called?"

The panic in his eyes wasn't lost on her. Her heart raced, and she gasped a little, trying to catch her breath. She had no idea why, but she was feeling his trauma, his fear. "Of course I do. That's not something a mother would forget." It was sad but so very true. "It had a long name. But they called it EV-118."

Pointing clumsily to the vial around her neck he croaked, "Where is the rest?"

She clutched the bottle tightly in her hand. "What?" What was he asking her? Why was he asking her? "That's why I came back here." Speaking the words seemed to rip through her but she managed to push them out, "I spread his ashes on the Mississippi. On Friday."

The room began to spin. Waves of nausea crept through him. It felt like hot needles jabbing into his face as he realized his blood pressure had spiked. Was he about to pass out? Unbelievable! Fortunately, the floors in the dining room were bare. He didn't feel so bad losing everything he'd just eaten on the floor. He'd clean that up. After he regained consciousness.

...

She knew she shouldn't have, but she did it anyway. After they cleaned Eddie up and got him into the guest room, Hana had gone back to help with the mess. His phone dinged. Trying to ignore it was impossible. She snatched the device up and unlocked it with a swipe. There was no code. The notification was a push from CNN. More of the same everywhere. Ignoring that, she opened his text messages.

Before getting a chance to actually read anything, she heard Queenie from behind whisper softly, "Are you sure you wanna do that, girl?" There was no judgment in her voice.

Hana set the phone back on the table and watched the screen go dark. "He must have been exhausted," she empathized.

"Everyone is," Morgan said, shuffling through the dining area towards the living room. The plush sofa was his claim for the night. "He's okay." Switching off the light over the living room, he called back, "Everyone needs to get some sleep."

Shari had missed the last bit of excitement as she had gone to bed just before. It made the most sense for Queenie to take the fold out in the den, which left Hana in the guest room as well. Fortunately, there was a full bath. The water was hot, and it was clean. It had been years since she had taken a well water shower but the soft feel as it rolled down her skin was unmistakable. It had that brackish almost salty quality that the neighboring swamp possessed. But it was nice.

How had she ended up here? All she wanted to do was close a door. Instead... Her thoughts were interrupted by the grumbling noise coming from the bed. Eddie was stirring. "Holy shit, my head," he groaned.

She was still wrapped in the bath towel and her hair was wet. Drops of water fell onto the sheets as she sat down next to him. "I think you may have banged it on the table." She leaned over and gently outlined the small knot on his forehead with the tip of her finger, careful not to actually touch it. "Morgan said it wasn't bad enough to worry about." Lowering her voice, she whispered, "It looks pretty bad though."

"It feels pretty bad," he tried to joke and laugh. That had been a mistake. His head was screaming. Tiny droplets of water dripped from the tips of her hair onto his face. A pleasing fragrance of coconut wafted around her as well as the clean smell of soap. His vision was a little blurry which made all the lines around her soft. He'd had a little more of the wine than he thought.

Not sure if it was the maternal instinct in her begging to come out, or something else, she kissed his forehead several times. Each time she leaned in, the tips of her hair bounced off the pillow leaving a damp ring on each side. Tilting his head back he caught her lips with his as she leaned forward again. "Sorry," he whispered, realizing his breath must smell terrible.

It had begun to rain outside, and the heavy drops hit the ceramic roof tiles creating a rhythmic pinging. The sound was almost transcendent for a few moments. "What time is it?" he managed to ask, although he didn't really care. "Oh my God." He realized how he'd ended up in this bed. "I made a mess."

"It's okay, it wasn't bad," she lied, then continued to kiss his face. He hadn't shaved in a couple of days. She liked it. He looked so much different right now. Defeated. Weak. Fragile. A completely different person than the man she met just two days ago. Maybe that man was a front. "We got it."

Outside the walls of the cozy swamp cottage, the world was going to hell. He knew he should text Rosalind back. Tell her about Ebrim's ashes. But that couldn't be it. Could it? The room was spinning a little. There were a thousand things he should be doing right now.

But when the little tuck she had secured the towel to herself with came loose and slid slowly off her body, he forgot everything.

She feigned protest, "You need to sleep." He did need to sleep. She needed to sleep. But she wasn't going to stop him.

...

The patter of the rain was cleansing. Just what they needed. Queenie sat in the middle of the fold out bed quietly praying. From what she had pieced together in her dreams, Brother Borre might not have been the first, but he was the first one they found. Something had carried on up the river. How it happened was neither here nor there.

The world had become a terrible place. No, that wasn't true. It was the people that had made it that way. She didn't have her altar, but she did enjoy the two-way fireplace that opened into the living room. She was able to watch the coals as they smoldered. The aroma was warm. It would do for now.

Addressing St. Michael, her first prayer was for her new friends. The second for herself. She wasn't even sure anymore if anyone was listening. But she had to believe. Very little light crept in from the night, but occasionally a little ray of moonlight tagged the blanket in front of her. She focused on that.

"You will not fear the terror of night. Nor the arrow that flies by day. Nor the pestilence that stalks in the darkness. Nor the plague that destroys at midday," she recited from Psalm 91. "A thousand may fall at your side. Ten thousand at your right hand but it will not come near you. You will only observe with your eyes and see the punishment of the wicked." Wicked? She mused. It wouldn't be so bad if they'd all been wicked. But that's not how a plague worked. It was indiscriminate. More often than not, it was fickle.

It wasn't that she was against science. But these folks were playing God. *Creating* life. Even if it was only visible under a microscope. That's what they were doing. When the Good Lord designed sickness, He designed a way for it to end. Let's hope these doctors had done the same. But more than likely this was all an accident. She shuddered as she thought about that poor girl. Even Judas was only a tool when it all came down to it. Destined to be the one. Hana had pulled that lot too.

It was how things balanced out. Take the good with the bad. The light with the dark. One will never weigh more. You just gotta see the whole picture. She saw the whole picture. And it still made her shiver.

END ACT 2

ACT THREE – THE SCIENCE OF IT ALL

Monday Morning

By the time the sun came up, Rosalind was back in the hotel. She was under guard. Obviously, they hadn't forgotten. All things in perspective. She texted Eddie, but he hadn't answered. She was worried about him, but she wasn't sure at this point if she even still retained that right. Olivia had messaged earlier in the morning that she'd managed to get a flight to DC this afternoon.

Her eyes were tired and felt like she'd been rubbing salt in them for the past couple of hours. Her stomach was rumbling, and her head was pounding. She hadn't eaten or had any caffeine in about twenty-four hours. She ordered room service and took a hot shower. Before she'd had a chance to completely dry off, room service had delivered her breakfast.

The croissant was warm and flaky. The coffee was fresh, and the aroma was a little overwhelming. She was exhausted. Local broadcasts of national news played all over the country. Reports from Georgia and New Mexico. Even as far as Ohio. It would only be a matter of days before it affected the whole world.

It sure sounded like something out of her most recent dissertations, Dr. Tedesse had insisted. "It would take *weeks* for a visible breakdown to occur," she argued. "Whatever is going on only takes *hours*. There is just no way this could occur so fast." And that's where they were. They were facing a possible global epidemic of a virus that presented no telltale signs until it... Until it what? Started dissolving the infected into water?

Going over any natural mutation was where they'd left off. Her eyes were blurry, and everything was confusing.

The other things puzzling them that needed to be solved quickly was how it was spreading, and why it didn't affect everyone. Those two answers would be the key to stopping it. If they could stop it. She was dozing when her phone dinged. The number displayed above the text said *Unknown.* All the text said was, *We need to talk.*

She was not interested in cryptic contacts. *Who is this?* she replied. It was several minutes before a response came. She figured maybe they'd had the wrong number and realized their mistake. When the notification went off again, she sighed. She was falling asleep.

The reply not only woke her up, it also made her shudder. *It's Noah.*

...

Olivia had a few things to tie up in Montreal before she headed out. She considered re-cluttering Rosalind's computer, but there wasn't anything on it. She would just say she couldn't sleep. Given what was happening all over the states, it was likely Rosalind would never even see a court room. She'd figure out what was going on, be the hero and everyone would forget. Which actually suited her. This whole thing had gotten messy.

What she should do is just forget about it. Walk away. But she wasn't sure that was an option. Instead, here she was heading out to Washington DC shortly. She just wanted to go home. No, that wasn't true. She wanted this win. No, she wanted to see Rosalind.

The flight wasn't until just after one o'clock, so she had plenty of time. Collecting Rosalind's things as well, she realized she was going to have to pay for the extra bag. She had to get her things back to her though. Slinging Rosalind's jacket across her arm as she was about to leave, a clear plastic object flew out of one of the pockets. It was the tip cover for a flash drive. The fury at which she ripped through all of Rosalind's belongings again was disturbing, even to her. Still no drive.

Slowly repacking everything as neatly as she could, she almost lunged when the phone in her own bag rang. Aside from Rosalind, she couldn't think of anyone who might be calling her right now. She fumbled around until she located it in the bottom of her carry on, but it had already stopped ringing. "Shit." The phone nearly slipped out of her hands as she was looking at the missed calls. Instead of Ros' number, which she was expecting to see, it said *Unknown*.

...

The aroma of fresh coffee wafted through the house. Shari had given Hana a few items of clothing last night to choose from and the fleece pants and the long sleeve t-shirt won. She was surprised that, aside from Shari, she was the first person stirring. But the coffee was so inviting. Shari seemed pleased to have company over her first morning cup.

"Is it wrong to feel relieved right now?" Shari broached the heavy subject way too early. But one mother to another, it was a valid question. "My whole family is here. And I've made some new friends. But so many people..."

Even with the cream she added, the coffee was hotter than she expected, and Hana made a face as she tried to cool her mouth. "There is nothing wrong with being happy that your kid is okay."

Shari was going to continue but saw the look of loss and pain in her eyes. She was obviously speaking from experience. A mother knew that look. Instead she jumped up and fiddled with a few items in the refrigerator. "Omelets!" she proclaimed.

"Why do you have to be so loud?" Morgan called from the sofa.

"Ungrateful child!" Shari laughed. Pouring a cup of the morning ambrosia she carried it over to him. He sat up and returned the laughter sleepily. "You hungry?" He nodded as he blew on the cup. The scene was beautiful, even if everything else was a mess. It was normal.

Eddie stirred just after Hana left the bed. He needed a shower. He could smell the coffee and hear the voices down the hall. Everyone was waking up. He felt almost guilty putting on the late Mr. Hall's clothes, but he didn't have any options. The flannel shirt felt comfortably worn, and the sweats fit well enough.

By the time he joined them in the dining area, everyone but Queenie had come out. Shari paused as he walked past. For just a moment, she saw Grant. As she shook the thought, she noticed the welt on his forehead. "When did you do that?"

"You missed all the fun, Mom." Morgan made light of the situation.

His phone was still on the corner of the table. No one had moved it. It still had a bit of a charge, and he noticed that he had missed a couple of calls. Shari was an incredible hostess, or maybe she just missed the family vibe. She brought a cup of coffee and set it down in front of him. "Normally, I have a no phones at the table rule," she playfully scolded. "I think today we can make an exception."

He smiled and thanked her for the coffee. As he connected to voicemail, he took in everything around him. It would have been an incredible postcard for family had the situation not been what it was. "Eddie. It's pretty early or late or whatever it is. I'm going to get some sleep." Rosalind sounded so scared. She almost pleaded, "Please just let me know you're okay."

Disconnecting from voicemail, he sent her a text message. *I'm OK.* He sent a second message. *Do you want me to come to DC?* There had been a couple of missed calls after hers. They were both from unknown numbers. Her voicemail was the only one.

It had only been a couple of hours since she left the voicemail. He was sure she'd still be sleeping, but a reply came immediately. *Dr. Patel isn't dead.*

That was strange. *What?* he replied. For a brief second, he paused then sent a second text, *Are you sure?*

I just talked to him, the black text on the screen faded to red then to black again. That happened every so often, when things didn't make sense. *Where are you?* she texted again.

He replied quickly, *Lafayette. Long story.*

Hana was sitting across from him. Talking to Shari. She was resting her chin on the palm of her hand. She sensed him gazing at her and looked his way and smiled. A look of stunned confusion on his face caught her attention. "What's wrong?" she asked. As though there wasn't a list of at least a thousand things.

"Have you checked your messages lately?" he asked.

Her phone had died last night at some point. Her purse was still sitting against the back wall of the dining room. She dug through and found the charger and plugged it in. "You were the last person to check my voicemail." She hung her head. That seemed like it had been years ago. It only took a couple of minutes for the phone to power up, but it took forever for all of the push notifications to come through as it vibrated constantly in her hand.

When she looked up again, everyone was watching her. Queenie had made her way silently through the kitchen and was pouring her own cup of coffee. Even she was watching. That was creepy. What was creepier was the text message she was looking at. The number showed as *Unknown* but the message was clear. *IM-V-4248. The files are in my safe. Get them to Dr. Rosalind Bélisaire. She should be in DC by now.*

Backing out of text messages, she pulled down on the screen to refresh it. She opened the text again and the date stamp showed the message had come early this morning. *Early this morning.* Was this from Noah? Her right ear began to ring loudly. As the pitch changed in her head, the screeching sound made her wince. Her face was flush, and she could feel her heart pounding in her cheeks.

Leaning against the wall for support, she realized she was still being watched. No one said a word as she worked out the situation in her head. Eddie made his way over to where she was almost crumpled on the floor. Looking up at him completely confused she turned the phone around so that he could see the screen.

Shari's concern overtook her as she exclaimed, "You look like you've seen a ghost, dear." She had no idea how right she'd been.

"That almost looks kind of like one of Rosalind's...." Eddie didn't have time to finish his thought before Hana nodded forcefully. "Is this text from..." he trailed off again. How could he ask her something like that?

"It's from Noah," she stated flatly. Then looking around the room she said to everyone, "I need Eddie to take me home." She *needed* to go home. She *wanted* Eddie to take her. No, she needed him to. How else would she get it all to Rosalind?

"Where is home?" he whispered. It didn't matter if she'd said Shreveport or Los Angeles, he would drive her. But he was relieved when she said Tiki Island. That was only about three hours west. He'd been there dozens of times with the firm. "Eat first," he told her as he picked her up off the floor. No one asked what was happening. She was glad for that. Shari gleefully brought her the first plate. She was starving. The omelet was incredible.

...

Although distant puffs of smoke still seemed to blend into the clouds, the fires were out for the most part. Small crews had busied themselves early this morning clearing cars, cleaning debris and patching up what could be patched. Nearly a quarter of city officials, officers and other public servants had not shown up to work. Nearly a quarter of the city was just...gone. It was possible some had just cut and run. But he was sure the death toll would be inconceivable.

Sgt. Denning sat at his desk taking inventory of the day. Someone had finally gotten the stain out of the carpet. But the spot was much cleaner than the rest now. It screamed failure, either way. He had spoken with someone from the World Health Organization early this morning and it seemed that the virus or whatever it was didn't have any lasting effects on the environment. What that meant was, it wouldn't recirculate. They hoped.

For the first time in...well, ever, Mardi Gras had officially been canceled. It was likely more people were going to be concerning themselves with Ash Wednesday instead. Either way, the city's revenue would tank. While the Sergeant didn't see a problem with that, the Mayor did. And she was already on his ass which was more than he needed on a Monday.

Iris' notes were still scattered across his desk. He wondered how many of these files were representative of people they'd never see again. Not the way he wanted to lighten the work load, that's for sure. The sounds of people talking, footsteps and other normal daily noises fluttered around him. It would be a long time before anything was normal again.

As he was shaking the thought, his phone began to buzz. The sound it made as it slowly skittered across the desk was unnerving. He didn't recognize the number. "Denning," he barked into the phone as he connected the call.

"Get any sleep last night?" It was Joaquin.

"Hell no," he wanted to laugh, but he was too tired. The smell of fresh coffee wafted through the office, someone had made a new pot. "Just another day in paradise though, right?"

With a heavy sigh, Joaquin said, "It's a mess here in Baton Rouge too.

226

Looks like we lost control before we ever even realized there was a problem."

Sergeant Denning nodded. He knew that Joaquin couldn't see him, but he nodded. "Isn't that how it goes?" Then added, "Do you have any new information?"

It took at least a full minute for Joaquin to collect his thoughts. "From what I can piece together, it's some kind of manmade catastrophe."

"Of course it is," the Sergeant agreed sarcastically.

"I'm on my way back. Wanted to check something out," Joaquin sounded like he had an idea. "Want to meet me at Lafayette 1 in about an hour?"

...

The morning had started out sunny but had quickly turned overcast. The gray of the sky bled all the way into the ground creating a scene that looked black and white. Joaquin arrived about ten minutes earlier than he thought. The area was completely silent. It would have been almost relaxing, but for the whole terrifying part.

Looking over the map of the plots, he located the one he was looking for. Fortunately, it was right off the lane. Nothing really looked out of place. The dirt had been disturbed, possibly when they collected the samples. Three years old. What a terrible shame. He didn't have the authority to even suggest such a thing, Denning probably didn't either. Lost in thought he almost jumped when he heard his name.

"Mr. Rivas," Sgt Denning called. "Why here?"

"Please. Joaquin," he jumped up and shook the Sergeant's hand.

The Sergeant returned the handshake and replied, "John." He turned to look at the tiny grave, "Is this where Mr. Borre was found?"

Turning back to the disturbed soil he answered, "Yes, that's what they said." Pulling up the photo he showed it to him, "This is the picture they sent."

"You're not thinking about asking to..." he paused. "You can't just go digging bodies up."

Lost somewhere in thought he replied absently, "Why not?" The smell of ozone preceding a storm was overwhelming. It always smelled so fresh and clean but today it was different. Or maybe he just thought it was different. Either way, it was about to rain.

"Jesus, man. How am I supposed to go about that?" He was rubbing his two-day beard. "This one was a little girl." Considering the idea, he felt he had come up with the best solution. "We need that guy from the WHO to get an order. What was his name?" He realized that Joaquin might have no idea who he was talking about. "Kanger?"

"Kainer," Joaquin corrected him. "Klaus Kainer." Then shook his head. "Never met the man. But that's pretty high up there." Adding hastily, "This isn't official. I'd lose my job if they knew I was even here right now."

Nodding with understanding, Denning assured him. "No one is losing any jobs. What exactly are you hoping you're going to find in there?" he pointed to the stone.

"Shouldn't we look to see if she's..." He couldn't even bring himself to say it because it sounded so unreal. Finding his voice again he continued, "...still there."

As much as he hated the idea, the Sergeant agreed. For whatever good it was going to do. This could just be a random grave on which the poor man hit his head. The samples could have easily come from Mr. Borre. But damned if he didn't want to know now.

"I'll call Mr. Kainer when I get back to the station," he said as he strolled back towards his car. "So, we weren't just here?"

"Please?" Joaquin nodded, relieved. "Thank you."

Prizes

They were just ahead of the rain on I-10 nearly the entire drive. By the time they crossed the state line, the grayness had dissolved into blue skies and huge fluffy clouds. They were fortunate to find a mini-mart style gas station that was still open, so they filled up and grabbed a variety of horrible, salty snacks. "Because...road trip," Hana had said.

The end of February was the beginning of spring this far south. The trees hadn't fully gotten over the freeze yet and were still bare. The deathly looking stalks whizzed by, even at only forty miles an hour. Although the speed limit was seventy through here, there was too much debris on the road. Even with the few little obstacles they encountered, he was surprised that there was moving traffic both ways.

They didn't talk very much. But as they crossed through Beaumont, the "almost home" adrenaline kicked in. Fiddling with the satellite stations, she landed on a classic. It was almost impossible to keep his eyes on the road as Hana began to sway to the music. Steve Miller punctuated his thoughts in the background, *"You're the cutest thing that I ever did see."* Shaking his head, he focused on the road ahead.

The severity of the situation had always been obvious, but it all seemed to catch up with him as they drove. He was able to gain a little speed, but it didn't last for long as they approached the first major city. Getting through Beaumont had taken longer than they expected, because the mess through here was still fresh. It was like they were intentionally crossing into an active combat zone, with no idea what they'd find. Fortunately, they weren't impeded, just delayed. The smell of fire grew stronger as they got in towards the ship channel. Occasionally the tart, salty scent of gunpowder tickled her nose and made her sneeze.

"I would be lying if I said I wasn't absolutely terrified right now," Eddie broke the silence. "I can't even wrap my head around what's going on."

She'd been wanting to ask since last night, but she didn't know how to broach the subject. Finally, she blurted out, "Did Rosalind do this?" It wasn't an accusatory question. Just an observation.

"That's what they think," he said sadly. "They also thought she killed Noah. There's no way she could have done that. And he's not dead." Of course he'd stick up for her. He knew it was true.

"How do we know that text was really from Noah? I'm still not sure it was him." She wasn't. She hadn't been at all. But the safe. The files? If they were there, it had to be him. But why did he have research that could help with this? "But I believe you," she sighed. "This research, this stuff... he was *obsessed.* Not one of those healthy obsessions. All he wanted was to win."

What did he possibly want to win? He had *Hana.* But he understood what she meant. "I'm sorry." He honestly didn't know what else to say.

The phone rang through the speakers on the van, interrupting their musical interlude. It was Rosalind. "Are you okay?" was the first thing he asked. "Where are you?"

"I'm fine. I think. Hell, I don't know." She sounded frazzled. "There are soldiers outside of my hotel room, Eddie. *Soldiers.*" Sighing, she added, "I'm in DC still."

"Didn't you tell them he's alive?" He knew that was probably the most ridiculous thing he could have said. "I'm sure you thought of that."

"Yes, yes of course." The volume in her voice dropped considerably and he almost had to turn the speakers up to hear her when she said, "But that's not why they're here. Do you understand? They think I did this."

He didn't know how to respond. Not wanting to miss the opportunity, he asked. "Did you actually *talk* to Dr. Patel?" At least he could get some confirmation for Hana.

"Yes," she shot back quickly. "I spoke with him on the phone."

"Where is he?" Eddie asked, wondering if she would wonder why.

"How the hell am I supposed to know that?" she spat out. "He said he had something that would help. He's asked his wife to get it for him. For me." The tone in her voice was still panic.

"Do you know what it is?" he asked her dryly. He didn't know what it was, but he knew what it was called.

"It's some of his research. Something that he said might help," she answered quickly.

Should he tell her what he was doing? He looked over at Hana and back to the road. "Do you have any idea what IM-V-4248 is?"

The tiny gasp played in stereo. "What?" It was obvious she was trying to collect her thoughts. "Why would you..." She paused. "Where did you hear that?"

"So you know what it is?" A car ahead slammed on their breaks. He swerved to avoid an impact. "Shit."

"Are you okay?" Rosalind sounded concerned. "Where are you?"

He passed the sign as she asked. "Almost to Houston, going through Anahuac." The signal faded a bit but they didn't lose connection.

"Why are you in Texas?" She sounded appalled.

Fuck it. "I'm driving Dr. Patel's ex-wife home to get you some files for something called IM-V-4248." Hana gasped; she couldn't believe that he had told her.

He expected a hundred questions that didn't come. All she said before hanging up was, "Oh Jesus, Eddie. I have to go."

...

"Do you know what it is?" Eddie didn't mean to be so abrupt. When the call disconnected, he felt the tension that remained. They had headed south, on the last bit of their drive. Passing through the seaside town was surreal. At one point, he had to drive around into the oncoming lane to get around a boat. Likely, it had fallen off a trailer, but it still seemed completely out of place.

"I think so." She answered after a few quiet moments. "Kind of at least. Some immuno research he was working on. I mean..." She trailed off for a moment. "I hate to admit it, but after a while I just quit listening."

He nodded in support, smiling a little. "Sounds familiar."

"We're horrible people, aren't we?" she sighed. "There!" She pointed towards the turn. She'd lived there for years and she almost missed it every time. It didn't help that they kept adding houses, but no roads. But where were they going to add roads? The houses were literally built on the bay. It used to be peaceful. Now it was just cramped.

The crisp musky smell of dampness assaulted their senses as she pulled the door open. Obviously, there was a window open somewhere in the house. No. Broken. The front window was broken. That was great. Now not only was her place tiny, it was disgusting. She almost changed her mind. Mistaking her hesitation for fear, Eddie slid his arm around her waist and said, "I got you."

Flipping the switches just inside the door, the lights in the entry came on. Eddie pushed ahead of her and slipped in first. It could have just been a broken window. The alarm keypad by the door was blinking power failure. He was jumpy, but he had good reason. "Everything look right?" he asked before letting her completely cross the threshold.

At first glance, yes, everything was as she left it. Except one tiny detail. She struggled with the whole surge of emotions bubbling up as she circled the room opening the curtains to let the light in. Every photograph that she had removed and put away had been painstakingly rehung. The entire family portrait wall. Why would he do that? Technically he still lived here, but she didn't think he'd come back recently. "It's fine." She pushed through and almost sprinted to the back part of the house.

Regret and guilt nearly consumed him as he stood staring at the pictures on the wall. The brutal truth was, whether they'd had insurance or not, medicine wasn't going to save Ebrim. Hana seemed to understand that too. He still felt a nauseating and disturbing contempt for himself for playing any part in it.

He couldn't help but take in the scene though. From left to right, the wall told a story. Hana hadn't changed in years. The sparkling tiaras, evening gowns, roses and sashes progressed through the years. The far left read Miss Teen Texas, then Miss Texas and the last one before the family pictures began said Miss USA. When had she been Miss USA? It made sense to him though.

Slowly, he made his way to where she had disappeared. It looked like a den at one point in time. Currently it appeared to be a storage room. There were boxes scattered everywhere.

There was a desk in the back of the room almost completely eclipsed by the items stacked on top of and around it, but the corner of a floor safe was peeking through. She had gotten distracted on her way to the safe by a small fluffy stuffed rabbit. He recognized the look. For a few minutes he stood there watching her, lost wherever it was she was lost, wishing he could join her. Feeling his gaze, she turned almost embarrassed towards him. "The safe."

"It's okay." He was genuinely trying to be supportive. "It can wait a minute."

Jumping up and tossing the toy aside she almost cried. "Can it?" She pushed the boxes aside enough to pull the chair out and sat on the floor. She had obviously been in and out of the safe more than once, she was able to unlock it without even thinking. It was stuffed full of envelopes of different sizes. She wasn't after an envelope, she slid her hand into the bottom of the safe and felt across the bottom until she found the storage drive. In crude magic marker someone had written across the blue plastic IM-V-4248.

"This was supposed to win the Breakthrough, then the Lasker, then the Nobel," she reflected. "That's what he thought." She handed him the drive and pulled herself up from the floor. "I don't know if it didn't work or if they just pulled the plug. But he was always weird about it."

"Weird?" Rosalind had her *weird* times. It was usually surrounding her research as well. But the awards, she didn't care about those. She was absorbed in the discovery.

"I don't know." She shrugged and headed towards the bedroom. She began picking through clothes and shoving them in a soft bag. Facing him frantically she said, "I don't want to stay here." Then thinking he might have intended to drop her off at home and go home himself she turned away, embarrassed. She realized that he was completely out of her league but had recently hit bottom. He wasn't going to keep crawling around with her.

"I'll take you anywhere you want to go." Leaning against the door frame, he smiled at her softly. "But I don't think we can outrun this."

She didn't want to run. As a matter of fact, she wanted to *stop* running. "I don't think any of Noah's stuff will fit you." She changed subjects clumsily as she pawed through what was hanging in the closet. Eddie was at least six foot two, maybe taller. Noah was just over five foot nine. "The shirts maybe..." Finishing her packing she changed the subject again, "How do we get this to Rosalind?"

...

"I'm telling you it will work." Dr. Patel looked much younger, even just three years ago. There was no doubt losing his son aged him instantly. But when he was whole, he was on fire.

"You're lightyears away from actual testing," Rosalind had protested. "There are still so many unknown variables here." It was a promising start. It was more than a start. But there was so much red tape, paperwork and approvals before they could ever think of moving onto the next phase of testing. So far everything had been done on such a small scale. At the molecular level. But the thing was, *it worked.*

By manipulating the genes, they were able to create resistances to all kinds of things. He had literally rewritten the protein codes in several viruses that would create new immunity that was not naturally available. He had effectively created an entirely new way to produce a healthy immune system. But it was all still so deeply rooted in theory.

Even at the time, she understood his overwhelming need to win. He didn't care so much about the advancement. Not by this time. All he cared about was being seen, being recognized. That made him dangerous in the eyes of his peers. It made him sloppy. He was moving too fast.

The promise was there. The proof. It would have been a lot different had she had time. But she didn't. It was a shame that only she and Noah really knew how well it had *actually* worked. Rosalind slowly shook off the thought as she tried to bring herself back to the task at hand. Unfortunately, the task at hand seemed to keep dragging her back.

Olivia had made it to DC yesterday, but Rosalind wasn't allowed guests. She was surprised they were still letting her use her phone. Since she wasn't a murder suspect anymore, maybe they just didn't care. *But could they be listening? What would they hope to hear?*

They did give her the things that Olivia had gathered up in Montreal. For some reason, she'd gone through her computer and rearranged everything. The note on the desktop said, "I couldn't sleep. You're welcome." But she'd completely mixed up several different files and now Rosalind had to go through and re-sort everything. It was a mess.

Olivia was brilliant, but she was so naive. She had no idea how life worked. It was brutalizing her by the time they met. She was way too overzealous and seemed to be following in Noah's footsteps. She wanted the notoriety. She wanted the fame. She wanted the prizes. Suddenly in dawned on her. *She wanted EV-121!* That's why she had gone through her computer. "Shit" Rosalind tossed the laptop to the side and rubbed her eyes.

...

It was disturbingly surprising how fast they were able to get the warrants to exhume the body of a child. Truth was, WHO could pretty much do what they wanted. It wasn't a bad thing, but Sgt. Denning was having a horrid internal struggle with the order. No one contacted the parents. They just dug her up.

Klaus Kainer had quite a bit of leverage already, being a global representative for the organization. But all it actually took was a signature from the mayor, and she was more than willing to sign off. She didn't even think twice. She was already panicked. Scared. She'd give them anything they wanted.

She'd also offered them the highest awards she could, if they could just stop what was happening. As though they would work faster, harder, or even solve this thing because she offered them prizes. Maybe that would have had more pull if it was the President offering rewards, but whatever. It wasn't like they weren't already trying to figure it out.

The crew arrived just after noon. They didn't need a backhoe as the ground was still soft. The rain had almost died off but there was still a light mist coming down. It intensified the fragrance of fresh soil as they dug. As they reached the tiny casket, the consistency of the dirt had become more clay than soil. But it was not completely seated yet, and they didn't need heavy tools.

Watching from a good distance, as not to get in the way, Sergeant

Denning made a call. "I still can't believe anyone agreed to this," he announced as Joaquin answered. "I mean, what if this has nothing to do with anything?"

Joaquin fired back, "What if it does?" Then added, "Are they already there?"

Watching them raise the small wooden box he said, "They're done." He was relieved that they didn't open it up right there. They had insisted that it would be better in a controlled environment. He figured he'd let Joaquin know where they were going so he could "accidentally" happen to be there. He'd like to know what's going on too. Joaquin seemed like a good partner. He seemed like a good person. Who could blame him for wanting to know what was going on?

At least for the moment, normalcy had settled into the parish. About as normal as it could be. But it was quiet. And that didn't seem right. Sergeant Denning shuddered as he asked his new confidant, "Do you get the feeling that this isn't over? Like maybe we're just in the eye of the storm?"

The Science of Faith

"In world news today, an unidentified virus, which seems to have started in South Central Louisiana just a few days ago, has found its way across the globe," the cable television news droned on in the background. The woman's voice was strained as she recited her lines, "We have very little to go on from officials, but viewers all over the world are sending in their own reports." Dropping her voice to a cautionary tone, she closed, "What you are about to see may be disturbing."

"Look at this," a man's voice sounded from out of view. The focus was on a scene in a small suburban neighborhood. At this point, it could have been anywhere. "They just started freaking out." There was an SUV wedged in the side of a home at the end of a cul-de-sac. As the camera spun around to show everything, the scene was familiar. Smoke and fire everywhere. "People are dying and then, I don't know. Melting? Dissolving?"

Another video clip crossed the screen, somewhere from the East Coast. An older woman, with a mane of silver hair, was narrating, "I hope I'm doing this right." She swung the focus around to what she was looking at. She described the scene in front of her, "Just over there, that big fire. There was a huge explosion a few minutes ago.

Now it's just burning". The frame advanced to the end of a gravel driveway as if trying to get just a little closer to the scene. "The truck stop went up. I think that's what I'm looking at."

She turned a bit so that the visual included what looked like a main road through a small town. There were cars abandoned in the middle of the street. Some had wrecked, some seemed to have just stopped where they were and been abandoned. Debris littered the roadway. "It's like something out of one of those movies." Sighing heavily, she said, "I don't see the heroes in capes anywhere though. They need to hurry."

Scene after scene from city after city flashed across the television. The narrative was the same. Explosions, fire, madness, then people missing. "It all happened so fast." Another viewer somewhere in the country was speaking, but there was no picture. "It was like he saw something that wasn't there. Ran right off the roof!" A still image of a six-story apartment complex flashed on the screen. "By the time I got down there, he'd literally..." There was a long pause, "He was melting."

Shari kept the coffee fresh. It was all she could do to not sit and fret in front of the news. But it was so hard. Obviously, they had been spared by whatever it was. But what about the long-term effect? How many people were going to get sick? How far was this going to go? None of it seemed natural.

Her new friend seemed to know more than she should. More than she wanted to. But it was obvious she did have a much firmer grasp on it than anyone else. She just *knew* things were going to happen. Her prayers were sweet and her faith was affirming. Shari needed that faith.

As if sensing the emotions in her, Queenie reached out and touched her hand. "It's all got a purpose. Don't worry yourself trying to understand."

"Do you understand?" Shari asked, with genuine wonder.

Laughing jovially, she had to catch her breath before she answered, "I haven't understood a thing for going on twenty or so years. Just gotta roll with it."

Morgan had moved off to the guest room and was sleeping. He needed to rest to heal. At least he'd heal. Shari found herself wandering to the room and standing at the door, which was open slightly, then made her way back to start another pot of coffee. She was going to have the jitters by evening, but it was okay.

The white noise of the television continued. Clip after clip of the same thing all over the country, and from what they were saying now, all over the globe. In some places, the "crazy" was dying down. In others it had just begun. Most everyone had the same story.

"It's crazy all the way from here to Galveston." The woman looked around as though she was taking it in for the first time. Behind her the historical building, now pizza parlor, seemed to be functioning at full capacity. "What else can we do right now? People need to eat." Someone else was holding the camera, and the shot was clear. "We're just lucky we haven't lost power, or worse." The banner at the bottom of the screen said, "*Midnite Slice, Owner*". The clip was obviously recycled from an earlier local news broadcast.

The five-lane highway was littered with cars, boats and other debris. But there was very little other movement. It was like whatever had swept through the town had made its exit already. "Didn't they have to go through there to get to Tiki Island?" Shari saw the name of the town flash on the screen. Adding with concern, "Do you think they'll be okay?"

Queenie laughed, looking around the humble but spacious home she'd been welcomed into. She was so grateful. "They still got a lot to do. Their part isn't over yet." Although most people would have asked her to explain, Shari seemed to accept the answer on faith as not only truth, but with sadness.

"What about our part?" The coffee had finished, and she absently poured two cups and sat down with Queenie.

"Much as I hate to say it," Queenie shook her head slowly back and forth, "It may be time to wake all of the saints."

...

"Why are we meeting here?" Olivia sat near the back of the massive cathedral. There was no mass or service on, but there were always people in and out. It was more chaotic today as the frantic, panicked and desperate had come to seek a blessing. The acrid sulfur smell of freshly lit matches continued to assault her senses as everyone was lighting candles for St. Roch.

It was only the second time she'd seen Rex in person. He looked much rougher during the day. Until now, all of their communication had been through vague texts and breathy quiet conversations. He reeked of stale cigarettes and last night's beer. "Seems like the place to be today." He sniffled a bit and lowered his head.

"I changed my mind," she said sadly.

"I noticed." The brim of his ridiculous hat covered his face completely. "What happened?"

She sat quietly for quite some time. The question was valid but seemed so ridiculous. "Look around you." It was Monday afternoon and the church was full. There were very few places to sit. Families and friends all consumed in their prayers to the heavens. Begging for their salvation. It would be pathetic if it wasn't so real. "What is going on?"

"You're the scientist," he scoffed. Then said, "This isn't what we're trying to..."

She cut him off quickly, "Of course not!" She was horrified that he thought they were after something destructive. "Everything we worked on was about saving lives. You know that. At least I thought you did until Dr. Patel..."

"That wasn't me," he insisted.

"The fire?" She knew he'd deny that too. She just didn't know whether to believe him or not. She just assumed he'd gotten sloppy. Or caught. Either way, it was evident he realized there was no money.

"Believe what you want. Doesn't change anything." He sounded tired of defending himself. Gesturing at the hopeful and desperate souls that had convened, he asked "Think any of this does any good?"

The afternoon shifted the sun so that it was coming through the stained glass, creating an eerie red aura across the floors and shadowing almost half of the people in the sanctuary in a red glow. It was an ominous sight. Olivia shivered. "Houses of worship are notorious for spreading plague more than any other structure in history," she spoke almost like a recitation. "People flock to their faith more than their doctors when they're seriously or mortally ill."

"So, that's a no?" he chuckled nervously. "What do we do now?"

Realizing what a contradiction it was, she shook her head as she said, "Now, I guess we pray."

...

Joaquin popped in just before the casket was delivered to the lab. It was almost terrifying seeing the mud stained white coveralls traipsing through. At least they weren't fully decked out in bio gear. It was a bit ridiculous. Especially with everything that was going on. It was all part of the protocol though.

The coffee hit him hard as he fought off the lurches in his stomach. He'd be sick about now if he had eaten breakfast. He wasn't squeamish. Normally a body wouldn't be an issue. But he was still having so many reservations over this one. He was deep in thought when the voice behind him startled him and almost made him jump.

"What a coincidence," Tannon said sarcastically. "You being here, and all." Even in the middle of a health crisis, she was perfectly polished. The soft scent of powder emanated from her. It crept through his senses overtaking the sterile smell and the most recent fragrance of wet soil.

Tannon Pyburn was a research microbiologist for the CDC. Most of her training had been in the field with the Marines as an Environmental Health Officer. Her reputation was impeccable. He respected her more than any other official in the organization. He was glad they sent her. As he was mulling these thoughts over, she asked, "You want to document for me?"

He did. "Thanks," he said quietly. Then added, "This doesn't feel wrong to you?"

She smiled at him. "Of course it does. But I wouldn't be here if it didn't feel wrong," she lamented. "Have you ever done an exhumation?"

"No," he admitted.

He was relieved when she replied, "Me either." They walked together to the elevator and made their way to the third floor. It was quiet, especially for a Monday. There weren't as many people around the building. There just weren't as many people around. They had gone overboard. They always went overboard. That was their job. The room they chose to open the little box in was in the containment lab. It wasn't as secure as ones at the facilities. But time was a factor.

The faint foul stench of sulfur had reached every corner of the room. It wasn't overwhelming, but it was there. Tannon was there to observe, mostly. The actual examination would be done by the forensic doctors, but her expertise was needed. She also seemed to have been briefed by someone at the WHO. They had a theory. He was hoping she'd let him in on it.

It was obvious that no one wanted to open the tiny walnut box. The shine hadn't even completely worn off. The mood went from curious to somber as everyone gathered to begin. Joaquin stayed back out of the way, but the room was small. He wasn't sure what he was expecting. He'd never seen a body after it had been buried. He had never *wanted* to see it. But here he was.

"That doesn't look right," the short stout doctor declared as soon as they lifted the top. He was almost difficult to take seriously as he had donned full hazmat type surgical gear. But the look on his face was *very* serious. "Right here," he held up the paperwork, "It says the deceased was buried three months ago?"

"That's right," Joaquin confirmed. "Um, girl three years old. Bélisaire."

"Wait," Tannon spoke almost off sides to Joaquin. "This is Édouard Bélisaire's daughter?" Almost all of the professional shine had worn off her face. As she clutched the gold cross around her neck, she nervously stroked the surface with her thumb. It almost looked as though she was saying a prayer.

The scene from the freeway played in his head. The people in the van. The woman had said the driver was married to the scientist. Mr. Eddie, she called him. "Holy shit," he exclaimed as he gasped for breath. "And Dr. Bélisaire."

"Do you know Rosalind?" It wouldn't be out of the question. It would make sense their paths might cross. But he shook his head, dispelling that idea. The foul odor in the room grew stronger.

"There was an accident on the freeway last night," he recounted. "We must have come up on it not long after it happened. He was already pulling people out of cars. They called him Eddie." As though he was pausing the memory at a certain point he said, "Apparently Dr. Bélisaire had some kind of research that had something to do this whole thing."

"That sounds like Eddie." They had been whispering and had missed the reasoning behind the man's incredulous protests. The way the lid was raised she had to walk around to see what he might be referring to. She recognized the dress, but the body was too far decomposed for only three months. Had it been August, maybe this would have made more sense but they buried her at the beginning of December. She had attended the funeral.

Her quiet whisper immediately rose to a stifled roar, "Did anyone call the parents?" She knew they hadn't. They weren't required to notify anyone in cases where public health was at risk. Before they removed the body from the casket, she stormed out of the room. The tiny heels of her shoes clicking at a frenzied pace down the hall.

...

By the time they made their way back to Interstate 10, it was already nearly four o'clock. There had been another accident on the main road leading off the island. Because the roads were surrounded by waterways, there were no detours. They had to move the cars themselves. There was no one else around. The salty air was thick and humid, creating a dense fog that eclipsed the island as they drove away.

Damp, tired and completely confused they headed east. The WiFi on the van worked great. The problem was the folder was too big to email. Hana sat with her legs crossed up on the dash. Computer in her lap. The whole scene made Eddie nervous. But he didn't say anything. Instead, he asked, "Where are we going?"

"I don't care," was all she said and busied herself with her task. She had figured out how to send just one folder at a time, but it was going to take a while. There were so many folders. She painstakingly went down the line as she sent message after message to Rosalind's email. Hopefully they were in order, but surely if they weren't that wouldn't be a problem for her. She didn't look up for quite some time. They didn't speak.

The radio station was barely audible, but the music had stopped at some point. *Weird*, he thought. But they were talking. From the few things he'd read on his phone while they were at Hana's house, he was able to put together that this was global now. His phone kept ringing, but he hadn't bothered to pair it to the van again, so he just let it ring.

They had crossed over the state line back into Louisiana by the time the phone rang a third time. Finally finished sending emails, Hana reached for it and recited the name on the screen, "It says Sgt. Pyburn."

"Answer on speaker." He almost felt like he was giving her orders. His head was throbbing, as the knot reminded him that just a few hours ago he had passed out. "Please," he added quickly as she hit the speaker button. "Tan. What's up?" It was obvious they were friends.

The soft voice was so low, Hana fiddled with the volume to turn it up. "Eddie, where are you?"

"Close to Jennings." He looked up at the sign they had just passed, then his voice turned to a gentle concern. "Are you okay? Where are you?"

"At the field office in NOLA," she answered quickly. The long pause and heavy sigh that came next was foreboding. "I don't even know how to tell you this. But I thought someone should."

A thousand scenarios went through his head instantly. He had known Tannon for a very long time. Longer than he had known Rosalind. As a matter of fact, she had introduced them. While they hadn't served in the same unit, when you're in a foreign country you pick your drinking buddies carefully. She had been his. There had been rumors about the two of them, until he'd gotten married. There may have been after that, but he hadn't heard any more of the jokes.

He hadn't talked to any of his "buddies" in a long time. Except Tan. The last time he saw her was at Dellie's funeral. "What are you talking about?" The freeway heading back east was clear. Had they not just driven through madness, it wouldn't have seemed so odd. Crews had been working around the clock since Saturday.

She stammered and sighed heavily. It was obvious she was trying to choose her words carefully. "The WHO exhumed Delphine this morning." The heavy breath said that wasn't even the worst part. "They are examining the possibility that this started..." She didn't want to keep talking. She wanted to be done. "Patient zero, or whatever they're classifying him as was found unconscious at her grave Saturday morning." She realized how terrible the whole thing sounded and added, "He was one of the grounds keepers." She realized it wasn't going to soften the blow, but it kept a thousand creepy thoughts at bay.

Hana nearly dropped the phone as Eddie swerved to miss the car that had slammed on its breaks in front of them. The sign indicating that Lafayette was only about 10 minutes away caught her attention. "Why don't we stop at Shari's?" she whispered.

"Are you okay?" Tannon asked nervously.

"I'll call you back." Eddie absently snatched the phone from Hana's hand and disconnected the call.

As Hana watched a range of emotions cross his face, she felt helpless. There was mourning of loss all over again, there was confusion but mostly there was anger. Why was he so angry? What was going through his mind that would have caused so much anger?

Putting the phone to his ear, he waited as it rang. Rosalind answered on the first ring. "Thank you, I think I've got it all," she answered instead of "Hello".

"What the fuck did you do?" he demanded.

Revelations

It was over, she understood that. This was *all* her fault. Somehow, she had done this. And whatever that meant for tomorrow, today she had to figure out how to stop it. "Eddie," she attempted to explain herself, but she knew she'd never be able to over the phone. "What do you want me to say here?"

The claustrophobia she'd been experiencing heightened exponentially. She was suffocating in the tiny room. He was clenching his jaw. She could hear it in his voice. "Why'd they dig my baby up?"

"What?" she was stunned. *What was he saying?* Is this why Noah wanted her to see his notes? The wave of heat started in the center of her stomach and washed through her slowly. "They didn't..." She wasn't able to finish her question.

"Why?" He wasn't yelling, yet. That terrified her more than the words he was saying. There was a slight hiss, and the call threatened to drop but did not.

"I'm so sorry." She didn't know what to say. Obviously, an apology was misplaced. Maybe she was sorry she didn't know what to say?

"You have to believe..."

"No. Fuck you. What did you do?" Now he was yelling. He took a short breath then snapped again, "What did you *do*?"

A woman's voice sounded faintly behind him. She whispered, "Exit, there."

"Where are you?" It didn't matter how angry he was, she was still worried about him.

"No," he shot back. "What did you do?"

"I'll tell you everything." She finally broke. There was no point in keeping secrets anymore. "But first I *have* to figure out how to fix what I...". She almost choked on the words. Steeling herself, she tried again. "I have to figure out how to fix what I broke. Before I can do that, I have to figure out *how* I broke it!" She didn't wait for him to answer. Instead, she disconnected the call. He wouldn't call back. She knew him too well.

The files that she had received were complete but were in random order. It took her a little bit of time to go through everything and sort it out. Once she had it sorted to the best of her ability, she started reading over everything. She had been dying to get her hands on this for some time. And now, she didn't want any part of it. She wanted to go home.

...

"What happened?" Joaquin found Tannon outside one of the doors, smoking a cigarette. She looked like she was done. It was getting cloudy again and the light humid mist clung in the air. Her hair had gone limp and her makeup was running. She had been crying. "Are you okay?"

"I wasn't okay before I got here," she admitted almost regretfully. "I wasn't expecting..." she stuttered just a bit. "I don't know what I was expecting. But that wasn't it." She puffed on the cigarette again. "Eddie is a good friend."

"I got that." He didn't know what else to say.

"Someone had to tell him." It almost sounded like she was apologizing. She looked around almost wildly. "Shit! I'm going to get fired."

There was no one around. She seemed so jumpy. "I don't think you have anything to worry about." It almost looked like she wanted to run. "Are you feeling okay?"

"Are you interviewing me?" she laughed. "I'm fine. I promise." Did he think she was affected or infected or whichever it was? There was still so much she didn't get. She knew he didn't either. "Dellie was my goddaughter."

He understood. She wasn't sick. She was mourning. Again. It was almost unsettling how close he seemed to be to the root of the epidemic. This family seemed to *literally* be the cause for all of this. He watched her as she carefully tapped the fire out of the tip of her cigarette, extinguished it on the sidewalk, then tucked the butt in the tiny pocket in her slacks. "I see you follow your bad habits with good ones."

"Only hurting myself," she joked. It wasn't funny. She had almost forgotten about the phone tucked under her arm when it buzzed. The notification was for a text. It was from Eddie. *Call Rosalind. This is her mess.* What could that possibly mean? She replied, *What?* Joaquin was looking quizzically at her.

The scenery seemed to have faded back into grays. Sunset was just a couple of hours away. It didn't seem like it would make another appearance before ducking down below them for the night. The cicada had begun to sing their song. It was almost at a roar already.

They both jumped a little when her phone rang. "Yes?" she answered without even looking at the display.

The voice on the other end was unfamiliar. "Can you come back to the lab? You might want to see this."

...

What a difference just a day made. Morgan felt much better. Still sore but at least able to move around. He was going stir crazy. The women were watching more of the same on the television and talking. Sitting there over their coffee, talking.

The television was on in the background. The volume was too low to make out what they were saying, but it was obvious that the cable news station continued to tell the story. So completely outrageous and ridiculous that if he hadn't lived it for the past few days, he would never have believed it. But here they were.

"I need to go into town and get some things," he announced as he snagged Shari's keys off the hanger by the door.

The aroma of fresh bread hung about the kitchen. They were baking! He shook his head and smiled. "Do either of you need anything?" If he went now, he could be back before dark.

Queenie smiled at Morgan and slowly shook her head. He was such a good young man. He was destined for greatness. If he made it through this whole ordeal. It was obvious that Shari was about to protest him leaving. She smiled about that too.

"What could you possibly need?" Shari protested. "I just went to the store Saturday." The scene was normal. Absolutely perfectly normal. Except for the fact that Shari just didn't want her son to...disappear. A chill traveled down her spine as the thought crossed her mind.

He opened the door and stepped out onto the porch. The humid air mixed with the damp coolness. A fine mist had settled low over the swamp. The air was fresh and smelled clean. He breathed in deeply and the smell of the salty air mixed with the smell of bread from behind him. A strange chill crawled down his back. Everything just felt so wrong. He stepped back inside and shut the door.

Queenie nodded. "You feel it too?" Thinking carefully, she added, "You should just text what you need to Mr. Eddie. I'm sure they'll be back soon."

...

Delphine was so tiny. So underdeveloped. The doctors said that she had a long fight ahead of her just to be released from NICU. As they had suspected, the development of her immune system didn't happen. Rosalind wasn't up for visitors and was almost upset when Noah showed up.

"I'm telling you it will work," he insisted.

"You're lightyears away from actual testing," Rosalind had protested. "There are still so many unknown variables here." She was exhausted. None of this was important right now. Was it?

"It works." He tried to go into the research, all of the variables they had tested. But the problem was they hadn't done any real testing. But it was so promising. If only there had been a little more time.

"What you're suggesting is..." She struggled for the words to punctuate how distasteful it all was. But the truth was, it wasn't distasteful, it was just "...unethical," she finished.

"What makes it unethical?" What did? He was on fire. Was it because he wanted to help, or because he wanted to be right? *Wanting* to be right and being right were two completely different things. Then again, what if it worked?

"What if something went wrong?" She was tired of debating.

The question seemed to fuel him. "Something *has* gone wrong." Breathing deeply, he promised, "But we can *fix* it."

The sterile acrid odor of hospitals made her nauseous. Being cooped up in a hospital room for three days was her limit. She wanted to hold her baby. She wanted to touch her skin. Feel her breathe. It was selfish. It was all selfish. "How would we..." She had no idea where her question was going. *How would we live with ourselves if something happened? How would we keep from getting caught? How would this truly affect Dellie?* "How would we get around the nurses?" Stunned when the words came out of her own mouth, she realized she had already decided.

...

The small motel room was musty. The damp odor was almost nauseating at times. He'd been here for a few days and he was ready to go...he didn't know where. But this is not where he wanted to be. The fire at The Queen Elizabeth had been a bit much, he knew that. But the distraction was undeniably perfect. It was already getting dark and he hadn't turned any of the lights on.

The people next door were already arguing. It had been going on the whole time he was here, but dusk seemed to be the point when things always got heated. He could hear the impact as he assumed the man punched the wall. It was likely by the time they checked out, the management would find holes everywhere. Between that and the constant noise from their late nights, it was all Noah could do to get a minute of sleep. But he managed. As he waited on the food delivery, he sat lost in thought.

The center of the room was slightly illuminated by the little bit of light that seeped through the dirty curtains. Other than that, the room faded into shadows. That's all he had intended to do, just fade into the shadows. He had one or two friends left up there and at least they were keeping him up to date on the spreading madness.

He had contemplated waiting to contact Rosalind, but it seemed important. It was just the *way* this virus was spreading. He had seen it in models and while no one else might have caught it, he did. He also knew she was the only one that would take it seriously enough. And the fact that it all started in New Orleans, he had to tell her.

Even if this whole thing turned out to be a coincidence, he knew at least Rosalind would have the best chance at figuring things out. She was an unpleasant woman. Arrogant and irritable. She had no patience and absolutely no compassion in her frozen soul, but she was brilliant. She would be the one that could figure this all out.

He had paid cash for everything up to this point. It was easy to disappear in Montreal if you were willing to deal with the garbage. That was probably true everywhere. He really wanted to talk to Hana. But what would he say? There were just some things you couldn't apologize for. No one knew where he was yet. He wanted to keep it that way for now.

The plan had been to slip back down to Texas when no one was looking. The whole murder thing, that stalled him. Dead men don't cross borders. Now, they probably realized he was responsible for the fire. For all of that disaster. There was no way he was getting home. But he knew he couldn't stay here forever. The smell alone would kill him.

...

It was a good thing they had some place to pull off the highway. As soon as they exited, Hana insisted that she drive. She didn't fully understand what was happening. He hadn't said anything yet, but it had obviously shaken him deeply. She didn't know what to do, so she drove the path they had come from, and they found themselves sitting in the drive at Shari's house.

"Is this where you want to be?" he asked. It would have been an odd question at any other time.

She didn't know where she wanted to be, but she knew she wanted to be wherever he was. That thought disturbed her a little. "What was that all about?" She wasn't sure how hard to press. But he had been so rattled he couldn't continue to drive.

"It's probably not polite to just sit in the driveway." He was deflecting. He was good at that. Eventide had arrived. The glow of the moon sparkled in places on the water in the distance. "I am so sorry." He reached across the console and clumsily took her hand. "I should have just gone home Friday night."

Friday night! It seemed the world had journeyed around the sun a million times since they met. "If you had, I would probably have died in that explosion," she whispered somberly.

He hung his head but did not let go of her hand. "Right."

He'd already gotten tired of crawling on the bottom. "You can leave me here if you want. I'm sure Shari won't mind." Hana tried to hide the disappointment in her voice. She wasn't sure how successful she was.

"Is that what you want?" The sorrowful place the question came from suggested he had been completely broken. They had everything in common but nothing worth fighting for anymore.

"What do you want?" She turned completely sideways, facing him.

The lines that furrowed deep in his brow relaxed. It was almost as though it was the first time anyone had ever asked him what *he* wanted. His eyes reflected surprise, sadness, joy and confusion all at the same time. All he could manage to say was, "You."

Whether anyone knew they were in the driveway or not, no one came out. The driveway lights weren't on. The darkness provided enough shelter that they were hidden by the night. Hana climbed over the console, into his lap. He reached around her waist and pulled her into him.

She whispered slowly, "Here?"

He fumbled with the seat release and the headrest slammed into the seat behind it. "Yes," he whispered back as she pressed her lips hard into his. The buzzing that had begun just before the sun set had grown to a frantic roar. The serenade of the insects, tree frogs and other inhabitants of the swamp surrounded them creating a rhythm that her movements swayed to. He ran his fingers through her long dark hair, unable to resist the urge to tug on it gently.

The electricity coursing between them was undeniable and created almost visible sparks. By the time she started to whimper softly, his head was already spinning. The world could completely go to hell as long as he could hear her whimper just one more time.

They had been parked in the drive for nearly an hour before they emerged from the van. As they stumbled up the steps to the door, it opened. Shari was smiling warmly. "Was wondering when y'all were going to come in. Dinner is almost ready." She left the door open and walked back towards the kitchen.

Resisting the urge to giggle like school children, they shut the door behind them as they went in. The roast that Shari was cooking smelled amazing. Eddie's stomach growled loudly. "Sorry we're late," he joked. There was so much to deal with. So much to sort out. But dinner with his new family seemed like the only thing that mattered right now.

END ACT 3

ACT FOUR – HERE IT COMES AGAIN

Second Wave

A sense of normalcy had returned to University Medical. Sort of. The plywood where the broken glass had been covered was still there, but it was clean. And it was open. Which was a good thing. It was nothing like the madness over the weekend, but there were some people in and out. It seemed that whatever had ripped through there had exited just as fast.

The strange thing was, no one had a clue what had happened. Kate didn't come in Monday. She wouldn't have had to come in today except no one knew where Morgan was. She vaguely remembered seeing him leave. And Mr. Elkins said that he saw him walking around too. But even if they could reach him, he still needed to rest. There is no way he'd be ready to care for patients now anyway. She didn't want to be here. The past weekend had made her seriously rethink her whole career path.

She'd been struck by patients before. Nurses usually got the worst out of their patients. They're the ones that got yelled at, knocked around, peed on or a million other disgusting things. But until this weekend she'd never thought about quitting. What happened this weekend had terrified her.

Her parents had both passed away a long time ago. She didn't have any siblings. The only person she was remotely close to had been missing for two days. She realized what that meant. She suspected she'd never see him again. That devastated her. But she had a job to do, and they needed her here.

Most of the emergency vehicles and other services had been directed to New Orleans East for the time being. They didn't have any more on staff, but they didn't have a huge hole near triage either. For the moment, the ER was quiet. The WHO had been in and out, just keeping an eye on what they might have incoming. She just wanted to get through the day with as little movement as possible. It was amazing she hadn't been injured when Bo tossed her.

Although it had been extinguished completely a couple of days ago, the smell of fire still persisted throughout the main entry area. As it mixed with the normal sterile odor of the air, it swirled through her senses. Kate sneezed.

"Don't do that," Dr. Schwartz had snuck up on her. She nearly jumped when she heard his voice.

"Don't do *that!*" she shot back. She was jumpy. They were all jumpy.

They were all tired. "Is this over yet?" she asked.

"Sorry." He leaned in so that no one would hear him. Not that there was anyone around, but the dramatic effect caught her attention immediately. "Got a call from Judy over at East. Something else is going on."

Something else? Wonderful. "What do you mean?"

"I don't know. But they're getting busy over there. She said it's almost the same but not quite." They were already short staffed, everyone was short staffed. Parts of the building were not ready to have occupants. But they had to be ready. For the most part, the hospital was operating business as usual. Except for the areas that were closed off, and the ones that were water damaged.

Kate sighed, "I'll see who's on call and who's still..." She had no idea how to finish that sentence. She thought about Morgan again. "I'll see who's available."

...

Joaquin had taken the Sergeant up on his offer. The couch was hard, the cushions were lumpy and the air in the apartment smelled like stale cigarettes. But he had slept so hard through the night. His trek to Baton Rouge had proven to be a bust. His sister was gone. His apartment was gone. Everything was gone.

Tannon said she'd get back with him when she had something to tell him. Whatever had happened yesterday while they were at the office was still completely a mystery. But he had a terrible feeling that something was really wrong when they asked him to "go ahead and head home." So, he was waiting for anything from her.

She was about ten years older than Joaquin but looked ten years younger. Marine, scientist, biologist. She was absolutely perfect. And beautiful. *And*...his mind wandered. What was he thinking? She was literally a superior in the chain of command. But she was beautiful.

His thoughts were interrupted by the gruff expletives coming from the kitchen, "Why can't this shit make itself?" Apparently, Sgt. Denning was having issues getting the morning coffee ready. The sun had pushed its way through the blinds a while ago. It was obviously time to get up.

Joaquin checked his phone. He had missed a text from earlier in the morning. He didn't have the number programmed in, but it was clearly from Tannon. *From bad to worse. Round two. Nosebleed, heavy vomiting and dementia. I know, it sounds the same but something's different. So far not fatal. I'll call you later.*

"Shit!" Joaquin shot up and called through the bar cut out in the kitchen, "Something is coming back around." He texted back, *Are you okay?* Her reply was surprisingly fast. *So far.*

"What do you mean?" John was obviously not a morning person. It was painfully aware he wasn't ready for more bad news. Turning on the television he said, "You want a cup?" Whatever Tannon was talking about hadn't made the morning broadcast. Joaquin told him about the text and watched whatever strength was left in the Sergeant completely drain. "Of course."

...

Queenie was up before the rest this morning. She quietly made her way into the kitchen and made coffee. Shari was likely to be stirring soon and she'd be grateful it was ready. The sunshine was glimmering on the water outside the window. It created swaying shadows through the pane and onto the counter. They whispered a story to her.

Up to now, they'd been hiding. Waiting to see what was going to happen next. That poor boy, Morgan, was in no shape to do anything but hide. But the rest of them? They needed to do something. Praying would only get them so far. As the sparkling shadows danced back and forth on the marble, the end was revealed. It would be brutal. And it would be final. But the balance would be restored. She just wished she could see if she'd be there to witness it all.

Her dreams had become more and more cryptic as her age had progressed. They used to be so vivid and so easy to read. But now they were more like symbols and there was always fire. Even if nothing burned. The fact that Shari managed to sneak up on her, that said a lot. She nearly threw the scoop of coffee on the floor but caught it before it hit. Even managed to keep most of the grounds inside. Most of them.

"Sorry," Shari giggled quietly as she reached for the broom in the pantry. "I didn't know anyone else was up." It was evident, that despite the world falling apart, Shari was enjoying the company. She kept her voice low as she swept up the almost invisible debris. "Something else is happening, isn't it?" She could feel it. Everyone could feel it. That's why Eddie and Hana came back last night. Certainly, they had some place to go. But they chose to come back.

"I would bet we should make the most of what we have here right now," Queenie answered her, obviously understanding everything that was going through her head.

Without waiting for an explanation, Shari decided that meant breakfast. She hadn't left the house in a couple of days. They'd need to, and maybe sooner than later. But for now, she'd feed everyone as though it was their last breakfast ever. In case it was. By the time the bacon began to sizzle and drift its fragrance through the house, everyone else was stirring.

Morgan had turned the television on. A local morning show was playing. Even with the rest of the world just now feeling the effects of what they had come through, the morning show host was ridiculously perky and annoying. He turned the volume down almost immediately. "I'll go to the store today," he called out from the couch as he sat up. It was almost as if he knew what his mother was thinking. It was possible he also realized she was cooking nearly everything in the refrigerator at once.

The store. That was an interesting consideration. What would there be at the store? It was too soon to know if livestock or crops would be affected by this. And when people panicked whatever they couldn't buy they'd steal. But someone had to be open for business as usual. At least, that's what he gathered from watching the silent display on the television. They weren't acting like it was the end of the world. At least not anymore.

...

Fortunately, he'd remembered to plug the phone in before he went to sleep. There were several missed messages. Eddie quietly slipped out of the bed and carried his phone into the dining room. Queenie was already sitting with Morgan at the table. Shari was doing her thing in the kitchen. He didn't feel even a little out of place. Which was a relief. He had felt out of place for a very long time.

Although they were likely very close in age, Shari greeted him like she did Morgan. Very motherly. It wasn't as odd as it should have been. He figured that she just flourished when she had people to take care of. His mother had been like that. Still sleepy and fighting off every emotional thought as it peeked out, he was surprised when Shari handed him a fresh cup of coffee and shooed him through the kitchen to the table. "Out, out, out." she teased.

He hadn't spoken much to Morgan. That was mostly because the kid had been in pretty bad shape when they found him on the interstate. But at least he was where he really needed to be to heal. Mom's house was always the best medicine. "How are you feeling?" he asked.

Morgan's attention was diverted to the muted television. And the silent picture that played in front of the hospital. At some point, the morning news had eclipsed the ridiculous morning show and taken over. Turning the volume up, they caught the end part of the story. "It isn't clear at this time if this is connected to the incident this weekend," the woman seemed to be wrapping up. "But we'll bring you more on this as it develops."

Queenie shivered almost violently. "Someone playing hopscotch on my grave this morning." Turning her attention to Eddie she looked him straight in the eye with as much compassion as humanly possible. "That was disrespectful. I'm sorry."

The prior evening was a bit of a blur. Shari had fed them way too much, then decided to try her own hand at picking the wine. She picked several. They drank them all. They talked until very late. A mixture of hysterical laughter and sadness rolled over and over again. They had definitely bonded but had he told them about Dellie? No. He couldn't have, simply because he still didn't understand.

Fortunately, she wasn't waiting for a reaction. He began flipping through the messages on his phone. There were three missed calls from Rosalind. She was desperate to talk to him. Her texts that followed were vague. *Call me,* and *Eddie, I need to talk to you.* He didn't want to talk to her, but he still needed to understand what was happening. He replied, *You can text me. I don't want to talk to you.* He didn't want to hear her voice, he didn't want to hear her cry. Not because he was afraid that he'd cave, but because it would make him sick.

The television had been reduced again to a low whisper. It had gotten very chilly last night, and the front room was brisk. A slight rattle of pipes echoed from the back of the house. Hana was taking a shower. The aroma of bacon and sausage swirled through the air. "You're okay." He finally answered Queenie.

Shari carried several plates. Breakfast smelled good but the lurching in Eddie's stomach started as soon as she'd put the plate in front of him. "Start a fire?" she asked. Well, she was actually *telling* him to. Jumping up he was glad for the request because the smell of food was making him nauseous. He wouldn't tell her that part.

...

Hana's feet were freezing when she stepped into the shower. The water was so hot, it actually hurt. But only briefly. The citrus smell of the shampoo invaded her senses and woke her up a bit. The pounding in her head reminded her that they'd drank entirely too much wine last night. At least she had. It seemed like the world was ending and they were playing house in the swamp. She didn't hate it.

The room was chilly, so she dried quickly and got dressed. The damp hair that clung to the back of her shirt was mildly annoying, but she wanted to get near the fireplace. She could smell it burning. As she made her way through the kitchen, she saw Eddie tending to the newly lit flames. Everyone else was devouring the huge breakfast set on the table. The food smelled okay, but the coffee was music to the senses. She slowly fumbled with a cup as Shari half whispered, "There's aspirin on the counter." She was a great hostess, an even better mom.

No one had ever discussed why they were all there together. It just seemed right. It was as though they had been expected to come back once they had gotten what they had gone after. Queenie was a curious woman, but she seemed to just know things. Hana suspected that Shari was much the same. She seemed to just know as well. The two women had spent many hours praying together and putting together what seemed to be a talisman. At this point, they needed all the help they could get. She hadn't even found it odd.

Hana thought about the conversation between Eddie and his friend, and the partial conversation between he and Rosalind. It was obvious that Noah was as wrapped up in this mess as she was. Maybe this was his fault, not hers. But how? It was like they were missing something. Or maybe they weren't missing anything. Maybe that was just her.

Her phone was on the hutch behind the dining room table. Someone had charged it for her. That was sweet. The coffee was sweeter--she'd put too much sugar in it. "Good morning everyone." Her voice was tiny, but she tried to sound jovial. The first message that opened as she started up her phone managed to drain every tiny drop of joy she still possessed, *Where are Ebby's ashes?*

Although she tried to clutch the cup as hard a she could, it still slipped through her fingers and crashed down on the wood floor. It shattered into too many pieces to count. She knew she needed to clean it up. She realized there was a wet, sticky mess of glass all around her. But she couldn't move. Whomever buzzed around her quickly and begun to clean was a blur, but someone had sprung into action.

The movement around her became a wash of color and light. Shadows and darkness. Her ears began to ring at a pitch that would become maddening quickly. Eddie's voice seemed very far away at first but came closer like a freight train through a tunnel. "Hana." She looked up and he was hovering above her. "What's wrong?"

Frantically searching Google for a map of the river, Hana gasped out loud as she realized what the implication had been. There is no way that Noah knew she had already released them. She hadn't told anyone but Eddie. She was almost horrified as the question slipped out, "Where was Dellie buried?" She turned the phone around so that Eddie could see the map.

Somehow, she realized he'd already come to the same conclusion. When had that happened? Why hadn't he said anything? He didn't take the phone from her or try to expand the screen. He just looked at her with a broken expression. "That's it," he nodded sadly.

Gasping for air, Hana's attention panned back and forth between the concerned faces in the room. Queenie was nodding somberly, slowly, mournfully. Pulling back on the map just a bit, she tapped the screen to mark the spot with a pin. "This is where I..." she couldn't finish the sentence. But she'd remembered watching them float on the breeze, down the river. Towards the cemetery where, yesterday Eddie's daughter had been exhumed.

Sleight of Hand

EV-118 had been so close. Once it had been introduced it was clean and thorough, picking out the cancerous or damaged cells and slowly breaking them apart from the proteins that fed them. Breaking them down to nothing but H2O. Leaving behind very little trace. But it had taken too long to start working. That was the only flaw.

Everyone was stunned when they got the green light for the first human trial. An advanced leukemia case that hadn't responded to any of the treatments. The perfect subject. But it didn't work. The cancer had spread much faster than EV-118 could. This had been their last option. Had they started with this course, maybe they could have saved the boy. But treatments don't start at the experimental level. Those are generally reserved for the Hail Mary. Which is why so many of these trials fail. They couldn't do anything to speed the approval process up, but there *had* to be a way to speed up the virus.

Rosalind had been working on it tirelessly since the failure. It had been a couple of years. Every one of the small-scale tests had brought her closer. But it still didn't work fast enough. Except the one test that progressed it a little too fast. That would be catastrophic as well. It seemed that is what was happening around the world.

The problem was instead of just binding to cancerous or damaged cells, this was attacking all of them. Impossibly so. There was an obvious mutation, something that had caused it to spread indiscriminately and destroy every single cell. *But how?*

The tiny plane bounced around a little more than she would have liked. The past few days it was as though Rosalind had been swallowing her stomach to keep it down over and over again. The flight didn't help. But at least they were headed in the right direction. She was getting closer to home. It wasn't that she was off the hook necessarily, but they needed her expertise.

By the time she'd heard from Tannon, it was already late. She didn't have much time to collect her things and meet the car waiting for her. She wasn't able to text Eddie until she was in the air. He didn't answer. There was a good chance he wouldn't. She just needed to explain. But he'd never understand. There wasn't a chance in Hell now that he'd ever talk to her again. It had been a long time coming.

Olivia didn't answer either. Not that she was surprised by that. She realized that Olivia's interests were not in her. They were in her research. Whatever she was hoping she was going accomplish, the whole thing was absurd. By the time she'd landed at the small naval air base in New Orleans, she realized she was alone. Completely alone. At least Tannon needed her, for now.

...

He'd had so much faith in Rosalind, but he didn't think that EV-118 was going to work. But because of the nature of Ebrim's cancer, he was a perfect candidate to test it. Of course, the doctors, insurance and even the FDA fought them on it but Noah fought harder. By the time they got the necessary approvals, it was too late. That's why he never told Rosalind that it was Ebrim. But he'd still hoped. Maybe it had prolonged the inevitable, but it hadn't worked.

He had been breathing the damp air for too many days. The musty odor of the motel room had finally become more than he could stand. It had literally devoured all of his senses. The fire at The Queen Elizabeth had been an accident. Sort of. The *plan* was just to make it look like someone had tossed the room. The fire was only supposed to consume the papers and other small flammables. He wanted to create the illusion that everything he'd brought with him had been lost. The sprinklers should have gone off. None of the sprinklers went off.

It wasn't really even a plan, it was just a spontaneous moment of sheer panic. The fifth of whiskey didn't help either. It was a colossal disaster. Everything had been since Hana had insisted he move out. He didn't actually move. He just left. But this disaster wasn't going away. No one was supposed to get hurt. Two people died.

It was interesting, that something else even more terrifying was happening right under his nose. It played into his plan to disappear. He hadn't meant for Rosalind to get in any trouble. As a matter of fact, that is what this had all been about. Making sure neither of them got in trouble. He chuckled dryly at the thought. *Trouble.* Were they children?

He had no regrets. What he had done, he did because he understood what Rosalind was going through. He couldn't imagine a life where he'd never gotten to hold his child. Even if he'd been robbed of every other milestone that a father and son were supposed to achieve together, he'd had that tiny little chance to be his father. Rosalind and her husband deserved the same chance.

It wasn't even that difficult to administer. Obviously, in her fragile state and only three days old there was no way he could have ever delivered the therapy intravenously. The quick aerosol delivery had proven to be the most effective anyway. It was surprisingly easy to get it to her. It had only taken a moment while he was talking to Rosalind's husband. No one even noticed.

After that he had become so wrapped up in the battle for Ebrim. The one the insurance company won. He had at least kept tabs on Delphine enough to know that it had taken two months, but she had progressed enough that she was finally released and sent home. She was still fragile and had a tough road ahead of her. But she improved, naturally. IM-V-4248 had worked. It had worked!

When he heard about the strange, rapidly spreading virus that had begun in New Orleans he collected as much information as his contact could get. It definitely mimicked the intended purpose of EV-118 but it wasn't attacking just the cells that might be damaged or affected. It was destroying all of them. The problem was, the virus couldn't move this fast. Something else had to be accelerating the process.

At the very least, a healthy body would recognize the threat and work to compensate for it. That wasn't happening. It *was* happening, but the virus consumed faster than the body could repair. It was almost as though the virus itself had developed its own immunity to the body's natural defenses. That was so familiar. How could that possibly have happened?

...

The cup of coffee she was sipping on had become cold long ago. The view of Georgetown Waterfront Park was beautiful in the morning. The sun had come full and fast. The bright cheery mood created as the sunlight glistened on the Potomac out her window was a lie. Despite the lack of cloud cover, today would not prove to be bright or sunny. Olivia understood that.

Rex still insisted he'd had nothing to do with the fire or the murder. The fire at The Queen Elizabeth had been perfect--that's what she needed. Getting everyone to look the other way. But it was so brutal. The whole point of getting hold of EV-121 had been to benefit everyone. Yes, it was Rosalind's work for the most part. But every single one of them had put everything into the research, the testing, everything they did to make it complete. They all deserved the glory.

So what had he actually *done?* It was obvious everything had gotten out of hand. They failed, people died and now something even worse was happening. Since their meeting at the church yesterday, Olivia had been staying out of the way as much as possible. Whatever this was that was spreading was definitely indiscriminate and she knew that she was as susceptible to it as anyone else. So far, she was fine.

She'd been texting Rex since last night. Either he wasn't responding or couldn't. Either way she was pretty much done with him. Rosalind had called her late last night. She'd already gone to bed, but she wasn't sure if she wanted to call her back yet this morning or not. She wasn't sure of anything at this point.

The media had done its job. Every living being that had access to some kind of media was sufficiently terrified. Because most of the networks had been broadcasting nothing but news all day every day, most of the footage was recycled. She'd started to recognize all of the images. They interrupted the news cast that had interrupted the morning show to bring even more tragedy from New Orleans. That's how they said it. *Tragedy.*

Whatever started just a few days ago had obviously mutated. The ignorant anchors had no idea what they were droning on about and they kept insisting that something else was happening. So far there hadn't been any reports of disappearing patients or pools of water, at least not that the general media had reported. The WHO was keeping a very tight lid on the details. It indicated that they hadn't come up with any ideas on how to stop it.

It was possible they truly had no ideas. But because they'd not been forthcoming, the wild suspicions continued to be aired across the world. So many different stories that all ended in the same, gruesome way. And now it was starting up again.

She was so deep in thought that when the squealing began, she nearly screamed out loud. It took just a few seconds for her brain to process the shrill, overwhelming noise. The acrid aroma of smoke assaulted her senses. It was the fire alarm. The building was on fire. *Of course.* Reacting quickly, she reached for the handle on her rolling travel bag and fled the room.

The sixth-floor hallway was clear of smoke, but the smell was overwhelming. It had to be either directly above her or below her. The stairwell door wasn't warm, and she took a deep breath as she descended each flight of stairs. The smoke hadn't seeped into the enclosed space. Nearly tripping on her own feet twice, she didn't break the quick stride down the steps. Although moving quickly, she was not panicked. Just irritated.

By the time she'd exited the stairwell into the lobby, she had joined a group of dozens of people evacuating. The scene played in slow motion. As the faceless growing mob of people surrounded her, she almost tripped again. Reaching the front exit doors, Olivia turned back to see the formation of people still filing through the lobby. The elevators had already been grounded, and as the people fled out from the side stairwell areas, the majority were coughing and wheezing. The billowing pools of smoke made it to the lobby just as she made her way out the door.

...

By the time Rosalind had arrived last night, Tannon was already exhausted and everything was blurring together. The security detail that had accompanied her had also returned to DC almost immediately. It wasn't that they weren't watching, but with all domestic and international flights completely grounded, she couldn't really go anywhere. Tannon's position had allowed her to accept responsibility. She also needed her there to explain...well, to explain anything she could.

It was unclear what had actually happened in the field lab when they'd begun testing Delphine's remains. No one expected the amount of decay and rot the body had succumbed to. In fact, after just three months there should have been only a little evidence of decay at all had the body been prepared properly. They should have been able to still see the makeup on her cheeks, instead the flesh was decomposed beyond recognition.

Death has one odor. It was unmistakable. While the smell of death was present, another pungent fragrance was more prevalent. It was the same odor that had wafted from the paper mill she grew up near. Through a process called kraft pulping, they used chemicals and heat to transform the wood chips into a pulp that was later refined into paper. The smell was a result of that process. It smelled like rotten eggs.

As they proceeded with the examination several pustules of what must have been rotting tissue within the body cavity and on the remaining flesh had ruptured. By the time they were done, the odor at the field office had become so unbearable that they vacated for the day. Everyone had been tested for whatever they could test them for, but because they had no idea what they were dealing with it was hard to determine if there had been any threat of exposure. Still, they quarantined themselves. Standard operating procedure.

Most of the base had been abandoned for a very long time. About five years ago, they had begun working on it. Their reason was to create a rescue and command hub for natural disasters, but that's not exactly what they were doing. The face of the massive building still looked worn and decrepit, but the small base of operations was planted keenly within the center of one of the structures. Even the lighting inside had been carefully placed so that at night they stayed eclipsed within the darkness. This worked well for a small-scale quarantine.

The barracks that were on the other side of the building made great temporary housing for the members of **WHO** and other officials that needed to be discreet in their appearance. And while everyone in the world knew that something was spreading, they still didn't need the panic that an incoming group of suits created. Tannon had convinced them that Rosalind would be secure here. So, they brought her here. She'd need to speak with her soon.

Joaquin hadn't been there when they did the examination, but he had been there when they opened the box. She was relieved when he replied this morning. She did give him a list of symptoms to be on the lookout for, even though it was almost exactly the same. Just in case he ran across it or worse if he started showing any symptoms. So far only two of the forensic scientists had acquired something unusual. She'd been keeping up with the local hospitals and learned that these symptoms were presenting randomly in patients. A lot of patients.

Realizing that the quarantine might not have been necessary, she was struggling with the decision to let these people go home to their families. Whatever this second wave was, it was already beyond containment. What they needed to do now was identify a way to stop it, or at the very least slow it down. The first casualty had been reported to the WHO. New Orleans East called in the time of death at 10:15am. The autopsy was performed immediately and as she had suspected, the cause of death was organ failure. The smaller organs such as the kidneys had all but dissolved into a gooey mess.

They worked as fast as they could, but some of the organs had continued to break down. And all they had been left with in some places was a gelatinous substance. Quite the way a normal break down would have occurred over a much longer period of time. But they were left with a corpse. A gooey, smelly, unidentifiable corpse. But at least there were remains.

...

You can't hide from the devil, Queenie knew that. But you could put up a good enough fight. However the boy had managed to find her exactly what she needed was a mystery, but he had. He even managed to get her not one, not two but *three* chicken feet. The butcher was happy to make a couple of dollars on them, instead of throwing them out.

The thing that they had all failed to understand is that this wasn't a sickness. It was a curse. A curse on humanity. Sure, it may have played out just like every other kind of sick, but it sure didn't end that way. Praying for protection wasn't going to do a bit of good, unless the curse itself was gone.

Uncrossing a curse wasn't an easy task. It took concentration and devotion. Both of which she had an abundant amount. The sage didn't hurt, neither did the coffee. Okay, the coffee wasn't for the prayers, but it helped. She prepared everything just the way it needed to be and hailed all the saints.

She called on Christopher for their protection, Raphael for healing, Dymphna to soothe their fears and she even requested the presence of Oliver for peace. She could have called on a hundred more saints, but these were the ones that would come running. As she sat quietly in the den preparing her altar, she was finally ready to make her request. Repeating the prayer over and over again silently, she wondered if it would be enough.

"There walk out during this day and night, that thou mayest not let any of my enemies, approach me, if they do not intend to bring me what was spent from the Holy altar. Because God the Lord Jesus

Christ is ascended into Heaven in His living body. O Lord, this is good for me this day and night."

She thought her recitation had been silent, it was a pleasant surprise when she heard Shari answered with "Amen" from the living room.

Where two or more gather, she thought to herself. She hoped it was true.

All Fall Down

By the time Eddie got Rosalind's text, they had already passed through New Iberia on Hwy 90. They had taken the southern route back towards New Orleans, hoping to avoid traffic that was kicking up again as the new threat had been announced. He remembered to pair his phone with the Bluetooth on the van and it offered to read the text for him.

Rosalind's words were delivered by the unfeeling voice. *I'm not asking you to forgive me or even understand. I'm just asking you to listen.* It was a relief that the voice had no inflection. He didn't want to hear her begging. It was glaringly obvious to him what she had done. Glancing over, he caught Hana gazing at him. The sadness in her eyes indicated she also understood.

Hana knew it was none of her business. Or maybe it was. It had crossed over into her business what seemed like several lifetimes ago. "I wish there was something I could say," she finally managed to squeak out. The chill in the air was beginning to burn off, and the dew had all but exited the morning scene. The places where the dampness had persisted swept by like glittering diamonds. They were driving well over the posted speed limit.

With both hands almost white knuckling the wheel, Eddie didn't take his eyes off the road. The Morgan City bridge was empty. Completely empty. That was unsettling. What was more unsettling is that Hana wanted to comfort him. As the events of the past few days played in his head, he realized that he was probably the worst thing that had ever happened to her. But she wanted to comfort him. "I don't need you to say anything," he answered softly.

Reaching for his right hand she clasped it between both of her palms. It was dry and coarse. But that didn't stop her from raising it to her lips and kissing it over and over again. "What do you need?" *Where had that come from? Why did she ask that?* But she really wanted to hear him say...

"Just you," he interrupted her internal dialog. She wasn't sure what she had expected him to say. Judging by the surprise on his face, he hadn't expected to say it, not again.

Ringing in surround, the phone call interrupted whatever path their thoughts had strayed down. *Sgt. Pyburn* flashed across the screen on the dash. "Sergeant," he answered the phone.

"Eddie," the voice sounded flustered, "where are you?"

"About ten miles out of Metairie." The roads were still clear. It was almost foreboding. "Where are you?"

"Belle Chasse." She wasn't sure if he knew about the base. She wasn't sure if it mattered at this point. "Do you still have clearance, Colonel?"

Hana sat up straight. She wasn't sure why. The Sergeant he was talking to wasn't a police officer. She was a soldier. Eddie noticed her slight adjustment in her posture and almost laughed. Instead he smiled at her and replied to Tannon, "I doubt it."

"How do you not know?" The jest was playful. As playful as could be in the situation.

"Just tell me," he almost demanded. Normally he wouldn't have ever asked her to put her job in jeopardy, but he was tired of guessing games and cryptic answers.

The heavy breath that preceded the information was well placed, "This is top level Eddie, I shouldn't even be telling you this but..." she paused, "You need to be here. I am at the NSA Navy base with Dr. Tedesse, and Rosalind." She breathed again. It was clear she didn't know how much to tell him. "Just come around to the back of the complex. I'll get you in."

"I'm not alone," he informed her. As the words slipped from his lips, he recognized the impact the statement had on him. Although what he had meant to say was that he had someone with him. But he liked *I am not alone* a lot better.

...

"It's not like it's even going to matter if we can't get a handle on this," Tannon shivered as she spoke the words. Disconnecting the call, she turned to Rosalind, "You're going to have to tell him everything."

Nodding solemnly Rosalind said, "I should have a long time ago." She sighed and added, "I should have told you."

Rosalind and Tannon had been friends their entire lives. Ursuline Academy was an all-girls Catholic School that had a rich history in New Orleans. They were both part of that, but while the other girls were participating in competitive sports and creative arts, they were dissecting earth worms and frogs to see what made them work. They both wanted to save the world.

"Rosalind, you don't owe me anything." It was a genuine response. "I can't say I wouldn't have done the same."

Her nerves were shot. The anxiety that had been building since the Sûreté escorted her from her hotel room had finally come to a frantic head. The tremors radiating outward from her stomach reached all the way to her fingertips and toes. Her scalp tingled, and her palms were sweating. She was freezing. "How did everything get to this?" It was a sorrowful, rhetorical question. She knew the answer.

While the facade of the base was deteriorating and looked like it had been abandoned long ago, the working areas were impressive. Although completely surrounded by concrete and steel, it felt more like they were on a flight deck of a space ship. Rosalind had never seen anything like it. She realized that she wasn't a guest here, but at least everyone was respectful. The worst she received were a few nasty stares.

Everyone was busy. Busy working to correct her mess. Although she still didn't quite understand how it happened. The files that she got from Noah's wife were incredible, but how it all fit still didn't make sense. It would have been a lot easier if Noah hadn't been so damned cryptic. The mutation was their first concern as the first wave seemed to have run its course. But it was clear now what it did. What a terrible way to die.

One of the scientists had a theory but they couldn't quite fit the pieces together. When combined, the effects of the viruses seemed to act quite like what they had been witnessing over the past few days. Broad spectrum antivirals had no effect. Without understanding what catalyzed it, answers were still out of reach. "Nothing could have spread this far this fast as a contagion. We're looking at something that was disseminated much more widely all at once. Like an aerosol delivery."

"What are you saying?" Rosalind was horrified to think that someone could have recreated this and intentionally infected everyone. "That this was a biological attack?"

Shaking his head almost wildly he said, "All we know right now is that this didn't originally spread as a contagion. We are still investigating if being near the deceased at the time of their..." he paused, obviously trying to find the least offensive way to say it, "...dissolution has any affect."

"What about the mutation?" she asked, then clarified, "The second wave. Do we know how it's moving?"

"We haven't been able to determine how any of it is spreading just yet. However, all signs point to a genuine contagion of biblical proportions. It has the possibility of being pretty catastrophic." Did he sound excited?

It seemed like the panic from the last thousand years had finally caught up with her. As the immensity of what he was saying hit her, Rosalind doubled over and vomited on her feet, and the immaculately clean floor in the lab.

...

"I'm fine," Rosalind protested as they escorted her to the infirmary. She was still shaking at her core causing her to sweat and freeze at the same time.

Reaching for Rosalind's hand, Tannon held it as they walked through the corridor. "When was the last time you actually got some sleep?"

"November," she answered without emotion.

Tannon understood. "Just let them do their thing. Please." No one ever talked to Rosalind with more compassion and love than Tannon. But she could hear in her voice that even Tannon was annoyed with her. "Hey." She turned from Rosalind as she answered her phone, which had been buzzing in her hand. "Are you here?"

The heels of her shoes tapped almost erratically as she strode quickly out of the infirmary to the back entrance. The tension was already overwhelming, and it was about to get worse. As she exited the soft, industrial lighting she was almost blinded by the sun. The rays of UV that assaulted her eyes made them water.

"What the hell goes on in here?" Eddie embraced his friend warmly.

Returning the hug with zeal she joked, "If I tell you..."

They both laughed. Hana had lagged just a few steps behind, hoping to give them a moment as it appeared that they hadn't seen each other in some time. The jovial moment passed quickly. Everyone realized the gravity of the situation but sometimes a little love went a long way. She was stunned when Eddie reached back and took her hand gently and pulled her beside him. "This is Hana Patel," he announced.

Extending her hand to greet her, Tannon asked, "Dr. Patel's wife?"

As the words slipped out, Hana tried to bring them back. But it was too late. "Ex-wife." They had been separated for well over two years. They just hadn't filed the paperwork. "It's a pleasure to meet you." She fumbled with what to say.

"He's in quite a mess, huh?" Tannon truly looked sympathetic. At least she seemed to realize that it was his mess and Hana wasn't involved. He was in a mess. Hana wasn't even sure she understood the whole of his situation. But the mess started way before he got to Montreal.

As they navigated the concrete hallways, Tannon and Eddie continued to talk. "I had no idea any of this was functional, except the port," he admitted. Their voices softly echoed. The tap of their shoes reverberated around them.

"It's not," she corrected him as they reached the area marked *Infirmary*. There were guards at each side of the door. As they went through the mood became solemn. "Eddie, promise me you'll just listen?"

"I won't kill her," he said solemnly. "That's all I can promise." It wasn't a joke. He did want to kill her. But that wouldn't fix anything.

...

The surroundings were cold gray. The fact that any color managed to make it through was a miracle. Rosalind jumped up from the bed she'd been ordered to occupy as she saw Eddie walk through the door. There were a thousand things she needed to say. Waves of nausea swept her over and over again as she tried to hold onto whatever she may have had left in her stomach. It rumbled loudly. The fragrance of toasted sugar overwhelmed her senses. Turning her stomach over and over again.

Before they even made it all the way into the room, she could feel the daggers his stare was throwing. He didn't come to comfort her. Not that she had expected that. What she hadn't expected was to see him walk through the door holding hands with another woman. Before she could speak, Tannon led the conversation.

"This is Hana," she gestured towards her. "She's the one that sent you all of Dr. Patel's files." Turning her attention back to Hana she added, "Which turns out may have been pretty crucial. Thank you, by the way."

Hana stood tall and let go of Eddie's hand. If looks could kill, Rosalind would have laid her out at that moment. Instead she looked away and said, "Thank you. I guess." Thinking about the situation as a whole, she squeaked out, "I am very sorry for..."

"No," Eddie almost shouted. "You don't get to be..."

"Calm down," Tannon stepped between them. "Getting angry isn't going to help anyone." The tension between them was palpable. She and Eddie had been through a lot together, but Rosalind was her best friend. She had every intention of defending her.

"What do you want from me?" Rosalind almost whined. Realizing how pathetic she sounded, she stood straight and defended herself. "You can hate me as much as you want, but I didn't do anything wrong."

It was obvious that Tannon's attempt at being the buffer wasn't going to work. She didn't intervene. Hana slunk back, realizing that her presence was probably more confusing than anything. Although she didn't have all the pieces, it was obvious that Noah and Rosalind had conspired to...what? Save her daughter? How could she fault her for that?

"You experimented on our child. My baby," Eddie snapped.

Maintaining her posture, she shot back, "I brought Delphine *HOME.*" *Why was she defending herself over this? It had worked. It had worked!* It was obvious by her internal dialog that she didn't even believe herself. "I didn't have time to think about what I was doing, let alone talk to you first. Noah was so..."

"No." Eddie lowered the volume of his voice, but the anger was there. Not anger. Hate. "Don't pretend someone else did this. You made a decision. YOU made a decision." He was shaking. The slow flush that had begun to creep up his neck had settled on his face. It felt like hundreds of needles prodding his cheeks simultaneously. The flow of blood roared in both of his ears like raging rivers. He almost didn't hear Hana's soft voice behind him.

"I would have done the same thing," she whispered. The realization that the experimental gene therapy treatment they had tried on Ebrim was actually Rosalind's cure had been swirling Hana's mind for the past twenty-four hours, but the full effect of the circle they had created finally hit her. "Oh my God!" she pushed the words out with as much breath as she could muster, interrupting the daggers shooting back and forth. The room started to spin. Attempting to steady herself she managed to say, "This isn't her fault." Gasping for air she almost didn't get the rest out, "I did this."

She stumbled a couple of steps towards the seat behind her and almost collapsed into it. "It was Ebby's ashes. The EV-118...when I...I don't even know how that's..." Frustration overwhelmed her as she realized she hadn't completed a thought. "It was his ashes. Wasn't it?"

Eddie knelt beside the chair, realizing that Hana might be having a panic attack. Slowly running his finger back and forth on her palm, he quietly whispered, "You're okay. Just breathe."

It was glaringly apparent that his loyalties didn't go to her anymore. Rosalind almost laughed as Eddie rushed to that Barbie doll of a girl. How did this happen? She couldn't even be mad. It took a moment for Hana's words to register. *EV-118? It was Noah's son?* Why wouldn't he have told her?

The only word that Rosalind could manage was, "Ashes?" Could that even be possible? There is no way any biological entity could survive cremation. Could it? Could EV-118 have?

Tannon was trying to keep up, but it was finally clear to her what they were looking for. No matter how ridiculous or impossible, they had a real place to start. "I'm sorry to be the one to ask." Her attempt at being the strong one failed. It would explain the dissemination, somewhat. What a horrible thing to have to ask a mother. "Did you keep any?"

She'd already been clutching the tiny bottle around her neck before Tannon asked. She realized she was going to have to give them up. Tugging straight over her head she pulled the cord from around her neck and extended her arm as far as she could. When had she begun sobbing? Queenie had been right. She was going to end the world. Sobbing harder, she handed Tannon the last piece of her life.

Eddie tried to reign the conversation back, but his anger had completely faded. The implication was that this entire mess had been created by two grieving mothers. If he had known, he would have agreed. He should have known. "You should have told me," he said warily to Rosalind.

Every bit of his energy had been sapped the minute they walked through the door. Hana was crumbling beside him as Rosalind crumbled before him. The heavy breakfast hit the lowest part of his stomach like a rock.

Rosalind watched as the only support she had in the entire world fled the room at breakneck speed, with purpose. She was terrified, which wasn't anything new lately. But this felt like she had walked into a pack of wild dogs and they could smell her. She waited for the brutal attack that didn't come. Why was she afraid? Why was she in this...where is this? Who were all these people? Why were they yelling?

She was panicking. Redirecting her thoughts into one focus, she watched Eddie stroking Hana's hair. She wanted to cry. Everything was starting to blur. At some point, she'd sat back down on the bed. She was wringing her hands in her lap. Attempting to make a conscious effort to stop the fidgeting, she looked down. When the two small drops of blood landed on her thumb, she reached up to her nose. Pulling back her hand, she saw blood on her fingers.

As the room begun to spin, she managed to squeak, "Eddie?"

END ACT 4

ACT FIVE – ALL THE KING'S HORSES

Broken

"Thank you for tuning in. If you're just joining us, let me recap what we've learned so far." The man sat alone at the news anchor desk. He was disheveled and looked like he hadn't slept in days. His tie was discarded next to the stack of notes he had in front of him. "The unidentified illness that has been spreading like wildfire has not been contained. Reports from the **CDC** and **WHO** have been sketchy at best, but at this time we understand there is no treatment available."

Shifting his position to face a different camera he sighed. The pageantry was even annoying him. "At this time people are being asked to stay in their homes and avoid contact with anyone that you believe might be infected." The look on his face was confusion. "How are we supposed to know who might be infected?" he mumbled to someone off camera. It was obvious everyone was tired, punchy and ready for this to end. One way or another. "Sorry." He straightened his posture and regained his composure.

From somewhere out of sight a man's voice stated, "Camera two." Off-camera conversations were being picked up ever so slightly by the active mics. Shifting his attention again in the other direction, it was apparent the words he was reading on the prompter were new to him. "If you are exhibiting any of the symptoms behind me..." he gestured towards the green screen behind him which displayed each symptom one at a time, "...please report to one of the CDC outposts set up at various locations. Please check with your local law enforcement for the one nearest you." Shifting once more, he read the final statement, "Authorities are requesting that you not report to local emergency rooms or hospitals unless you have a physical injury."

Several video clips played silently behind him. CDC tents billowed in the wind like bleached out circus tents that had been in the sun too long. Representatives receiving the flood of patients that thought they might be infected looked like space creatures with their full hazmat gear. People of all ages gathering around officials, begging for answers. It was the scene at every medical outpost set up to diagnose...and then what? There was no cure.

Shari lowered the volume on the television and sat on the floor across from Queenie. They'd been praying all morning, but everything still felt so bleak. Whispering to her new faithful friend, the sound of sorrow from her own voice nearly devastated her. "I expected the rapture to be a little more peaceful."

Without raising her head Queenie replied, "That ain't what this is."

The tattered leather-bound tome beside her was opened to Ezekiel chapter sixteen. "Now this was the sin of your sister Sodom: She and her daughters were arrogant, overfed and unconcerned; they did not help the poor and needy. They were haughty and did detestable things before me. Therefore, I did away with them as you have seen." As she read part of the passage aloud, a chill crept down her spine.

As she lit the tip of the absolutely gourmet cigar that Morgan had brought her, she exhaled a thick cloud of smoke. "Comes around every so often. Never in the same lifetime." Tapping the tobacco wrap against the corner of the clear glass ashtray she punctuated, "We forget to live, we forget to give, we forget to love. And He take it all away."

Nodding with conviction she continued to speak, "I don't know if the saints are even listening. They mighta turned the other way by now." Drawing heavily on the cigar she puffed two rings above their head.

"What do we do?" Shari asked. As the smoke swirled above her head, she caught the scent of dark cherry and burning wood. It was a pleasant fragrance.

With a thick masculine tenor Queenie almost vibrated the words out rather than speaking them. "What do your senses tell you?"

The vibrato created as the long "u" sound was carried out way too far caused the tiny bones in Shari's ears to rattle. Shuddering just a bit she whispered, "Which ones?"

The ember from the cigar reflected back from her dark eyes, as she released the words as slow as molasses, "All of them."

As the soft glow of the fireplace danced behind Queenie, Shari focused on the display. The sweet smoke of the cigar mingled with the acrid odor of burning oak and swirled into her sinuses allowing her to almost taste the fire. From the kitchen the aroma of maple still lingered as well as the smell of burnt coffee. They had left the pot on too long. A chill had settled in. Although traditionally by this time of year things were warming up, the temperature had dropped again below fifty degrees. From where they sat the warmth barely reached from the fire and as Shari exhaled it appeared a plume of smoke was escaping.

Although the volume on the television was completely down, the nearly undetectable squeal it created was still audible, if only barely. Shari continued to shiver as she watched the flame dance. It was the black and white scene that somehow played only for her which caused the violent sudden shudder. Was she seeing the future or was her mind just playing tricks?

Queenie leaned forward with anticipation. "What are you seeing?"

"Death. All I see is death." Shari sat motionless, attempting to clear her mind. But it was no use. She'd already seen the end.

...

"I know how this works," Rosalind snapped as the phlebotomist tried to explain the process while attempting to locate a vein to draw from. The thin sheet on her arm glowed green. There were plenty of choices. Soldiers, doctors and scientists hovered around in various degrees of protective gear. No one honestly believed any of it did any good.

That was clearly apparent as Dr. Tedesse himself observed without so much as a mask. The concern in his eyes was accompanied by the macabre excitement that every doctor had when it came to something new. "I am sorry we have to do this, but you understand."

She understood. Of course she understood. It didn't make it better or easier. She winced slightly as the exaggerated pinch hit the surface of her skin. Either the girl was clumsy, or it was deliberate. It was probably deliberate. The cloudy confusion that had almost swallowed her whole had subsided. But panic stayed around the edges.

Although Bo Cane had been listed as patient zero, Rosalind was the first *living* patient they'd had any chance to test. Realizing the speed and nature of what the virus was doing, moving quickly was imperative. The clumsy young woman dabbed at the puncture site with a small cotton ball and quickly exited with two vials in her hand. She was obviously annoyed that Rosalind had snapped at her and didn't speak again.

"How are you feeling?" the soft, clearly genuine voice echoed slightly.

Rosalind looked up from the tiny puncture wound to see Hana standing close by. She wanted to be catty, but she didn't have the energy. It also occurred to her that Hana wasn't the enemy, *she* was. "I had no idea that the trial on EV-118 was Noah's son. They don't tell us who..." Why was she explaining herself to this Barbie? "...they just tell us the results." Her tone wasn't angry, condescending or judgmental.

 "I can't imagine why Noah didn't tell you." Hana slowly walked towards the bed where Rosalind had now been completely confined. "He seemed to know everything about the treatment they were offering. Once it got approved...they said it wasn't that the treatment didn't work. It was that it was already too late."

Nodding, it was obvious she had been informed of all of this. "That's why I wanted to speed the process up," she lamented. "Because..."

Hana was close enough that she reached out and put her hand on Rosalind's. It was shaking. "This isn't your fault." The shocking reality was that, although Rosalind and Noah had set the stage, this was her fault. She knew she wasn't supposed to release ashes in a river. Everyone knows that. But she did it anyway because she wanted to take him back to Butterfly Park. Even though she didn't cause this tragic event, she's the one that set it all in motion. That's the part that mattered.

"Isn't it though?" Tears were pouring from her bloodshot eyes. "I just wanted to hold my baby."

"I'd let everyone die if I could hold Ebrim just one more time." The words slipped out before she'd had time to process them. That was the darkness Queenie had seen. She did not know it existed. But it was there. She could never see Rosalind as the enemy. All she could see is a woman that would do anything for her child. She wasn't the bad guy, she was just a mother.

A chorus of machinery and wheels on concrete preceded the frantic entry into the infirmary. The roar seemed to go on for quite some time as several portable laboratory machines were wheeled through. Tannon filed in behind them. "We have a problem," she announced. "The blood didn't..." pausing she tried to find the right words, "...last long enough. From the moment it was drawn, it started breaking down." Motioning towards the equipment that had been hastily shoved into the room she clarified, "Maybe shaving off the travel time we'll have a better chance."

Hana hadn't let go of her hand. That was interesting. What was more interesting was that it hadn't been five minutes since the nurse had left, had it? Glancing up at the clock she was startled to see that almost an hour had passed since she last looked. Just before the snotty specialist stabbed her. How had that happened? "Did you learn anything at all?"

"Enough to understand what's happening," Tannon sounded defeated. "May even have a theory on *how.*" Her demeanor announced without words the truth that understanding what was happening and how it happened did not bring them closer to a way to stop it.

Hana sat and listened as the friends talked. She had retreated back a few steps and taken a seat near the end of the bed. Eddie should really be here, but he was still teetering between the grief he hadn't dealt with, the hatred he knew he shouldn't have and the duty he had to his wife. She could see it in his eyes when he walked out and headed down towards the docks. She didn't try to stop him. He needed time to sort it all out.

What they were saying was terrifying. Somehow EV-118 had survived the cremation process. After testing the remaining ashes, they had determined that each particle of ash that had been spread across the Mississippi on Friday had the potential to carry the virus. It was impossible, but that is what had happened.

After subjecting Rosalind to several tests, they determined the tissue in the brain seemed to be affected the quickest, leading to confusion and ultimately complete dementia. Rosalind shuddered violently as she realized that is what she had to look forward to.

"It's still not fast enough," one of the scientists was obviously frustrated and as he spoke, accidentally dropped the tools he was holding. He shook his head. "It's essentially dead before we can get anywhere."

It was obvious that Hana was the only person in the room that didn't completely understand everything that was going on. But she understood enough. It all sounded so familiar. Years and years of being subjected to Noah's rattling, even though he knew she didn't understand, but still he told her everything. After a while she couldn't even stand to hear his voice. At one point in their lives, watching him go on and on about some new discovery brought her joy. Now it only brought blinding terror.

Eddie had quietly slipped into the room some time ago and had been standing back listening to the whole of what was happening. He watched as Tannon repeatedly checked her phone, texting someone.

He watched as the people busied themselves with their appointed tasks. He watched as Hana offered compassion and understanding. He watched as Rosalind crumbled. She was going to die. He was glad no one noticed his presence until after he'd had a chance to wipe the tears out of his eyes clumsily with the back of his hand. He then dried it on his sweats.

Crossing the room, he silently acknowledged Tannon and smiled at Hana. For a brief moment he considered sitting next to her, instead he sat at the foot of the bed. Rosalind looked relieved. "I am so sorry," she pleaded.

"Why?" The look in his eyes was softer, the hate had disappeared. It was the emptiness when he looked at her that crushed Rosalind's soul. At least the presence of hate had suggested he still cared. "What part are you sorry for?"

Hana wanted to interrupt. Everyone was hurt. He was being unreasonable under the circumstances, wasn't he? But she couldn't form the words. As her eyes darted around the room, she realized that just about everyone was holding back the same. Instead she held her tongue. This was between them.

"I am sorry that anyone got..." How was she supposed to finish that sentence? *Got hurt? Died?* It all sounded so crass.

Holding her hand for the first time in almost a year, he could feel the tremble that had settled deep inside her. "I've blamed you for a lot of things, Ros." Relaxing slightly, his attempt at comforting her appeared to be well received. "This isn't your fault." At some point in time, he would have died for her. He would have killed for her. Breathing deeply, he pushed the words out as fast as he could. "What happened with Dellie wasn't your fault."

Although most of the people were pretending not to listen, they were. Only the four of them understood the reference to a past event. By the time he had spoken the words, all three women were weeping. Rosalind's sobs were almost hysterical and uncontrollable. "I'm okay," she tried desperately to regain any composure she could to assure the worried faces staring at her. "I haven't lost my mind yet." To try to prove to them or herself she turned to the doctor and interjected, "So what you're saying is that we need a better way to manipulate the live cells..."

Realizing his previous rattling had been heard, he stepped closer to her. That excitement in his eyes again. It made her nauseous. "The problem is, just like at death, the process seems to be accelerated. As soon as we draw it, it's too late."

"What about hemodialysis?" She looked around the room at the doctors and scientists for validation. It was a brilliant idea. Was it possible?

Obviously not following her train of thought, the weaselly little man shook his head. "Filtering it wouldn't fix the problem."

Moron. Rosalind shook the thought off as she shook her head no. "I mean can you effectively run the tests through dialysis?"

Stammering to decide he replied, "I...well maybe." He scratched the bald part of his head. "I mean we might have a better chance." It was glaringly apparent that thinking outside the box was not his strong suit. "But how would we do that?"

Waves of nausea as powerful as storm surges swelled in her. Rosalind gasped for air, hoping to not throw up again. The room had begun to spin a while back and her thoughts were assaulting her, creating a barricade of confusion. If she could just focus on her thoughts.

The smell of rotting eggs tickled her nose and it took a moment for her to realize that she was smelling her own breath. Gagging, she again forced whatever was still trying to work its way back up, back down again. The taste of bile and whatever that heat was continued to creep up her throat, causing a burning sensation behind her sternum.

There was that ringing again. She tried to shake it off, but the pitch only increased. She could feel her pulse racing as the pressure behind her eyes became almost unbearable. Covering her ears, she tried to block out the sound of roaring voices. She felt crowded and continued to struggle for air. "If you'd all stop talking at once..." Cutting herself, off she realized that everyone was staring at her with concern. "I don't think you have much time to figure it out."

Painful Truths

Joaquin was surprised when he got the first text from Tannon. *Just checking to see if you're okay,* it said. *I am. Are you?* he replied. Did she want to chat? That seemed odd. The next text came through very quickly. *Are you Public Trust?* She was asking about his security clearance. That was odd as well. He responded, *Collateral.* As soon as he tapped send, her reply came again. *How far are you from Belle Chasse?*

The drive only took about fifteen minutes. As Joaquin approached the abandoned complex, he chuckled to himself. He'd been back and forth through here countless times, always wondered why they were letting the complex sit empty. This made more sense. Tannon was at the end of the road, outside the gate smoking a cigarette. Climbing in the passenger side, she didn't toss her cigarette out before she got in.

Normally that would have bothered him, instead he rolled the windows down and smiled at her. "Where are we going?" Tired, worn and worried, she was still stunning.

She briefed him as they made their way onto the base. "Why did you invite me?" he asked after she had indicated that she was done. The day had blown by so fast. Twilight was coming, and dusk would cover the bay and inlet swamps with darkness. The salty air was thick, and he breathed in deeply, tasting the crisp bitterness.

A guard waved them through the almost invisible checkpoint. She didn't speak again until they parked. "You're the only investigator on the report," she said almost coyly as she slipped out of the SUV and walked around to the front. "You were the only investigator present at the opening of..." She paused. These were truths, and it's how she got him cleared so fast. Those weren't the only reasons. With an almost agonal gasp, she stepped towards him and confidently leaned into him. In her heels she was about an inch taller than him. Her breath smelled like stale cigarettes. He didn't stop her as she began kissing him urgently and whispering, "I don't want to be alone."

By the time she stopped and was regaining whatever composure she had left, Joaquin chuckled softly, "That bad?" The look of absolute terror in her eyes killed whatever laughter he still possessed. This entire ordeal seemed to have stretched out over lifetimes when in fact it hadn't been a week.

"I'm sorry," she said as she led him towards the back of the building.

"Don't be sorry. I'm not complaining." The sidewalk was cracked up the entire walk. The building appeared to be condemned until they stepped through the interior door. "Impressive." He whistled slightly, and it echoed down the halls. Mr. Bélisaire and the woman that was with him in the van were waiting in the small break area. "We should really stop meeting under such awful circumstances." Extending his hand first to Hana he introduced himself, "Joaquin."

The introductions were clumsy, and the mood was that of a funeral procession that had been stalled at a train. Eddie sat, fidgeting with the wedding band he was holding in his hand. It was obvious everyone was waiting. They all snapped to attention when the woman in hazmat surgical gear appeared at the door. Without addressing anyone else in the room, she waved Tannon to follow after her. He didn't mean to say it out loud. But his sadness was equaled by everyone in the room as Eddie said it, "There's no way that's good news."

...

Morgan watched the sun creep slowly across the sky. As it finally began to dip into the swamps behind the house, he'd grown restless and wary. His ribs still screamed every time he moved, and he was sure that the accident had broken one of them. The bruising on his chest had finally begun to fade to a disgusting wash of yellow and green smeared together. He'd live.

The sliding door was open completely and the chill of the air outside battled the warmth of the fire inside at the threshold. His mother and her new best friend were seated on the edge of the sofa, effectively mesmerized by the evening news. They weren't saying anything good. The warm smell of stew skated along with the smoky aroma of burning oak. His stomach rumbled loudly.

The distant sound like turbine engines indicated that there were air boats nearby. At least two, maybe three. The fact that he couldn't see any lights over the water didn't mean they weren't there. He slowly sunk back into the house and drew the blackout curtains. It wasn't unusual to hear the boats, but this evening it was unsettling.

"You do right to be wary," Queenie announced reverently as Morgan sat beside her, "But they ain't coming here." For a few moments, the sound increased to nearly a roar and then rolled away as fast. Wherever they were headed, they were in a hurry.

Queenie had her arsenal on the floor by the coffee table. It looked as though she had added some saints. The cards were stacked on the other side from the ones they had laid out this morning. His mother used to tell him stories of all the saints, and he recognized some of the names. The three she added this evening were the most familiar to him. St. Agatha was his mother's favorite for obvious reasons, she was the patron saint of nurses. The trio also included St. Luke for physicians and St. Dominic, the patron saint of scientists.

The pleasant aroma of burning sage overtook the other fragrances in the air. Pointing at the display he tried to joke, "God not coming?"

...

University Medical was a graveyard. Not literally. But since the news reports came out guiding everyone to the outposts, no one was coming here. They wanted to be where the answers were. For whatever answers there were right now. That was alright. The hospital could use a little quiet.

Kate sat behind the nurses' desk, almost dozing, when her phone began to rattle across the pressboard veneer. It was a text from Morgan, *Sorry I bailed.* Relieved she texted back, *Are you okay?* The sound of muted footsteps from somewhere down the hall reached her. *Had a little accident. I'm okay. I'm at my mom's.* Whoever was coming down the hall must have turned off before they got to her. No one appeared. *Stay there. We're all going to die anyway.* It wasn't an attempt at humor. She quickly sent another text. *Dr. Schwartz is gone. Half my nurses are gone. Just gone.*

Do you need me to come help you? Morgan was a sweet guy. Too bad he was so young. She replied, *No. Stay at your mom's. As long as you can.* The quiet throughout the halls had surpassed eerie a long time ago. About two minutes passed before his reply. *You should come to Lafayette.*

...

"It's not a contagion, it's airborne," the fat little man announced too loudly as he came through the doors.

Rosalind's head was throbbing, and she was becoming easily irritated. Well, *more* easily irritated. "It can't be just hanging around," she muttered.

"No. No." He nearly rushed to her bedside. The sudden movement made her nauseous. Everything made her nauseous. "It's in the, I think the word we settled with was, dissolution."

She nodded. The bobbing motion created more tension behind her eyes. "What about this?" she gestured at the equipment that had crowded her space. It wasn't that she wasn't fascinated, but this was the part that mattered right now. "I'm not..." she paused as she realized what she was about to say. She exhaled deeply and the taste of saline and a slight metallic odor that were being delivered through the IV crossed her breath. "I'm not sure how much longer I can be helpful." Her mind was wandering constantly.

It was poetic, she thought. Her entire life all she wanted was to save lives. All she wanted was to cure disease. Instead, people were dying. It was clear that it wasn't just her fault. There were several factors that weren't her doing, but ultimately, she was the one responsible. She dozed off and on between thoughts.

People were buzzing back and forth as her blood ran through the artificial kidney. They had removed the membrane filters and created a small testing platform behind the machine. "It's still moving too fast," one of the doctors announced frustrated. "If we could slow this whole thing down a little more..." She paused as she realized all of the color was gone from Rosalind's face. "Are you okay?"

She wasn't. But she had an idea. "What about biologics?" she asked...her speech was slow and slurred. The doctor was looking at her with some confusion. Was she swaying? Voices around the room were muffled and Rosalind strained to make out any one conversation. "You need to suppress the immune response, so..." She fidgeted with the fistula in her arm, which contained both needles. It itched so badly underneath. What was she doing? Oh, yes. That's right. "What was I saying?" The buzzing feeling in her hands made her jump before she realized that she was still holding her phone. She had received a text. *Where are you?* It was from Olivia.

The fear that she had been choking down threatened to all come up at once, as the betrayal finally hit her. She hadn't had time to deal with the little things, but suddenly it was immense. *What do you care?* she typed out, backspaced and retyped *Where are you?* It didn't matter, she didn't even care. Should she tell Olivia she was... she shook the thought off. Surely, they'd figure something out in time, right?

...

"That little fucking weasel," Olivia slammed her fists down on the dresser.

The motel room was gamey and smelled like an entire football team had just packed in after the big game. The humidity was way too high for the end of February and her hair fell like mop strings that hadn't been wrung out completely. She hated the South, but here she was.

The events of Friday night played over and over in her head. Rex was supposed to do the dirty work. The idea was to get Noah's computer, make it look like someone tossed the room, not torch the place. But he had been telling the truth. He didn't start the fire, and he didn't kill Noah. Noah wasn't even dead!

She had no idea that he would have reacted so over the top, but all he cared about was himself. Maybe telling him he'd been caught was a bad idea. He hadn't. As a matter of fact, Rosalind had drunkenly confessed all her sins the first night they spent together in Munich. Told her everything about Noah's little experiment. No one else knew. She hadn't told anyone. It was just supposed to serve her purpose. Did he actually torch his own room?

The phone skittered across the water-stained dresser top. She had replied to Rosalind over twenty minutes ago, but for some reason she wasn't texting back anymore. The words *Unknown Number* flashed above the message. It was Noah. *Did you get what you were looking for?*

Of course she hadn't. He knew that. He was baiting her. She didn't reply. It took about five more minutes for him to realize she wasn't going to reply. Instead he texted, *Rosalind's infected.*

...

It had been nearly two hours since they had shooed all non-essential persons from the infirmary. Eddie paced back and forth in the small but comfortable lounge area. Hana had fallen asleep on the hard sofa and was snoring ever so lightly. She must be exhausted from being dragged through all of his personal drama and the self-acquired weight she'd recently placed on her own shoulders. His phone had died about an hour ago. Finally plugging it in, he waited to get enough charge to check on Morgan. It was moving so slow. Everything was moving so slow.

A few times a stationed guard or doctor or someone would come in, get coffee and leave. No one spoke to them. Joaquin seemed to be just a little offended by that. Eddie chuckled, "They're just being good soldiers. They're trained not to see us." That seemed to make sense to him. He wouldn't tell him that he also was getting a little offended. He really wanted to see Rosalind. He didn't want her to be alone.

As soon as she brought Joaquin in, Tannon had completely disappeared. She loved Rosalind more than anyone else ever had. It was likely she was holding her hand, if she was able. Lost in thought, Eddie didn't notice that his phone had turned back on. The notification created a steady buzzing in his hands. There was one text. It was from Morgan.

Mom wants you to check in when you can. As weird as the statement looked, it felt like the most natural thing in the world. They had literally abandoned Queenie there. But she had not only been welcomed with open arms, it almost seemed like she already knew that's where she was going. *We're okay. Physically,* he tapped the words out. Before he sent the text he added, *Queenie keeping you safe?*

While he was waiting for an answer, he sent Tannon a text. He just needed to know something. The reply that came was from Morgan, *She's been going on for the last hour about that poor Missus Rosalind. What's going on? Isn't that your wife? No judgment.* It was odd that he ended the text that way. But he understood. He wasn't sure how much to tell them, but it seemed like they already had an idea. *They're doing everything they can, as fast as they can.* Morgan's reply came quickly, *I'm so sorry.* Without responding to the last text, he set the phone aside.

He was sitting in the chair, next to Hana with his head cradled in his hands when Tannon came in. "It worked." She was excited, but not as excited as she could have been. That could only mean that "It worked" didn't mean they'd cured her. It meant her idea to isolate whatever it was that they needed to isolate had worked.

Too wary to stand, Eddie looked up. "How is she?" He hadn't eaten since breakfast, but something kept flipping over and over in his stomach. Maybe it was the mass amounts of coffee he had ingested. When she hung her head, his stomach flipped again.

"They're working as fast as they can." As though she was gasping for air she added, "I don't know if it will be enough."

Although they had been speaking at a very low level, Hana stirred. Her eyes were cloudy, and it took just a moment for the room to come into view. It also took just a moment to clear her mind, to remember where she was. "What's going on?" She sat up way too quickly which made her dizzy and she wobbled just a bit.

"I should be in there." He jumped up and began pacing again.

"It's airborne," she said absently.

"So, we've already been in there." He was unclear on why she was telling him this now. Was this new? Did they just learn this?

"Not communicable," she corrected. "Airborne." He was a brilliant lawyer, an even more brilliant leader but he was clueless when it came to biological science.

"Whatever." He was irritated. Incredibly so. "That just means we could all already be infected."

"But you're not, right?" She wasn't really asking, she was telling him.

Had she just imagined she'd spoken? She was still half asleep. Her lower back was on fire. Her joints were screaming at her. The pounding in her head had become more intense. Her neck hurt from the angle she'd been laying at. The arm rest made a terrible pillow. "How long have I been asleep?"

Eddie hadn't meant to ignore Hana, but his head was spinning. He wasn't sure how much more of this he could handle before he broke. He didn't have that luxury. Not right now. Without looking towards her he answered, "About an hour." He fumbled with the coffee machine, figuring that she might need a cup.

Tannon crossed the room and sat down next to Joaquin, who up to this point had been silent. He was an outsider, in a glaring way. He realized that. He had no idea who these people were. He had no idea why he was even still here. Yes, he did. It was that kiss. It was the realization that they could possibly all... His train of thought was interrupted as the Styrofoam cup Eddie had prepared bounced up from the floor, the hot liquid spraying both Tannon and Joaquin in the face.

Eddie had turned to Hana but stood frozen. Hana's expression was pure confusion as a deep groan crept up his throat. The thump his knees made as they hit the hard-polished floor in front of her was far less painful than what he was seeing. He reached behind him, hoping to get Tannon's attention. He couldn't speak.

As drops of blood rolled down her lip, Hana realized what was going on. She wiped her nose and leaned forward into Eddie who was still on his knees, toppling him backwards on the floor.

A Whisper on The Breeze

The sun was already creeping up from behind the bay. Had it not been the end of the world, it would have been the most beautiful sight. Instead, the rays burned through the mist like napalm as they assaulted Eddie's eyes. The fog from the gulf burned off as it reached the bay, but still hovered over the body of water, making it impossible to see more than a few feet out.

He should have slept, but instead he had been sitting on the dock staring out over the water since about three A.M. Whatever they did for Rosalind was able to at least slow the whole thing down, but the clock was still ticking. She was sleeping. Tannon promised to text him when she woke up. He'd found the crushed pack of stale cigarettes at the bottom of Hana's purse. He'd only seen her smoke two, so no telling how old they were, but they tasted terrible. He smoked three of them.

He watched as Comfort sauntered into the bay. USS Comfort was a naval hospital ship. Designed to treat mass injuries and sickness. Why were they bringing her in? They were holding back just a little bit, out in the distance. But even through the mist and fog, he could see the bold red cross and white surface.

As the sky turned from a dark blue to a brighter hue, he drove back up to the base. The sweatpants he'd been wearing for the past three days were stained, his shirt was crumpled and spattered with coffee and a couple of drops of blood. He wasn't even sure who's blood it was. It was so quiet. The terrifying silence only existed on the outside of the inner door. Once he walked back inside, the chaos would resume. He considered walking away and driving as far from New Orleans as he could, but he shook the thought off and opened the door. Everything he cared about was inside.

"Sergeant Pyburn said to give you these." As soon as he walked through the door he was greeted with clean clothes. It was the first time any of the enlisted had spoken to him. "She said you need a shower. I'll show you where it is." The young man's face was battling terror and composure. The true face of any soldier during war. As far as wars went, it looked like they'd lost this one. Everyone seemed to recognize that.

"I'll take the hint." Eddie followed him to the area they called the barracks. It was more like a small housing complex complete with private living areas and private baths. Although sparse, the room looked comfortable. He had no intention of sleeping, but the shower was welcome. And necessary. He could use a shave too, but there were no razors. Just soap. That was good enough.

As the water pulsed down almost too hard, Eddie stood with his head pressed into the shower wall, quietly sobbing. From the moment he had pulled his little girl's body from the pool, he had felt nothing but anger. He had directed every bit of that towards Rosalind, who was mourning too. He should have been there for her then. At least he could be here for her now. Whatever good that was.

He had plenty of beer at the house. When he'd gone out Friday night, he wasn't looking for a drink—he was looking for human contact. He hadn't realized that until now. It could have been anyone, but it wasn't. He'd seen the same need in Hana. No matter how he played it over in his head, he realized that nothing had been chance. Forces that he didn't understand had guided them all together. Without Hana, they wouldn't have Dr. Patel's research. At least not as quickly. Without Hana, he would have run. Maybe he should have.

Because of Hana, Queenie and Morgan were safe in Lafayette instead of sitting in a rocking chair or struggling on the road with broken ribs. Because of Hana, Shari had her son close. Because of Hana... His thoughts drifted off as he fell asleep for a moment standing under the lukewarm spray. He roused as the water began to sputter ice cold, and almost slipped as he quickly stumbled out of the stall before reaching back in and turning off the water.

The steam had already dissipated, but tiny streams of water continued to roll down the mirror. Whose face was this? His eyes were completely bloodshot, and still welling with tears. The lines on his face seemed to have doubled in the past few days, deep craters of sorrow and emptiness carved a path across his brow and forehead. The lines at the corner of his eyes appeared deeper and his gaze seemed hollow. *When did I get so old?* he wondered.

He was so lost in his sorrow, he missed the first knock. The second was a bit louder. Hana was standing just outside the private room. She had been crying. "Why are you up wandering around?" The soft, almost whisper was all he could manage.

"I can't just sit around and wait to..." She shuddered. All of this was her fault. She caused this. So many people had died. So many more were still going to die. Eddie stepped back from the door, clutching the towel around his waist and invited her in. Before the door was completely latched Hana stood on her toes and leaned in against him. As he wrapped his arms around her, he kissed her forehead. Lifting her face to meet his lips, she breathed him in as he returned her kiss over and over again. "This is wrong," she announced between kisses. But she didn't stop.

"Which part?" He knew which part. He wasn't waiting for an answer. Softness replaced the sorrow. The cinch on the towel threatened to let go just as he pulled her back towards the twin size cot. The need and desire that had been burning him alive shifted as he softly cradled her face between his palms and gently pressed his lips to her forehead. Pulling her into his lap they both fumbled to remove her clothes. She was dirty, sweaty and it smelled like she'd thrown up recently. He didn't care.

For just a short time, the entire world disappeared. Hana was dizzy, and she realized it was probably the virus. The fire that was radiating from her wasn't because of that. It was Eddie. She swayed with the music playing in her head. It serenaded them as they moved together.

...

It was almost three A.M. when Tannon finally left Rosalind's side. The same biologics they used to slow the virus a little had been administered to Hana. Hopefully that would give them time, which was a luxury these days. Several other personnel at the base started exhibiting symptoms and they'd been treated the same and sent to rest. She was exhausted. Joaquin could see that. But she denied it over and over again.

"You should get some sleep." He didn't know much about her, other than their professional relationship, but for some reason she chose him to...end the world with? That thought almost made him chuckle, except the whole devastating part. She was beautiful. Thick hair, long legs and big blue eyes. They were puffy because she'd been crying on and off all day. He hadn't seen her crying, but it was obvious she had been. He still couldn't help himself from staring into them.

She smelled like bubblegum. He wasn't sure if it was traces left over from perfume, or just her. Either way it was intoxicating. He hadn't slept since he left Sgt. Denning's apartment. He hadn't been able to reach him either. John was a good man. A little rough around the edges, but good. He hoped that he hadn't... His wandering thoughts were interrupted as Tannon took his hand and led him towards the barracks. She didn't speak. She didn't need to.

The awkwardness faded quickly as she closed the door and pushed him against it. Her kiss was urgent as she pressed her body to his. Her breathing was frantic but fit the mood. Although there was no music, the slow waltz they did around the room ended at the tiny bunk. "What are we doing?" Joaquin asked. It's not that he didn't understand where this was heading, he just wanted to give her a moment to think about it. She slid her hands up his chest under his shirt, sliding it over his head. "Are you sure?" he attempted again.

"Shut up." The force that her lips met his with was almost catastrophic. The panic in her soul translated in her movements. She was abrupt, almost maniacal. He hadn't expected her to be so rough, but he returned the same. Finally managing to drift to sleep, they clung to each other for dear life.

...

It was almost three o'clock as Kate turned onto the gravel road. She'd been here once, just after Morgan's dad died. They had a house full of mourning family, she felt out of place. But Morgan had needed a friend. She couldn't stand the idea of just sitting around, waiting to get sick and watching everyone die. At least she finished out her shift first. But she probably wouldn't go back. It's not like they were actually helping anyone at this point.

It was dark tonight. As the moon peeked ever so slightly through the clouds, the rays glittered on the swamp. She was almost relieved that someone wanted to spend some time with her. Morgan's invitation was exactly what she needed. She didn't want to be alone. She sat in the drive with the car idling for about five minutes, trying to decide whether to go up to the house or not.

There was just enough light to see the walk to the stairs. As she started up the steps, she caught a whiff of cherry tobacco and saw the red glow from a cigar. Just before she made it to the top of the steps, she heard the woman cough. It was that old woman, Queenie. Why was she *here*? "I should be done with these," she giggled. "Morgan said you was coming. I'm glad you made it safe." Kate paused at the door. "I don't think you gotta knock, baby."

The warm glow of the fire was the first thing she saw as she walked through the door. There were no lights on, but the fireplace from the living room illuminated the dining area well enough that she could navigate through. Morgan had fallen asleep on the sofa. She almost felt bad for disturbing him, but she sat on the edge of the couch beside him. "How are you feeling?"

He was shirtless, and his chest had a bluish green tinge from his collar bone down to his hip on the left side. Sitting up a little faster than he should have, he clutched his side. "Oh, you know, ready to run a marathon." The words came out slowly as he shook off the sleep he had just awakened from.

"I see the Eye of the Quarter is watching over you." She was referring to Queenie's presence on the porch. "How did that happen?"

"I have no idea." He shook his head. He had no idea how any of this had happened. "I know mom thinks they must have been separated at birth." Sighing he added, "I guess we all need one good friend right now."

She was nearly sixteen years older than him. She'd passed forty a few months ago. She was almost old enough to be his mother. "Is that what you need?"

Kate was one of the most beautiful women he'd ever met. He wasn't sure she realized that. He had no idea why he'd invited her, not until she was sitting beside him. In fact, he was surprised when he leaned towards her and kissed her. Even more surprised that she returned it with the same passion. Even though his breath was ripe from sleep, she didn't flinch.

They didn't talk as he took her hand and led her through the kitchen to the guest room. The queen size bed was made up with a gaudy floral comforter and all of the matching linens. Even the curtains matched. The mattress was over soft but moved with them like a cloud. As the hue of the sky went from dark and ominous to bright and blue, they were both finally overwhelmed by sleep.

...

The rental car was musty, but it was all they had. As she made her way south towards the bay, her phone alerted her that she had arrived. Before her was a huge complex of run-down buildings and dilapidated roads. It looked as though the place was completely abandoned. But the manned gate proved otherwise. They must have been expecting her, because one of the soldiers waved her through before she came to a complete stop.

Olivia hadn't expected to hear from Rosalind. It was way past midnight by the time she did. The sun would be up soon, but she couldn't sleep. The fact that Rosalind wanted to see her at all seemed very foreboding. Even more devastating was that she said "please". Rosalind never said "please". She said it was too much like begging.

But the text said, *Please come see me.*

By the time they escorted her to where Rosalind was, the sun had started to creep up over the bay. Even at such an early hour, she needed sunglasses. It was as though the sun was announcing its entry into the day with a scream. The infirmary was packed with portable machines, and they had to navigate around some of the clutter but as soon as Rosalind saw her, she reached up for her hand. Olivia pulled one of the chairs as close to the bed as she could. "I am so sorry Ros."

"No need to be," she answered slowly. It was painful to watch her struggle to breathe. "We've all got our own reasons for what we've done." Was that forgiveness? That was another thing Rosalind didn't do: forgive. The realization that she knew she was going to die hit Olivia harder than she'd expected. The fragrances of medicine and other sterile odors assaulted her and made her nauseous. Or maybe it was seeing this strong powerful woman this way.

"What can I do?" she asked as she squeezed hard on her hand.

Rosalind had been holding the small flash drive in her other hand for the past several hours. She had been clutching it so tightly that releasing her fingers and loosening her fist was a chore. As she struggled a bit to extend her arm, she handed it to Olivia. "I would have shared it with you. All you had to do was ask."

Regret and a lifetime of trying to prove her own worth caught up with her. "I am so sorry," she sobbed out the words. She didn't know what else to say. And she was. She was sorry for using her, she was sorry for being so selfish and she was sorry that it was Rosalind and not her. "I would take your place in a heartbeat if I could." She meant that. She genuinely did.

Rosalind seemed to appreciate the empty platitude and received it with as much love as it had been delivered. "Just sit with me," she requested. They were quiet for some time. The sounds of people working had faded into the background. They were still busy and working, but it seemed as though they'd moved hundreds of feet away.

The small television close by was airing the news. Every channel was airing the news. It was likely the whole world was. The volume was down but the same story played over and over again, like a bad nightmare that they couldn't wake up from. Olivia stared at the small plastic gadget in her hand. This was what she'd been looking for. This is why The Queen Elizabeth burned. This is why Noah disappeared. None of which she'd done. All of which, was pretty much her fault. She was stunned to realize that she didn't want it anymore. Setting it on the small bedside table she began to weep.

"Stop crying, please." There it was again. Rosalind had said "please".

She slowly shook her head, as though to clarify her thoughts. "I'm not mad. I'm not..."

Interrupting her gently, Olivia sighed, "You should be."

"Takes too much energy." She pulled Olivia's hand to her mouth and kissed her palm. "You are so very brilliant." Breathing hard she continued, "I don't know why I've never told you that before."

"Stop." The emotional display was too much for her. "Where is Eddie?"

She chuckled which turned into a horrible cough. "He's here. Sleeping I hope." Attempting to clear her throat caused her to cough more violently. Her breathing was labored. She was shaking.

"You should be too," Olivia chastised lovingly.

"I've had enough of that. I'm sure I'll have a lot more soon." For the first time in her life, Rosalind admitted she was mortal. She was going to die. There was no sense sugar-coating it.

Olivia's heart was breaking. There is no reason that she should be here. Rosalind should hate her. But she didn't. She wanted to spend her last breaths with her. "I love you. You know that."

"I know." She smiled. As hard as she tried to fight it, her eyes were heavy. As she dozed off, she felt Olivia squeezing her hand.

These Foolish Things

The sound of singing was floating on the air. "Oh, will you never let me be? Oh, will you never set me free? The ties that bound us are still around us. There's no escape that I can see." Who was that? The smoky, beautiful voice echoed down the hall. Morgan stumbled to the kitchen only to see Queenie swaying to the song in her soul as the coffee brewed. "A cigarette that bears a lipstick's traces. An airline ticket to romantic places..." She paused as she saw Morgan standing with his mouth agape.

"That is beautiful. You don't have to stop." He retrieved two coffee mugs and shooed Queenie away as he poured them full. "You don't take anything in it do you?"

"It's all good, however you make it." She sat, smiling at him. Such a good boy. That sweet nurse Kate was a lucky woman. It was just too bad it took such horrible circumstances. "Thank you," she whispered as he handed her the warm mug. "You feeling better?"

"I'll make it." He smiled. The house was quiet except for the occasional tick from the warmer plate on the coffee maker. The sun had made its grand entrance through the sliding doors, which faced east. Queenie sat humming the song she'd been singing. He was stunned at such a sorrowful melody, even without the vocalization.

As if she understood all the questions in his eyes she spoke, "Seems like lifetimes have passed since those days." It was the first time anyone had looked at her with adoration in a long time. But the boy was smiling. "I was just a girl when I first got a taste of that spotlight, the black velvet curtain. It was all so glamorous." She reminisced with such love. "I was feeling like a star. They made me change my name all those years ago. Said that Etta would confuse people. They be thinking they be seeing The Queen, not me. So I became Queenie," she chuckled "You know, to make sure they knew who I was."

He remembered seeing her real name at some point. When he'd cared for her at the hospital. He didn't know what queen she was referring to. She seemed to know what he was thinking. "Ah, they just didn't want folk to be thinking they were coming for that Miss Ella. Oh, but I could hold my candle up to hers." She paused. "Not that it mattered to me. I just wanted to sing." Sighing, she continued her story. "They ripped that place down in 1966, and any true jazz went with it. Don't get me wrong, that zydeco is where it's at now but the jazz, that was born in NOLA. I was born for the music."

"Is that when you stopped singing?" Morgan was leaning with both elbows on the table, listening intently to her story. "When they tore the club down?"

"Naw. I moved around to the other places too," she recounted. "I think I may've been about your age when I had to stop. Not that I wanted to. No." A sadness overtook her face. "Lotta ugliness back then. Bad things. Bad people. Guess that never really goes away." Attempting to regain the jovial mood she had been in before she said, "Not that it matters much now. Like I said, it was lifetimes ago."

They sat quietly for a short time. The fire that had been burning all night had almost smoldered out and only a few glowing areas of ash remained. The smoky aroma still lingered but was fighting it out with the smell of coffee. Slowly, Queenie started shaking her head. "You got a way to reach Mr. Eddie?"

That came out of nowhere. "Yea, I have his number." He didn't ask why. He'd gotten to know Queenie well enough over the last few days to understand that nothing she did or said was random. She always had a reason.

Nodding she explained. "Something bad where he is." Her eyes looked vacant. Was she *seeing* where he was? No, there was no way. She seemed to know things, but up to this point it was all just intuition. At least that's how it all seemed. But to be so direct. "Let 'em sleep for now, but you should be reaching out in a while."

...

Olivia stayed by Rosalind's bed while she slept. The open room wasn't dark, but the glow of the laptop screen still managed to burn through her eyes. Her head was pounding, and the aspirin hadn't started working yet. She needed caffeine. It was almost painful to listen to Rosalind laboring to breathe while she slept. The past few hours crawled by like years.

The files on the drive were just like the ones on her computer. An absolute mess. She almost giggled as she realized that Rosalind had her own system—it wasn't a mess. It was brilliant. Like Rosalind. Everything was arranged as a timetable. The entire process was mapped out from beginning to end. For all intents and purposes, she was looking at a cure for lymphoma. A few things didn't seem to make sense, but she wasn't a genius. She was just a research scientist. A glorified assistant.

Rosalind was the first person to even recognize her contributions. A couple of years of collaboration and sharing of ideas had led to their meeting up in Munich. And now they were lightyears away from all of it. So much jealousy for nothing. So much conspiracy, for what? The thought made her begin to sob, but she reigned it in. For once, she was going to be the strong one. Hopefully.

Every so often, someone would whiz by, but they never stopped. Whatever they were doing, they needed to figure it out. Rosalind wasn't getting better, she wasn't evening out, and she was digressing. It had to seem like a horrible nightmare to her. She had to be silently screaming in her sleep for someone to wake her up. What a horrible way to die. Would everyone eventually succumb?

Suddenly, things that mattered didn't matter anymore. For all the prizes, all the money, all the glory out there; eventually everyone was going to die. Rosalind had been right. "Discovery doesn't belong to any one of us. It belongs to all of us." It was her central argument for insisting that they collaborate without separating who's was who's. She believed that the collaboration was more important than the individual. She had delivered it much more eloquently but for the first time the words actually meant something to Olivia.

It was obvious that by slowing the process down, they had prolonged the horrible parts too. Rosalind had to have known that would happen when she suggested it. But it was a good idea. Hopefully it wasn't for naught. Hopefully it would give them the time they needed to isolate a cure.

...

Your wife is sick. The text came through a little after four in the morning. He'd backed himself into a neat little corner and was desperately attempting to figure out how to get home. That research scientist, Olivia, had pretty much screwed him. No, he did that himself. At least she had the decency to let him know.

All commercial flights domestic and foreign had been completely grounded, but somehow, he was able to rent a car. He realized that he probably wasn't supposed to cross the border in the rental. He wasn't even sure if they'd let him but when he got to the bridge it was evident no one was watching. Eighteen lanes at the west New York crossing and not a single customs officer.

At the rate this virus was destroying the host, he wouldn't make it to Hana in time. It would take over twenty-six hours of driving with no stops to get there. It was a straight shot, but he couldn't do it without stopping at some point. He'd go as far as he could.

The only person he'd had any contact with at the WHO wasn't responding anymore. Noah wasn't sure if he'd just bailed or had died. Either way, he was completely out of the loop now. With Rosalind working on it, they had to have made some kind of forward progress.

Everything fit, down to the way that EV-118 was protecting itself from the immune system. Hana had been talking about releasing Ebby's ashes for two years. The fact that the virus not only survived cremation, but how it stayed alive all that time was the part that didn't make sense. But with everything they understood about disease, there were always variables that remained a mystery. Had that annoying little Brit not sent her thug to scare the shit out of him, he might not have put it together.

As the black of night faded behind him, the daylight screamed from in front. The scenery was a canvas of destruction and disorder. The worst of people at the worst of times. That's how it worked. There is no way that the whole of the mess was from those dying. Although that seemed to be what sparked the fire, the threat of the world ending had fueled it. People were animals.

Hana had been his prize at one time. But his obsession had convoluted that fact a long time ago. The lifelong search for glory, for prizes...he'd already had his. Instead he turned on her when she needed him the most. Whatever happened to him, he needed to get to where she was.

...

When Kate woke up, she was alone. For just a moment she was confused, but as the last bit of sleep faded, she remembered where she was. Was it fear that had motivated Morgan to invite her? Was it fear that motivated her to accept? Did it even matter? Fortunately, she'd gotten her things out of her locker before she left work last night, so she had clean clothes.

The water was soft. She was used to the harsh city water, so this was pleasant. She stood under the shower and let it roll down her face.

Ever since she was a little girl, she just knew she was going to be a nurse. For some reason it looked glamorous. For some reason she thought she was going to get to save lives. Whatever ridiculous fantasies she'd had about the profession were extinguished years ago.

But the truth was, more often than not, what she got were drug addicts looking for any kind of fix, gang fights ending in one or more bullet wounds, drunken brawls turned violent or the worst of all were the countless women who had "walked into doors" or "fallen down the stairs" *repeatedly.* She wasn't saving lives, she was protecting degenerates.

Morgan had just started down this path, so his innocent and almost naive concepts were what made him such a good person. He genuinely cared and took the time to get to know some of these people. After seeing enough patients die, you quit trying to make friends. But she was sure that Morgan would keep doing his thing. That's why she came.

The smell of bacon and coffee had filled the room. She hadn't smelled it until she got out of the shower. Someone was cooking breakfast. As she came through the kitchen, she saw Morgan's mom at the stove. "Well, hello..." Shari said warmly, but paused. "I'm sorry, I've forgotten your name."

Awkwardly, she responded, "Kate." It was no surprise she hadn't remembered her name. She had been here for a short time, to support Morgan after his father passed away. She didn't really say much to his mom. She just hadn't known what to say.

"That's right!" she exclaimed as she opened the cabinet to pull out an extra plate. "No one told me you were here, or I'd have been ready for you." Shari shooed her out of the kitchen insisting she sit down. Not once did it seem that she questioned why she was there. It was obvious where Morgan got his personality and such accepting heart from.

Behind them, the television was on but there was no sound. The media's dream come true. *Pandemic of global proportions* is what the banner said. How long had they been waiting to actually use "pandemic"? But that's what it was. She was squinting to read the closed captioning. *Finally, something concrete from the World Health Organization.* "Can we turn up the TV?"

Morgan moved fairly quickly, he seemed to be reading it too. "...that you avoid contact with recently dead or dying individuals." Turning to a different angle, the woman repeated herself, "Again, it has been determined that the virus is airborne. You cannot contract this from living persons. However, it can be transmitted at time of death. Finally, something concrete from the World Health Organization. Authorities are asking that you avoid contact with recently dead or dying individuals."

"Don't have to tell me twice to stay away from the dead," Queenie shuddered.

...

After just twenty minutes of sleep, Eddie was wide awake again. He was exhausted, but the adrenaline wouldn't stop coming. He sat in the dark in the only chair that occupied the room. It was sparse, a single twin bed, a small desk, a lamp, a chair and no window. It was likely the barracks hadn't been occupied since they had begun the interior renovations. He sat in the dark because he couldn't stand the idea of the light right now.

His phone was on silent, but he'd been holding it since he woke up. It buzzed in his hand. The message was from Morgan. *Queenie said to check in with you.* It didn't even surprise him anymore that she was always on time. He messaged back, *We're alive. For now.* He didn't know what else to say. *That's not very reassuring.* The reply made him chuckle sadly. It wasn't supposed to be. It was just the truth.

If he wandered the halls he'd end up with Rosalind, and he couldn't bear to see her right now. He just needed a little more time. If he stayed in this room Hana would eventually wake up and he couldn't bear to see her either. It was selfish. He knew that. But why couldn't he be selfish for a change? At least for a minute.

Tannon wasn't answering her texts, which meant she was probably sleeping, which was way overdue. He had no idea what to do. Life had turned into a complete shit show years ago, this was just the end of the road. All of the fighting and anger over all of the years, for what? Maybe this whole thing was mercy from the cosmos. Just end it all.

He couldn't accept that, no matter how much he wanted to. But he felt so useless. He wasn't trained to fight this enemy. There was a whole building full of people that were though, and they seemed to know what they were doing. Kind of. The realization that no one ever really knew what they were doing came to him.

The big house, the fast cars, the toys...none of it mattered. They had both been placating their needs with things for so long that they had forgotten how to just *be*. He'd felt truly alive for the first time in a very long time on Friday night. It seemed like every one of them understood that their lives had been a lie. But now it was way too late. Wasn't it?

He finally slipped out of the room as quietly as possible and headed down the hall towards the infirmary. The two enlisted he passed nodded. There was someone sitting by Rosalind. He didn't recognize her. As he got a little closer, he realized that she was sleeping in the chair. He stood next to the bed and gently took Rosalind's hand.

"Now I've seen everything," Rosalind whispered weakly. He'd been lost in whatever thoughts were still lingering and didn't realize she had stirred. "Édouard Francis Bélisaire, are you crying?" He hadn't heard that playful lilt in her voice in a very long time.

"What can I do?" He attempted to pull it together, to regain his composure. But the waterworks he had allowed to start earlier took over again. He squeezed her hand a little tighter than he meant to and she winced. "I'm sorry." He was. "I'm sorry for everything."

"You don't have anything to be sorry for," she spoke slowly and deliberately. As though she were struggling for the words as much as she was the breath. "You have always had the patience of a saint." Her slow, almost forced laughter caused her to cough. At some point, the blood had just become part of the cough. The look of horror in his eyes broke her heart. "Nothing new." She tried to reassure him that she was okay for now, but that didn't do it.

"That's not supposed to be comforting is it?" The last twenty-one years overwhelmed his thoughts at the same time. He had spent so long reminding himself of the few little things about her that drove him insane that he'd forgotten the million things that made him love her.

The look in his eyes was one she hadn't seen in a long time. It wasn't pity, it was...it was love. "Don't make me cry. Please." Looking at his hand holding hers, she breathed in heavily, "You were right."

He didn't even blink as he was concentrating on her eyes. "About what?"

"I am an ice bitch," she chuckled.

"I didn't mean that." That is what he had said to her before he'd stormed out. On the night Delphine drowned.

"Of course you did. But it's true. I just wanted you to..." The look of confusion crossed her face again. Struggling to recognize her surroundings, she only saw one familiar sight. "Eddie?" It was definitely a question. Scanning the room wildly she asked, "Where are we?"

Sacrifices

The frantic rapping at the door jolted Tannon from the first sound sleep she'd had all week. There was no way to get out of the tiny bunk that wouldn't disturb Joaquin. When the knock sounded again, he stirred as well. "Sgt. Pyburn," the voice from the other side of the door sounded urgent. She fumbled to dress and stumbled towards the door as she watched Joaquin collect his clothes and head to the shower.

"I'm coming." She slipped out of the room and shut the door behind her.

Filling her in as they walked, the soldier sounded excited. She hadn't had near enough sleep for his level of alertness. "Dr. Tedesse asked me to come get you. He said he's got something."

"What is it?" she asked. Her mind was racing. It could be a million things.

"Sorry. I don't know." Shaking his head, he added, "I just work here." The jest was playful. But she understood.

Almost doubling her pace, she was amused when he seemed to

break into a jog to keep up with her. As soon as they arrived at the lab he broke off for another appointed task. Tannon found the Director General in a small office surrounded by several laptops and other devices. Without looking up he asked, "What's your blood type?"

"A positive," she answered, with no idea where he was heading.

"Me too." He sat back and focused his attention on her. "We've been investigating everyone we know that received medical care from the hospitals." It was apparent he had been at this for hours. But he did have a point. "The first several patients reported all showed to be type O." Shaking his head he continued, "I thought I was onto something, but this second wave seems to be all over the place. Dr. Bélisaire is AB. Mrs. Patel is B."

Tannon had no idea what he was getting at but he seemed to be going somewhere. "What is the significance of all of this?"

"How would you like to donate some blood?" That wasn't what she was expecting. Carefully scanning the doctor's posture, she realized his left sleeve was rolled up and saw the tiny discarded cotton ball with one drop of blood on the desk beside him. "None of the patients reported were A positive."

"Of course I will," she agreed before asking, "What are we doing with it?" The room was cluttered. Obviously not ready to be used as an office. Several boxes lined the walls and there were two desks crammed in the room. The musty smell of wet concrete seeped in from the outer walls. She hadn't noticed at first, but now that she'd recognized the odor, she couldn't shake it.

"At the least, buying a little time for everyone." There were thirteen people on the base that had begun deteriorating. Buying a little time sounded wonderful. But were they buying time for the patients or for the world? Either way, he'd already contributed. She was happy to as well.

It was an interesting thought, Tannon mused as she winced when the needle punctured her vein. Squeezing the little foam ball, she considered the science. EV-118 had been engineered to attack cancer cells in the blood. Whatever they were battling appeared to go after all of the cells. Why a specific blood type might not be affected would be a huge discovery.

Breeding certain immunoglobulins naturally required specific proteins that weren't created by the red blood cells but instead delivered from the plasma. That's what they were going to use it for. It wasn't until they had finished drawing her blood that the realization came to her. "We're doing this backwards," she announced.

She had everyone's attention. "By the time we know someone is sick, its already too late because it spreads too fast, right?" Dr Tedesse nodded slowly, gravely. He was brilliant, and it seemed he understood where she was going. "We need to catch this as close to the end of its gestation as possible. We know that can't be more than a day, right?"

The nod turned to protest as he shook his head gently. "What you're suggesting is out of the question." No one else in the room seemed to be on their page. "Besides, who would volunteer for that?"

Before he had even finished asking, Tannon boldly spoke. "I'll do it. You said there was a possibility we were immune anyway."

The slow shaking became more furious. "No, I never said that. I said no one with A positive has been reported as..." The scientist in him awoke. He took several breaths as he absorbed what she was saying. "I hate that I'm even saying this, but you're right. The advantage we could gain from..." The doctor in him took over again. "I can't approve something like that. It's like asking me to watch you commit suicide."

The truth was, if they could catch the virus as it woke up and started moving through the blood, they would have a much better chance of isolating it. Once symptoms presented, this process would be far too advanced. This was literally their *best* chance to finally gain the upper hand. "I'm not making a formal request doctor." She motioned towards the infirmary on the other side of the wall. "People are dying. Lots of people, thousands of people. And that's all the family I have left over there."

"I'm a doctor, Tannon." The familiarity with which he was speaking to her punctuated his point.

Nodding she said, "I'm a scientist and a soldier."

He turned away and retreated from the room. Without looking back, he said, "I'm not here to make military decisions."

...

"Are you fucking insane?" Eddie was almost yelling. When Hana came around the corner to the lounge for coffee, she saw him sitting next to Tannon.

"Hear me out," Tannon defended herself.

Hana wasn't sure they were aware of her presence, so she quietly walked past them without looking their way. She really needed coffee. Eddie didn't stand but spoke to her, "How are you feeling?"

"I'm okay. How is Rosalind?" She couldn't bear to look either of them in the eye, so she focused on the machine as it over zealously spat out the black liquid from above the cup. She didn't tell him that it took her about five minutes after she woke to remember where she was, and why she was here. She didn't tell him that she was terrified. He didn't need to hear those things.

"Sleeping." Eddie hung his head. Whatever had caused the outburst seemed to have been forgotten. For a moment. Regaining his thoughts, he redirected his attention to his dear friend. "Please don't do this." He knew her better than anyone. Once she made her mind up, there was no way to convince her otherwise. "Hana, tell her..." he stopped, obviously frustrated.

"I'm sorry, I don't know what's happening." Had something else slipped her mind? She regretted admitting that she was lost.

Obviously recognizing the fear in her eyes. Eddie said. "No, you weren't in here." Wringing his hands in his lap he explained, "Tannon has this brilliant idea that they should use her as a test rat."

"Stupidest thing I've ever heard." The blonde that had been sleeping next to Rosalind's bed walked through the door. The accent was familiar. This is the voice he heard on the phone Sunday morning when they arrested Rosalind. She had been with her. "I need coffee, sorry to interrupt."

"You're Rosalind's..." He wanted to say friend, but he had no idea who she was.

"Colleague." She nodded at everyone around the room. "I already know your names." As boldly as she walked in, she sauntered out. It was obvious she didn't care to become acquainted. It didn't matter, Eddie thought. Whoever she was, Rosalind had wanted her here. And it dawned on him. He'd wondered for a couple of years if there was someone waiting for her on one of her many trips. They were all genuinely work, but there were times she almost seemed excited to go. He just thought she wanted to get away from him.

He chuckled to himself and whispered under his breath, "Way to go, Ros." There was no sense being angry, plus he had no right. Remembering his protest from just moments ago he turned his attention back to Tannon. "Why does it have to be you?"

"Not going to ask anyone else to," she said as though he was being ridiculous.

"Why couldn't I do it?" He hadn't even entertained the idea before the words came out. The look of surprise on his face gave that away.

Hana sat quietly watching them. As each spoke, she turned her head to focus. For a moment, she felt like she was at a tennis game. The motion caused her to become nauseous. Swallowing hard, she tried to concentrate.

"You're not A positive," she announced as though it were the ultimate conversation end. Instead of arguing, she stood and strode confidently out the door.

Hana sat, completely confused. Unable to focus on anything but the anguish that had settled on him. "I'm sorry," she sobbed. She kept remembering how this was all her fault. Struggling to breathe, her chest tightened. She was having another panic attack. "I'm so sorry," was all she could manage to say.

...

Noah was somewhere in Ohio when the car started smoking. As he pulled off of the freeway he chuckled at the sign "Bellville Dam Landing Strip next exit". *That was convenient!* Slowly making his way to the private airport, the car wheezed and sputtered out. From where he was, he could see people and watched as one small craft took off. He hadn't taken a shower, was completely disheveled and unshaven. As he approached the three men at the end of one of the small runways, they became defensive.

Raising his arms high above his head he called out. "I just want to pay someone to fly me to New Orleans." He realized he didn't look like he could pay for a flight, and it was possible he couldn't. He was afraid to reach for his wallet, in case they misinterpreted his intentions. Everyone was jumpy, and he didn't want to add to it. "I'm a doctor. My car broke down." He stepped forward one step. "They need me at the naval base," he lied.

Whether eager to believe that doctors were en route or just being a good person, one of the men stepped towards him. "There is a possibility I might be heading that way." Judging by his boots and the way he stood, he was probably enlisted. "Just waiting for orders." As soon as he finished talking his phone rang. After just a brief one-sided conversation, the man looked at him again. "What's your name?"

Shit, he thought. Had he backed himself into another corner? "Dr. Noah Patel." He stepped forward without hesitation now. He was either getting on the plane or not, but no one considered him a threat anymore.

He listened to the man repeat his name into the phone. There was no way they were going to take him. He almost missed the instructions that were directed at him. "We take off in twenty minutes, doctor. Please clean up."

The locker room was no more than a couple of pipes with aerators and some plywood stalls, but the water was hot. He scrubbed all of the grime of the motel out of his skin and hair. His soft suitcase was easy enough to tote so he'd had that with him. Fortunately, a clean pair of jeans and t-shirt still existed in his world. He almost sobbed, realizing that suddenly everything was going his way. That couldn't last long.

As the small plane bounced way too low, Noah sat holding a faded photo in his hand. Worn by age and constant pawing. Back when there was an actual reason to live. He had met Hana at a black-tie gala when she was representing the state of Texas. A fundraiser for this or that. She had seemed as bored as he was. Her smile sparkled brighter than the tiara she was wearing. She was absolute grace and beauty. He had to have her.

It wasn't her fault that he couldn't bounce his ideas off her. That she couldn't grasp the magnitude of the things that he was saying. But it always frustrated him. After a while, somehow, he came to resent the fact that she wasn't as enthralled as he was. She said he was obsessed. She said a lot of things that were true, even though he didn't realize it at the time.

She forgave him for every horrible thing he ever said to her. For treating her like she was a child. For not being there. She forgave him for all of that. What she couldn't forgive him for was hitting her. He didn't mean to. He didn't even realize what he was doing. Not until it was over. That didn't change what was done. It was likely she wouldn't even see him. But it was necessary for her to know he tried.

"What are we delivering?" Noah asked as he tucked the photo into his pocket. They were in a small cargo plane. The boxes were unmarked but appeared to be cold packed. It was loud and due to the rapid increase and decease in altitude repeatedly, his ears popped over and over again; making it difficult to hear.

"Plasma," the man replied. "Heading the same place you are."

"Who did you talk to?" Noah had to know who had given the okay for him to be there.

"No one was expecting you, by the way." He leaned forward, "As a matter of fact, they were pretty surprised you were coming. Apparently, you're in a lot of trouble."

Yes, there it was. He knew the good luck couldn't possibly hold for long. He slumped his shoulders and leaned back against the seat. But at least that would put him wherever Hana was.

...

Queenie sat on the back balcony, looking out over the delicate ecosystem that was the swamps. So much life, so much death and all in the blink of an eye. And it all served a purpose. Even now, all this death...she had to believe it served a purpose. As she communed with whichever spirits would listen to her, she knew what she needed to do.

She must have recited the Rosary more than fifty times, clutching the beads between her fingers. She didn't feel any closer to Mother Mary than she had when she started. Mary wanted nothing to do with what she had on her mind. Even Mother Teresa had turned her back.

From somewhere in the unseen distance the sound of an idling air boat resonated through the trees. Humming softly, she matched the deepest tones, which rattled through her ears. She'd been going about this all wrong. She knew she was going to have to cross the line. But she knew Santa Muerta would be listening. If she could help at all, this was going to be it.

She wasn't even sure she still had it in her but when she opened her eyes, there she was. It took a few moments for her to adjust to the scene around her. She had walked between the worlds before, but it wasn't one of those things you got used to. It was easier this time, than all those years ago when she'd been lying in the grass waiting for death. She'd made a deal with Death then. It was time to pay up.

She followed the spark that started just over her head. As it spread and guided her, it created an intricate grid above. It was pure energy traveling on pure energy. Although she could see her hands and feet and own self in vivid color, the surroundings were smoky at best. The faces were indistinct as she followed the fire. She could see the people around her, bustling. They were all working at their tasks to save the world. They couldn't see her.

As she moved forward the grid dissipated behind her, reminding her abruptly that this was a one-way trip. She'd best make the best of it. At first, she thought she might save them both. But as she found herself looking at Hana and Rosalind, sitting there unaware of her presence, she realized how very tired Missus Rosalind looked. If truth was known, Queenie was tired. So very, very tired.

She could hear the voices, but only barely. There was something big going on. What she hadn't expected was for anyone to see her. That only meant that Missus Rosalind was close to death herself. As clear as though they were occupying the same space, she heard Rosalind say, "Does anyone else see that woman?"

The muffled replies sounded one by one. All saying there was no one there. It was Hana's voice that nearly stopped her heart. "It's Queenie." Raising her finger to her mouth she looked Hana straight in the eyes and said, "You don't see me here."

Rosalind's voice sounded so small, so full of fear. As she looked out from the strange tunnel that the old woman had pulled her into, she realized she was looking back at herself. "What is this?" Surveying the darkness behind them and the glowing sparks above, a wariness washed over her. "Am I dead?"

Queenie took her hand. "Not yet." It was a bold statement from either side, but for some reason Rosalind felt comforted.

They stood for moments, or maybe it was hours, time seemed to stop where they were. "I have some things I need to say. Before I..." She should have been terrified. She should have begged for her life. Right? Why did she feel like she was about to go home?

"We got time," Queenie smiled. "I need to save the girl." She pointed towards Hana through the haze.

Redemption

Eddie looked around the room almost wildly. There is no way Queenie could be here. But Rosalind had seen her first. No. Rosalind saw a woman, Hana saw Queenie. They were both deteriorating. Rosalind looked so fragile, so far away. Fighting tears, he chastised himself. He wasn't going to do that again. He took a deep breath. "There's no one here," he whispered to both of them.

He had hoped that Tannon's new friend would have helped talk some sense into her, but apparently until this weekend they were just colleagues. It was all too much for him. *For him?* He was being so selfish. But it was...Just. Too. Much.

"What is this?" Rosalind chuckled weakly. "A funeral?" It wasn't funny. She knew it wasn't funny. But she couldn't stand the weepy looks everyone was giving each other. She didn't have much time, and the old woman was waiting. "So, it doesn't look like I'm going to see this whole thing out." She ignored the protests from around her and pushed through. "Shut up, please." She was already struggling to hold her thoughts together, she needed to get through this.

Because things were so critical, everyone that could had shoved their work into the infirmary. It was crowded, and Rosalind hadn't intended on everyone listening, but they were. She had to make this count. But all she wanted to do was confess her sins. The ones they didn't know about yet. "Mrs. Patel," she looked sorrowfully at her.

"You can call me Hana." She was trying to be supportive, but what could Rosalind possibly have to say to her?

"I'm not going to do that," she said snidely, but smiled warmly. She had to maintain some of her dignity. "Let me tell you about the arrogance that comes with incredible discovery." She sighed. She was sure that Hana was well aware of it, but she had a reason. "I just wanted it to work. I just *knew* it would work. When the FDA gave us the green light, and the approvals came rolling in...I thought we'd won."

For just a moment, her mind wandered. *Focus,* she scolded herself. Everyone sat in quiet reverence, waiting to hear how this story ended. "Where did I leave off?" She was grasping to remember. *Approvals.* "We didn't expect the insurance company to say no." The appropriate confusion on everyone's face stalled her.

Hana shook her head. "No, they didn't. They paid for it."

Hanging her head Rosalind corrected her, "I paid for it." Straightening a bit, she added. "I just wanted it to work. I just wanted to show the world that it would work. I had no idea they were going to..." It hadn't just been the therapy she'd covered the costs on. She had actually paid a couple of people a large amount of money to help with some of the paperwork. She didn't tell them that part. The look on Eddie's face at least showed that he'd been paying attention. It was her fault in the first place that there was even a loophole in the policy for Eddie to find. He understood the words she didn't say.

Hana sat at Rosalind's feet on the bed. The compassion that was spilling from her was undeserved. "By the time anyone even suggested it, it was a last resort." She nodded. "You don't start with the experimental stuff. I mean..." Shaking her head she tried to find the right words. "We weren't at the end of the money, we were at the end of the..."

"I didn't know it was Noah's son," Rosalind defended herself needlessly. "He didn't tell me."

Hana nodded. "He didn't think it was going to work."

"It didn't," Rosalind reminded her. Hana scooted forward just a bit and reached for her hand. What was more surprising was when Rosalind reached out and took hers. The sweet fragrance of cotton candy hung about Hana. She smelled like Eddie. The room began to wobble a bit. The bright lights that were assaulting her had dimmed. A haze settled around her.

...

Olivia had become annoyed at the display that was transpiring before her. There were a thousand other things that Rosalind could have been thinking about right now, but everyone was allowing her to crumble into a weeping mess. She realized the anger that was bubbling up from somewhere deep inside her wasn't because of that.

Rosalind wasn't the only one that had made a mess, Olivia mused. She'd really managed to screw things up too. That's why she had spent so much time sitting here going over everything. All the words, all of the information had begun to bleed together. She had been getting nowhere. She wasn't a problem solver, she was a fact gatherer. Rosalind was the problem solver, and she was sitting there weeping with the woman that was obviously sleeping with her husband.

I should be holding her hand. Jealousy? Wow, Olivia stunned herself. Instead of speaking she buried her face in the glow of the laptop. She couldn't really see much at this point. The tears that had been threatening to escape clouded her eyes. It wasn't so much that she saw the answer, it just kind of jumped out after her mind had a chance to absorb what she'd been reading. "Bloody fucking hell," she exclaimed much louder than she meant to.

Whatever reverence there was hanging in the air suddenly vanished. The problem with EV-118 is that it hadn't worked fast enough. That was Rosalind's path. That's the avenue she had pursued. Every bit of her energy had been poured into creating a stable, instantly visible change. Something they could at least track on the cellular level. In order to do this, the cells had been manipulated by messengers that had instructed them to double certain protein productions and eliminate others. Not an unfamiliar concept. What was amazing was that the success rate was so high. Why hadn't they been testing this?

It wasn't that she *genuinely* had a cure for certain types of cancer that was so overwhelming, it was the fact that this solved their immediate problem too. Theoretically. "Rosalind already found the cure for this...whatever this is," she announced, and bolted from the infirmary to find Dr. Tedesse and that stupid lab rat soldier girl.

...

He'd obviously missed the excitement because by the time he arrived, Dr. Tedesse had whatever scientists they had there working on something important. No one had filled him in. He should have been detained. He should have been...he didn't know what should have happened. Apparently, the end of the world, rules were different. What *did* happen is they brought him to Hana. Not just Hana but a room full of sick and sobbing, slobbering people. Rosalind looked so bad. He should have felt bad for her but all he felt was the stare of death that Hana had bored into him. She was not near as relieved to see his face as he was hers.

He was aware that it was his presence that caused such an uncomfortable silence. What he wanted to do was get on his knees and grovel. He wanted her to forgive him. Instead he sat down in a small chair furthest from the group. He wasn't surprised when Hana got up and walked out. What did surprise him is that Rosalind's husband chased after her.

"What is that all about?" he asked, stunned at the grin on Rosalind's face.

Rosalind laughed. For whatever cynical reason, it made her hysterically giddy to see the look in Noah's eyes when he realized he wasn't going to be reconciling with Hana. She wondered if he had expected all of this madness to wash away his sins. He didn't have to confess them, they were boldly tattooed in his expression.

"Was it all worth it?" she asked. So much deception, so many lies. And while she wasn't excusing her own, she recognized the difference between them. She had only wanted to hold her baby. She had only wanted to save the world. He wanted to be famous. He wanted to win the prizes. And the only prize he'd ever actually won couldn't even look him in the eye.

"Did they figure this out?" No one was telling him anything. He didn't expect Rosalind to, but once she started talking, it was like she was unable to stop. She told him everything up to Olivia having an epiphany and running off to save the world. Rosalind was aware that Noah despised Olivia. So, the fact that he knew that she had her paws all over his work now was a little delicious to her.

It wasn't that she wanted bad things to happen to Noah, she just realized that Olivia was right about him. He was a tiny little man. Not in stature, but in character. A weasel. He was absolutely genius but had no social skills or compassion. Whatever redemption he was hoping for wouldn't happen today.

...

"Are you trying to prove something?" Joaquin had his arms wrapped around Tannon as they sat against the wall in the bunk. He didn't know her as well as he'd like to. But what he did know, he really liked. Except the whole being crazy part. No, he liked that too.

"If the whole thing works like Olivia thinks it will, I did this for nothing," she chuckled. "I trust Rosalind." She leaned back putting her weight into him. "Thanks for coming."

"Can't think of anywhere else I'd rather be." It was a bizarre thing to say. But had things not been so terrifying, so doomsday...he would have still wanted to be wherever she was. It had been a long time since he'd even thought about how alone he was. It had become a little more evident as he only had one loss to mourn. So many people had so many more.

It was almost a bittersweet irony that by the time he realized how very alone he was, that the woman filling that empty space might be dying in his arms. Shaking that thought was so hard. In less than a week the earth had shattered opened, leaving behind such a devastating path of death. In spite of all of that, there was no place he'd rather be. "Do you want to talk?" he asked.

Except for Rosalind who was slipping away, Tannon had no family. It was something she never regretted until this moment. The past few months had been agonizing for all of them, but none of them had talked about it. She did want to talk. She wanted to tell him everything. She wanted to share her triumphs, her sorrows and her dreams. She wanted to know that if she didn't make it through this, someone would miss her. She wanted to pass on her life to someone else.

"No," she said quietly. "Just sit here with me."

...

Life had been coming at them fast ever since Saturday morning. Hana hadn't given much thought to the injury she had sustained from the broken glass in Eddie's study. It had been minor, but it hadn't been cleaned or treated properly. They weren't doctors. The dull fire she'd been ignoring for at least a day or two had become a stabbing pain. It was infected. Not seriously, but enough that it finally needed a little attention.

Olivia was rough. She was harsh, and she was realistic. Sometimes she could come off as a little snotty. *Okay, a lot snotty* she conceded to herself. Even she winced after she heard herself say, "How dumb do you have to be to not know you have an infected cut on your foot?" Before she had a chance to apologize, she had one of those "aha" moments. "That's why you haven't..." for the first time she wanted to consider her words before she spoke them, "Seemed to have as many symptoms as fast as Ros."

"Because I'm dumb?" Hana understood what she meant, but she was looking for humor in the dark.

That was the case. The infection had created a distraction for her immune system. Its attention was split between two things. It gave them a good chance to try out the recently discovered information, as soon as they could implement the idea. As the world whirred around her, busy with the parts she couldn't understand, she felt like someone was watching her. There was no one there that shouldn't be. But she couldn't shake the feeling.

...

The day had gotten away from them. Shari was stunned to realize it was almost four in the afternoon and she hadn't done anything today but sit and talk. She liked Kate. Didn't even mind the fact that she was closer to her age than Morgan's. She was genuine, sweet and definitely the girl she would have chosen for her son to end the world with. She shivered at the thought.

There was so much going on out there that she had no idea about. She had chosen to tuck herself away and hide. But that was okay. Was someone working on a way to stop this? Were they going to see their new friends again? What would happen tomorrow?

As she mused these things, she walked through the house. The rooms still had so much of Grant in them. She hadn't changed anything since he'd passed on. Maybe it was time for a little change. She was already envisioning Morgan taking over the guest room. She'd leave the wine.

There were so many memories that she had made here, but that was a different lifetime. There were more memories to be made, right? She'd spent so much time praying and worrying that she'd almost missed the beautiful things. There would be more beautiful things.

Her thoughts drew her out back to the balcony. It was a beautiful place to sit and watch the swamp live. She had originally wanted a staircase leading down to the back, but Grant had insisted it be inaccessible and just a balcony. That's why she was taken a little by surprise when she walked out and Queenie wasn't in the chair. She had watched her go out there.

The chair was empty and there was a cigar burning in the ashtray. It appeared to have been lit and discarded. The coal hadn't gone out completely. Except for a small bit at the end, it was a single long ash.

...

"Why her?" Rosalind was in the tunnel again, standing next to Queenie. It wasn't that she was jealous, it wasn't that she didn't agree. She just wanted to know why it was so important that Hana live. For a moment, she wondered if she'd just gone mad. Had this horrible virus that she had given birth to finally taken her brain? Maybe she deserved this.

"Not her." Queenie still pointed towards Hana, "HER." Looking at Rosalind's confused, wary face she said, "Do you see?"

As vivid as a movie on a grand 3D screen, a life played out. It was like watching a home movie that hadn't been filmed yet. But was about to be. A baby being born and growing to a beautiful little girl. A brilliant young woman. A college graduate. A Nobel Prize winner. A healer. She had Hana's beautiful face, but she had Eddie's eyes. "I do see." Rosalind replied. What should have been sadness was joy. What should have devastated her brought her peace.

As the haze around them lightened a bit, they were able to see everyone in the infirmary. The audio was still muffled, as though there was a blanket carefully placed over the speakers. But she could see they were already preparing some kind of shot. Possibly for the infection in Hana's foot, but it seemed like they had skipped ahead a bit. This was something else.

"That cure ain't gonna work on her. Not the way they're doing it." The old, tattered and mangled woman that had been standing beside her slowly morphed into a stunning younger woman. It was still her. "Didn't need that ugly part anymore," she announced after realizing that Rosalind was staring with her mouth agape. "Nothing left in here but our souls."

Rosalind stared at the beautiful woman standing before her. There was an air of familiarity that she couldn't place. "I know you," she whispered.

Queenie nodded, "You do."

"Do we tell them how to make it work?" Rosalind was a little overwhelmed as the secrets of life flooded in and all of the beauty of what was next was presented before her. The tunnel grew brighter, as the sparks of energy came closer. She could see every color.

"They'll figure it out." Queenie reached for Rosalind's hand. "Are you ready?"

The love in Rosalind's eyes spilled out like rivers. She understood that Queenie was trading her soul for Hana's. No, not for Hana's. "What are they going to name her?"

Chuckling, Queenie reported, "That little Rosalind Bélisaire will cure more than cancer. But you can see it all where we're going."

Ashes to Ashes

Rosalind was getting weaker. It was made painfully clear by the machines they had monitoring her. Eddie wanted to be near her and was overwhelmed by the emotions that kept assaulting him. He had been holding her hand as the squealing began. The tones the apparatuses were emitting had bored through his ears into his brain.

At some point the sun had set on them, but no one had seen it. There were more important things to do. The faint squeeze he felt from her hand jolted him out of whatever pity party he was settling into. She had deteriorated so fast that before him was a woman that seemed years beyond her age. As the tears welled in his eyes, she whispered almost inaudibly, "It's okay. I get to hold my baby again." Rosalind had abandoned any faith she'd had a long time ago. But the peace in her beautiful eyes was reassuring.

Kissing her forehead just before the heart monitor flat lined, he stepped back and watched as they quickly shuffled her out to a place where they could contain whatever happened next. He couldn't move. He couldn't think. He couldn't do this again when it was Tannon's time, or Hana's. What was the point of all of this? There had to be a reason. As his legs threatened to buckle underneath him, he sat in the middle of the floor where Rosalind's bed had just been.

He hadn't even noticed until she reached out and took his hand, that Tannon had taken a seat next to him on the floor. They had been closer than sisters. This had to be so very hard for her. "I thought we would have figured it out before..."

He squeezed her hand but didn't speak. There was no way he could put together two words right now anyway. By now, the best and brightest in the field were here. The ones that were left, anyway. They'd solve it. Wouldn't they? There had been talk of a possibility of wave after wave as this resilient virus mutated. Would they all eventually die?

At some point, he'd gotten up and stumbled to the room he had slept in before. He didn't remember walking there, he didn't remember seeing anyone on his way. As memories both good and bad washed over him, he wept as he succumbed to the darkness of sleep.

...

He may have been a pariah at the moment, but even he could be useful. It wasn't that they had it wrong, they were just going about it all the wrong way. "Even if you can stabilize it enough to deliver it through plasma, how could you possibly inoculate the whole world?" He finally had to say something after the rushed tests kept failing.

Noah insisted that they needed to work on a different way to deliver the, for lack of a better word, cure.

The word "cure" had been grossly misused throughout his career. Cure indicated that they'd attacked the disease head on and eliminated it. That isn't what they were doing. They were effectively re-writing genetic coding, introducing it into the virus and using the virus to deliver the message. The message is what told the cells how to react. And it would work. But not the way they were going about it.

Although the infection in her foot had slowed the process down, it hadn't stopped it. Hana was still slowly, painfully going downhill. He would have been there to comfort her, but that obviously wasn't his place anymore. At least he could do something here. If someone would just listen to him. As they struggled to piece the puzzle together, two more of the patients had died. The biologics had done the best they could do, but you don't put a band-aid on a gaping wound. They were running out of time. Not just in here, but out there.

The breakthrough they'd been working so hard on didn't jump out like they'd hoped. It nagged. It persisted, and finally they saw it. "What about a pulmonary delivery?" Olivia suggested. It might be a lot more stable and even work faster. Nebulization would be ineffective on any grand scale but it was a great place to start with individuals on the base.

It was brilliant. Noah was a little annoyed that she came to it before he could. But suddenly, she wasn't nearly as grating. Even less so when they were able to at least administer the test on Hana. Of course, it wasn't going to work instantly, if it worked at all. He felt better knowing they'd at least done something.

The night crept by silently. Those who could keep their eyes open kept working. Those who couldn't, slept. They took turns. At some point before dawn, Dr. Tedesse was up and looking for any progress. During the night, two more of their patients at the base had died. The first wave had finally made its way across the globe and the second one was moving outward. A third wave would devastate the world. They had to get ahead of this.

The ray of light that made its grand entrance Thursday morning had no connection to the brilliant sunrise they had missed. Hana seemed to respond faster than the other patients. While it wasn't miraculously cured, the messengers had delivered their message and the healthy cells were taking over again. It would be a day or two before they could call it a success, but it was definitely presenting that way.

It was a victory. It was a win. They had cleared the first major hurdle. The next one seemed daunting even to all of the scientific minds that had come together here. How to deliver the message to the rest of the world.

...

Rosalind had never been very generous with her affections, but she had really seemed to like Olivia. Whatever it was about her, Eddie was willing to try to make friends. She was smart. It was her that caught whatever the link was, it was her that figured out how to make it work. She may have very likely saved Hana's life. It was also a little entertaining to see how much Dr. Patel very obviously disliked her.

It was a relief to learn that the ridiculous test that Tannon had started had failed. It was probably also a relief to everyone with A positive blood. Tannon's system had isolated and destroyed the virus naturally. Like it was supposed to. That had to be another award-winning discovery. He mused almost sorrowfully at who would get that prize.

He watched back and forth as Tannon, Olivia, and Dr. Tedesse discussed ideas. They all sounded good. But what did he know? They just kept shooting each other's ideas down with long-winded explanations as to why it wouldn't work.

Hana had been quiet throughout the exchange. It's not like anyone expected her to actually contribute. But the simplicity was so overwhelming that no one could find a way to shoot it down. Not completely. "Why can't you just use ashes?" She clutched for the tiny bottle around her neck that was no longer there.

That is how this all started. But the forward momentum of the virus was also spread through the deceased at the time of death. It wasn't the method that was in question, it was the logistics. Tannon was the first to finally speak as they all sat considering the idea. "Even if the ash could carry the..." she paused. She hated the idea of using the word. But that's what it was. "Even if the ash could carry the virus, how would we deliver it?"

Everyone was a little uncomfortable when Eddie threw in his two cents. "You could explode a series of bombs over strategic areas." Okay, so this part *was* his department. After everyone got over the word "bomb", it didn't really seem like such a bad idea.

Tannon was following, but she felt like she'd missed the finer points. "Anything that could create enough ash to do that would have to be huge. It would be way too destructive."

"No. Use fly ash with the pay load. Then you only need enough boom to crack them open. Send them up far enough and at the right points, you could effectively cover the whole globe. Minimal debris." He had no idea if the science would work but he knew a little about strategy.

The rest of the day was spent feverishly trying to determine how to coordinate such a feat. There were world leaders to notify, alerts to be put out, press conferences to be held and all as quickly as possible. By the end of the day, orders from somewhere came down to secure the base again to only essential personnel and contributing scientists. Business as usual.

...

The darkness seemed darker tonight. The cloud cover had completely eclipsed everything. Hana and Eddie found themselves sitting at a park just north of the base. Neither of them knew what to say. They weren't sure if the treatment had actually worked or not, but if it didn't the whole thing would be a failure anyway. Then what would it matter? They decided to drive around for a while. But didn't talk.

After realizing that going home had been a mistake, Eddie found himself asking Hana again. "Where do you want to go?" There is no way he could sleep here. Not just because the house was a bit of a wreck. Broken windows, missing things. He didn't care. He just needed clothes. He'd take her anywhere.

She understood the urgency to get away from New Orleans. She didn't want to go home either. The van was out of gas, and it did bring him just a little joy to leave it behind and take his car. They didn't talk at all as he entered the interstate and headed west. They knew where they were going. Hana dozed on the drive. Occasionally a tiny snore escaped from the passenger seat.

He was almost sorry to wake her. But he didn't want to be rude and sit out in the driveway. Again. It was late, but the light was on. "Queenie must be expecting us." He chuckled as he opened the door for Hana. The darkness that had settled over NOLA had reached here as well. The backdrop that should be glittering with moonlight was black. Invisible.

The front door was ajar slightly so they didn't knock. They weren't sure what to expect as they went in, but the heaviness followed them here. Shari had been crying for quite some time. Her eyes were swollen and sad. Morgan seemed so shaken and confused. Despite the obvious devastation in the air they were all seated around the table as though they were waiting for their guests.

Shari spoke first. "I am so glad to see you both." Motioning over to the woman sitting by Morgan she said, "This is Kate."

The smell of coffee hung in the air. Hana and Eddie felt it but neither wanted to ask. Finally, Hana broke the uncomfortable silence, "Where is Queenie?"

A sorrowful moan crept from Shari's soul. There was a folded note in her hand. Shaking, she handed it to Hana. The script was messy and shaky but easy enough to read. Easy enough, except for the tears in both of their eyes.

The end of the world didn't come with a bang. It came as a whisper on the breeze. There are no accidents. Everything that happens has its reason. People just be where they need to be when it's time for them to be there.

All the wonder of the world don't hide the fact that the world can be terrible place. The true disease is darkness, and there's no cure. That is why it is so important to look for the light. It's there, if you look. Don't even have to look too hard. I saw the true light in my darkest hour so many years ago.

I was laying in the grass. Them boys had had their fun and had left me for dead. Don't know where the young girl came from or why she was out so late. But she saved my life. Never caught her name or saw her again, not until well... you can imagine how surprised I was to see Missus Rosalind again after all these years.

She done good. Don't forget that. I never did. Lord didn't either apparently. We going home.

Hana and Eddie had been reading at about the same pace and they both gasped.

"I told you she was there," Hana whimpered between sobs.

They sat around the table filling each other in on what had happened. They watched the news all the way through the night waiting to hear any announcements. None came. No one slept. No one wanted to miss another thing. The coffee, the food, the wine, would likely not be as easy to get hold of after everything that had transpired. But tonight was a celebration for Queenie. Even if it was a little weepy. It was a celebration for Rosalind and everyone that had lost their lives so far.

Eddie almost didn't see the text from Tannon. *So, I know it's none of my business, but Hana?* She wasn't asking him how Hana was doing. He chuckled. *I don't know. Why?* The text from Tannon had been sent nearly thirty minutes ago, but she must have been sitting on her phone. *Pretty sure she's pregnant.* That is not what Eddie expected to see. He didn't know what he expected, but that wasn't it. *Why would you think that?* Her answer was pretty clear, *Blood tests. Scientists. LOL.*

Should he tell her? She seemed so peaceful sitting there by the fire with Shari. Maybe he'd wait until tomorrow. It was getting close to dawn and nothing on any of the news stations had carried any announcements from the World Health Organization. He was afraid to ask, but while they were talking, he might as well ask Tannon, *Is it going to work?* It was back to business as usual--he'd almost forgotten. *Don't know for sure. Just watch the news in the morning.*

...

The morning news began at six A.M. and just as Tannon had advised, the story broke around the world. Dr. Tedesse was standing behind a bank of microphones, press conference style. "Over the last week, we have learned that for all of our advancements in medicine and science, there are so many things we still don't understand. A great many brilliant minds have been working tirelessly to contain what you've seen. We are sorry that there are so many questions that have been unanswered to this point as we attempted to solve them."

The press that were surrounding him were silent. There weren't twenty people yelling over each other to be heard. No one moved. It seemed as though no one breathed. The Director General continued, "Although there is still so much we don't understand about how this happened, we are at least relieved to finally announce that we have figured out a way to stop it."

He was jovial with his explanation of the discovery of the immunity. He was urgent calling on everyone with the marker that made them immune to donate blood in the interim, to prolong every moment they could for everyone. He was sorrowful as he explained the process and mutation of the enemy.

He was eloquent as he explained the plan to distribute the cure on the ashes across the globe with a series of incendiary containers. It was a lot more comforting than the word "bomb". After he was finished a field of questions came pouring in. Of course, they couldn't insure that every region of the planet would be completely covered, but it would be enough.

No promises had been made, but they could almost feel the sigh of relief that humanity exhaled all at once. A little bit of hope could go a long way.

...

It could have been any day on Bourbon Street, but it wasn't. It was Ash Wednesday. Instead of plastic beads, discarded clothing and other debris left over from the annual celebration, the streets were clean. Locals had spent most of the weekend cleaning up the French Quarter, preparing for their party. And the party went on. Not as rowdy, not as crowded, but it went on.

It only seemed fitting to stop by the little shop to pay their respects for Queenie. The musty smell wasn't so annoying, Hana mused to herself. They made their way up the stairs to see if she had left anything important behind. But she had so few belongings. Most of what she owned was at Shari's.

They found themselves downstairs again. Where Queenie had read the cards. The table was still overturned, but underneath one of the legs was a small crudely wrapped brown paper package. Hana's name was written on it in magic marker.

The alarm went off on Eddie's phone, indicating the time they'd announced for the ash distribution. It was possible they wouldn't see it. But they still wanted to be looking up. The roar of the jets as they flew by was almost deafening.

As Eddie stood with his neck craned up, she unwrapped the tiny box. There were only two things in it. A Tarot card from the deck she had read from the day she'd chased them out. On it was a beautiful woman seated on a lavish sofa that said Empress. There was also a tiny pink ribbon. As she looked to Eddie for his opinion, she heard the far-distant muted sound of two explosions. They hadn't expected to see the ash, but it was likely whoever gave the orders wanted to make sure it was thorough.

As the tiniest remnants of the fly ash reached the ground, Eddie took Hana's hand and led her back to the car. "Where do you want to go?" he asked her reverently. It was probably time to explain the gift that Queenie had left.

FIN

About the Author

While other girls were reading Teen Magazine, Angela Daniel was devouring copies of Popular Science. (Her dad insisted!) Being the granddaughter of a devout Southern Baptist minister also exposed her to faith at a very young age which bred an exigent curiosity in Theology.

Combining these two passions from opposite ends of the spectrum and drawing from her own unique sensory perceptions, Angela incorporates her view of the world into a tale designed to hit every sense on every page.

Angela is not a scientist. The mathematics were waaaaaay too hard.

Formatted 11/12/2018

No one ever inspired me more than you did. Rest in Peace Stan Lee.

Meet you on the other side.

Made in the USA
Middletown, DE
09 August 2019